CEMETERY KID
by
Alexandria May Ausman

This book is a work of fiction. Any references to historical events, real people, or real places, are used fictitiously. Other names, characters, places, and events are products of the author's imagination, and any resemblance to actual events or persons, living or dead, is entirely coincidental.

Copyright © 2022 by Alexandria May Ausman

All rights reserved, including the right to reproduce this book or portions thereof in any form whatsoever.

Book design by Jon M. Ausman
Cover photo by Christian Axel

Library of Congress Control Number: 2022911888

ISBN: 979-8-9862745-0-8 (ebook)
ISBN: 979-8-8396324-6-2 (paperback)

Dedication:

To the survivors of childhood neglect, abuse, and torture. To the memory of those who did not make it.

Characters: Book One

Amy: A schoolyard ally of Kelly.
Bob: male foster parent
Boyd: a deputy sheriff
Cathy: a deputy sheriff dispatcher
Cindy: granddaughter of a dead grandmother
Coach Crouch: Nickname for school athletic coach
Crystal: a classmate of Freak
Dennis: the county sheriff
Freak: the main character (this name will change over the years)
Jacinda: leader of the Denim Brigade
Green, Mr.: school principal
Gretta: member of the Denim Brigade
Higgs, Dr.: a contract psychiatrist to the sheriff's office
Keith: a jailer at the county jail
Kelly: a schoolyard bully
Maria: a girlfriend at age seven
Mary: female foster parent and Freak's grandmother
Michelle: a now dead foster child to Bob and Mary
Norma: member of the Denim Brigade
Opie: a rumor spreading student
Pat: member of the Denim Brigade
Patty: principal office secretary
Phillips, Mrs.: school teacher
Sandy: a child protective service caseworker
Scott, Dr.: new psychologist at mental health center
Stephanie: a schoolmate teased by Kelly
Tom: member of the Denim Brigade

Chapter 1: The Lesson of Death, a Halloween Story

Good evening Beautiful People! Oh, how I have missed all of you! Since my early retirement it has been a bit to adjust to a new way of life. Now, I have done "adjustments" so many times in my short existence you would think I had some kind of template or plan at least for it but alas, no. It has never gotten any easier with each major life event. Change is something that just gets harder as we get older. For some, we lose our elasticity, like that comfy pair of undies that has been stretched so far out that there is no grip on our person at all. Luckily, I have not gotten quite that far, yet. However, it was still a chore to get used to not working 24/7.

Now that I have gotten that out there in the open, on to writing my biography. I have had a lot of time to think about what I would talk about here in this book. Coming up with new ideas is not a hard thing, but deciding which ones will matter to you, beauties, now that has been a chore. I decided that you may find interesting and helpful to just let you get to know me better. That means I need to tell you more about who (or what, depending on your point of view) I am. So, let's start where all of us do, at the beginning. I will spend the next few chapters telling you more about how it is that I have arrived at this point in my life. A bit of a journey through a person's soul, through their own eyes, may be fun, or boring. Either way, you can choose to read on, or end it now. If you decide to stay, I hope that through this little bit of insight you can find at least a bit of entertainment, maybe a bit of understanding, perhaps even a smile.

I started out like everyone else did. Just a kid trying to make sense of the world I was born into. I had a father, a mother, and a home. That was not going to last very long but I did have one for the first seven years of my life. I can indeed still recall it. Nothing really stands out in those years. I was, like most kids, trying to fit in and wanted to grow up to be a veterinarian because I loved animals. I had a best friend named Marie and she and I got into trouble like best friends do. She wanted to grow up to be a princess. I wonder if she did. It was through Marie that I learned my first lesson that put me on the path to being a lifelong Goth a few short years later. She taught me about death.

It was Halloween 1977 and I was five years old. Marie and I were out trick or treating with all the neighborhood kids. Back then, I did fit in. Nobody saw me as anything other than just one of the pack. Back then, you could roam the streets with other kids without fear of kidnappers and often doors were not locked. It was a different time. No cell phone, no computers, and only three channels on the TV. Cable was really not around yet. Halloween back then was as big as Christmas. Getting a boatload of Halloween candy was a child's dream come true and if you were industrious you could collect enough to get you through most of the year. Costumes were mostly handmade and stuck to the classics like Dracula, the Mummy, Princesses and the occasional superhero like Wonder Woman or Superman.

That year of course Marie was a Princess. I was stuck with a crappy attempt at a Pumpkin. As usual Marie and I ran fast as we could from house to house trying to trip each other so we could beat the other for the first handful of whatever golden treats lay behind each unopened door. Ah, the sweet smells of the fallen leaves, smoke from fresh lit bon fires, and coolness of the coming fall hung in the air like a foreboding perfume adding to the exciting spookiness of the most Hallowed night. Only the heart of an innocent child can truly understand how that mix of "safe scary" made your heart beat faster in breathless anticipation of what was sure to be both frightening and exhilarating at the same time. By the time we reached the creepiest house on the block, Marie and I were breathless and ready for the "big scare" that sure was to come on such a glorious Halloween night. One that we could tell when we were old and grey, like I am telling you right now.

That house was supposed to be haunted by a witch and no kid ever went there unless it was Halloween night. It was just the typical rundown two-story house seen all over the country in every small and large town alike. Every neighborhood had this house or something like it and every town had an old lady who every child was sure ate children and flew on a broomstick late at night with a black cat hanging round the porch.

This was that house, and the old lady inside was actually just an elderly lady who once was like all of us. But to a five-year old kid being old was a scary thing, especially if you did not age well. This poor lady had not aged well. An old widow with no family and a severe case of osteoporosis was what she really was. To the kids of my neighborhood she was a witch pure and simple.

Marie and I arrived at house together laughing until we had hit the porch. Then a silent reverence overcame us as we used our eyes to dare each other to ring the doorbell. Finally, we rang it together and stepped back with fear making kitty biscuits on our spines. When she heard us at the door she growled and gurgled as she came out. She threw our treats in to our bags. She was so hideous to us. Long white unbrushed hair, several long silver whiskers poking out of her chin, one lazy eye, and forever bent looking at her feet with a hump in her back.

We barely mouthed "thank you" as we ran like the devil was after us. We kept running far down the street sure she had sent her flying monkeys to swoop down and take us back to her house for her Christmas Dinner. Both of us were out of breath and ready to collapse.

Marie asked me to look to see what she had given us in the bag. I did not want to look. I felt as if I needed to pee and my fingers were numb. I was certain she had thrown in the arms of babies as I had seen something white and slender go into the bags before we took off on our wild sprint. She was scared too and so we both sat down on the ground at the end of that street and went pawing together through my bag. She found it first and let out a yelp which scared the hell out of me. She pulled out a small skeleton figure with a sucker attached with tape to its back. We looked at it. I had never seen a skeleton up close before. I was fascinated and could not tear my eyes from it. She glared at it her eyes so wide I thought they would pop out of their sockets.

I asked her, "what is this"?

She dropped it on the ground finally breaking her gaze and immediately went through her bag. As soon as she found hers, she threw it far as her little arm could yelling "Skeleton! It is dead people!!!" She was visibly shaken.

I did not understand "dead people?" I asked still looking at this weird but very cool skeleton of mine.

"Yeah, dead people! She is a witch told you! Only a witch would give kids dead people for Halloween!" She then grabbed mine and threw it too. I was pissed but Marie was a year older than me so if she wanted it gone then so be it.

She then went through her bag ignoring me making sure there were no more "dead people" in there. We went home without much more chatter. This little surprise had upset her a lot. I did not ask any more questions. However, when she was going through her bag, I had retrieved one of them and hide it in my pocket. I wanted to have a closer look later without her disapproving comments.

When I got home that night, I pulled it from my pocket and took it to my bedroom to examine it without interruption. I stared at it in the mood light and tried to understand it better. I knew what dead was. I had a gold fish and a hamster that died. However, until that night I did not know people died too. I looked at its fingers and ribs and legs and toes (they matched up) and fear suddenly gripped me tighter than a vice. The room grew cold as I realized people die, this is what dead people look like. My dad is a people, Marie is a people, I am a people. We will die and this thing will be what happens to us!

I must have cried all night long as that horror gripped me as I thought of the goldfish and hamster laying there lifeless and buried. I somehow knew this would hurt a lot and the pain I felt in my heart at losing those pets, well I knew that would be the pain death would bring. I was far too sensitive as a kid I think as this burden bothered me so much, I actually spoke to my dad about it the next day and he verified my deepest fears, we all die. For weeks after that I cried every night trying to imagine what death was going to be like. I tried to come to grips with the inevitable even though my dad said it would be a long time for me. Time would pass and maybe not that day but someday I would be a skeleton too. I just could not wrap my tiny little brain around such a concept.

Until that horrible day I had never been afraid of the dark, nor of cemeteries (I did not understand them) but from that time on for several years to come each day as the sun set I would become so afraid I had to have a light on. Darkness represented death itself. If I had to walk past a cemetery I would scream and cry. Not for fear of the dead returning to life or of ghosts, but of my returning to death.

There is a famous line in the Crow, where one bad guy says: "my dad gave me this as a present and said, you know childhood is over the moment you realize you are going to die."

In many ways, I think that line is correct. Marie was older than I was, and she knew about all about it. We never discussed death again by the way. She was like the older sister who tells you there is no Santa Clause and over time I started to resent her for bringing me the ill tidings of a brutal truth about our existence. I was never close to her again and our friendship began to fade away until it was no more.

So, that old woman did in a way give us a kind of death for Halloween that night. It had caused the friendship to die, but it also started me down the road to the death of my childhood and sowed the seeds for the future Goth too. I also gained a true hatred for Halloween. Yeah, you read that right. I hated Halloween and became afraid of the darkness. It would be a few years to come before those two and I were reunited as allies. Had I learned it a bit later, or when I was better able to understand it, perhaps I would have come to grips with it with a bit more ease. As it was, like death tends to do, it was the catalyst that tore my inner world apart and it took a long time to rebuild it.

Why? It marked the beginning of a quest for understanding and obsession with death that would define me and ultimately lead to my Gothic lifestyle. However, that my beauties (if you are so inclined to hear more) is another story for another chapter.

Think about when did you discovered the truth of mortality? Do you remember how old and how you handled it? Do you wish to hear more about my journey to Goth or the ravings of a madwoman? If you do, then read on.

Chapter 2: Despair, Depression's Evil Step-Mother

I hope you are ready to take the next leg of the journey. I had just discovered at a very sensitive age that eventually I would die and the world would go on without me. I had also decided (and rightly so) that this death would be painful, too soon, and forever. A bit much for such an inexperienced mind to take in. I had not even begun to learn to enjoy life and now I was ruminating about the end of it! I had learned to fear the darkness, and all things that were connected to this natural progression of my mortality.

I even banned the word dead from my vocabulary. If I heard anyone else say anything remotely related to it, I would quickly cover my ears and run away trying like hell to keep the thoughts of being no more from my fevered mind. It had become an obsessive compulsive disorder (OCD) in which I began to develop rituals all designed to ward off the inevitable.

Now OCD disorder in a child so young is very rare but if seen it is related exclusively to genetics, brain damage or something just as bad, child abuse. I had become obsessed with death because just after this horrid Halloween incident I had also become aware of something else, my mother's treatment of me was not good and my fathers was not any better. The obsession was not because I was fearing a fantasy, it sadly, for me was a real possibility. The nightly beatings and forced starvation prior to understanding death were painful and hurtful, but I did not know that they could lead to the end of me forever.

I had been functioning pretty well. I had made a friend and managed a somewhat normal existence despite my dangerously small size and weight, and my chronic and very visible bruises. Making friends had always been a bit of a chore. We moved a lot. Every six months or so we packed up and ran from state to state. I was too little to understand why we were running. I now understand when Child Protective Services got too close, we packed up shop and left town. A sad fact that not only kept the law from helping me out of a very desperate situation but also kept me from making any real connections.

Children are naturally distrustful of new people. I was constantly a new person. For every new town, I was the tiny underfed bruised up kid with trouble keeping my bladder under control (nerves are such a bitch, you know?). That made me a target for more torment whenever I was sent to daycare and eventually to the horrors of public school.

It was in kindergarten (the second one since school had stared in August and this was November) that I had met Marie and this whole fear of death obsession began. She herself was very poor and had to wear big thick glasses. The other kids bullied her too, so we formed an alliance out of sheer desperation. However, now I hated Marie for telling me about death so I would not speak to her. Easier to blame her than the real cause of my pain (my parents). I was quickly drifting deeper into the hell that was my inner thoughts.

My parents were not religious people (go figure) and so I had never really been to church or knew anything about a God. Marie had told me about this fellow and said he looked after children in a special kind of understanding and love. I thought on that too, a lot, during that time. It just did not make any sense. If this guy was good to kids, why did he forget about me? I decided all the same I would try talking to him. Maybe he just did not know I was around, right? It did not seem to be working but I had to see if she was right about this one too.

Every night especially after a very nasty beating, I would talk to this God person and ask him if maybe he could help me to live forever or at least till I could grow up and kick my parents asses. If he could not see fit to do that, maybe he could see it in his heart to take them away to the cemetery so they did not send me there first. Yeah, at five I was praying for God to please make my parents die. I can safely say we were neither a close knit nor loving family.

It is here that I must tell you that Marie forgot to tell me about a heaven. That may have calmed some of my fear about death had she included that important information. She never mentioned death at all till that night. She had made God out to be a superhero, like superman, who saved the good people from the bad ones. That is what she had told me actually and since she was right about death, she must be right about this God person. For a little child this made perfect since and the possibility of a SuperGodman was a very realistic belief. Now that was a bit of an error because when God did not come and save me, I thought it was because I must be a bad person. Oh wait, now I am getting a bit ahead of myself. Actually, it was a particular incident that led to that belief.

Understanding all that as the months passed and the rituals (if you do not know what OCD rituals are, then look them up) and weird behaviors designed to ward off death seemed to be working while the talks with God were not, I began to wear out. I finally gave up asking for help. The rituals became so complex that I was almost paralyzed by them. This brought further fury from my parents who were already very annoyed by my existence. The severity of the beatings increased. That in turn brought the attention of the public schools as my weight plummeted and my bruises got bigger. We had to move yet again.

The day before we moved away, I went back to that old woman's house. You see I blamed her just as much as I blamed Marie for this new type of hell I had found for myself. In my anger and despair, I went there one day after walking home from school. I rang her doorbell and I head the same growling and gurgling (now I know she probably had COPD and couldn't breathe).

As she came to the door, I looked her right in her face and yelled WITCH!!! I HOPE YOU DIE!!! and I threw my books at her.

The poor thing was so confused she stopped, with the screen door still held open with one old bony arm. Thankfully I was too weak to do much damage as the books and pencils went flying in all directions. I waited to have her retort and give me a reason to attack further. Instead, I could see what looked like hurt in her eyes, even the lazy one. She did not say a word just looked at me.

Her refusal to say anything made me even angrier. I felt the fire in my belly rising and from somewhere deep down, maybe my toes, I began to growl. The anger was swelling and for a moment I almost felt like I was transforming into the wolf from the Three Little Pigs story. I admit it felt pretty good and that, to be honest, scared me.

"I hope you die! I hope your house burns down and I hope that God comes and makes you into a skeleton!" I yelled spiting like a wild creature at her. I couldn't think of anything worse to say and of course at the time my experiences with curses were very limited.

She just stood there all bowed over in that horrible pose that she was forever frozen into thanks to the ravages of calcium deficiency. I defiantly stood there; tiny fists balled up ready to attack. I was ready to bite, tear at her with whatever I had so that she could feel the pain I believed she had caused me. I was daring her to take a step, say a word back, but instead she began to weep.

That stopped my wrath in its tracks. To my absolute astonishment she stood there, old grey cloudy eyes filling with water and streams of tears now making their way down her wizened face like small creeks flowing down dry riverbeds. I watched as the first drops fell to that old wooden porch.

My fire inside went out and now I felt the heat of a different kind, that of shame. I wanted to run away from that spot, to hide in a deep hole, maybe even in a cemetery grave where at this point, I realized I probably belonged. But I could not move all I could do is stand there and stare back at her. It was then that the knowledge that indeed that I was a very bad person washed over me. It all made sense now, God knew I was bad and now here was the proof of it. I had just made an old woman cry, for what? For giving me a Halloween treat when I asked for it!

Her old cat came up just then onto that porch and began to rub itself on my leg. It meowed but to me is sounded like the cat said "meownster." I had to agree. I was a monster, albeit a baby one but definitely well on my way to hell in a hand basket or rather a Halloween basket.

I opened my mouth to say "I'm sorry" but nothing would come out but air. I felt my own rainstorm brewing behind my eyes. I knew in a moment, had you been a fly on that old porch, you would have seen two people, the very young and the very old, crying silently while staring bewildered at each other. I try not to laugh at the thought but there it is.

Then the old woman finally spoke. She said, "poor child. Do not despair. Whatever you think of me, I swear I would never harm a soul. I have little grandchildren of my own. I know I must be ugly and scary to you, but it is not because I am a witch, little one, it is because I have lived a long and hard life. Please believe me I am not a witch and would die before I would hurt you on purpose." She then tried to reach out to me as if to wipe away my newly emerging tears, but she was left reaching out to the nothingness I had left behind.

When she reached out, I ran away. I ran as fast as my little legs would go never looking back and I never went back for my books either. After all, I did not need them. We were moving away tomorrow. As I ran back to my house, I could hear her words ringing in my ears louder than my heartbeat as it raced to pump the blood needed to keep up my pace. "I would rather die than hurt you on purpose."

I ran till I could run no more and fell to the ground crying and gasping, feeling both like a shithead and also like a lost soul. I had never been so angry; I had never been so ashamed. I had wanted to hurt someone who really had not hurt me. I was a bad person, and death was actually her choice rather than hurt someone, unlike my evil little ass.

What a heavy lesson she had laid on me. It was something that would haunt me for a long time and just as the old woman (or at least I believe she did) had cursed me with the knowledge of death which led to an OCD hell, she took it all away in that single afternoon confrontation. I stopped the rituals and the compulsions that very night. I also stopped bothering with God too. Do you know why? Because that little episode had convinced me I deserved to be dead. It was a belief that did not ward off my fear of the dark or of cemeteries, but it certainly did stop the blaming of other people for my situation. Right or wrong, I believed I was getting exactly what I deserved.

Fixing that little error was going to take a lot longer than a few months but that, my beauties, is yet another story destined for a future chapter.

If you are still here after this horrible confession, here are my three questions for you. What was your home life like? Did you grow up in a rough environment or was your home a stable and loving one? If it was an ugly one, did you believe you deserved it too or did you lay the blame where it belonged?

Chapter 3: Why do Cemeteries have Walls?
Because Everyone is just Dying to get Inside

My family moved again. I thought a lot in the coming months about my behavior that day with the old lady on that porch. I also thought a lot about death, life and what it all really means. I thought about what is a "good person" and what makes a person "bad." The rituals and compulsions had stopped but my hunger to know the answers to my many questions nearly drove me nuts.

We moved again, and again, and yet again. The beatings and punishments, of being locked up or starved continued and often were quite vicious. However, by now at the age of seven, I was a seasoned abused child.

I knew just how to hide the bruises and what not to say. I even learned how to steal food, beg for it, or even look for change to buy it when it was withheld. I learned how to hide that too when I could get it, for the harder times. In a sentence, I was becoming very skilled at surviving my brutal childhood. I had even managed to keep a sunny disposition and a positive attitude about life in general.

How? Well, I am so glad you asked! I had been seeking a lot of answers and knew right where to find them, the library. When the other kids went to play for recess I would sneak into the library and scour the books. Some were too far advanced for me to read, but I did look at the pictures and read what I could. Mostly I read about mummies, myths, legends and above all, anything that remotely had something to do with death. I wanted to understand my nemesis.

What I mostly encountered were the stories about the Ancient Egyptians and their take on death and dying. They were not obsessed with death at all. They were like me obsessed with life, eternal life to be exact. I devoured the books about that culture because they seemed to me to have beaten the grave or at least the fear of it. At this time in the late 1970's, King Tut was still all the rage and the old Hippy culture still dying its last breaths. It was a good time to seek out an answer that would suit my troubled mind.

When things were darkest at home, I could escape into the ancient world of gold, silver, desert Kings and Queens, amazing legends, and above all a land where death was just a leg of a journey but not the destination. It was during this time that I saved all the money I could find or make doing odd jobs for neighbors and bought my first Ankh from a little junk seller on the side of the road in the city we lived in. I gave up the possibility of buying food that week to have that little cheap tin charm. It cost me all I had. I thought it the best purchase ever. I made the necklace it hung from out of a broken cheap necklace my mother had thrown away. For me the Ankh, (which actually means "life force" not "eternal life") was my homespun protection.

I actually convinced myself that as long as I wore this symbol, no death could ever take me away. If my parents killed me then I would simply meet up with the good old dog headed Anubis. He would know me because I wore the sign of the Ancients and he would lead me to a land where life was the same, but better! My body would never be a skeleton because it would mummify instead. It all seems very silly now to think I ever thought that, but to the mind of a little kid with big problems it made a hellish existence bearable.

At school, the kids really bullied me very badly. The old "new kid" curse continued and now as I entered this phase in life kids were splitting off into same gender hordes of what would soon become cliques. Being an outsider was killing my shot at such valuable socialization. No one wanted me in their group, their home, or their world. So, I spent all my time with my colorful friends that had the heads of dogs, ravens, and hawks and escaped into a land that was far away and the sun was a God. Darkness could never beat a God! I had learned to live inside my own head and forget about the cold, nasty, unforgiving world outside of it.

It was this year of my life that my dad up and left. He never came back. I did sort of miss him in the beginning. He would only hit me when he was drunk and sometimes, he was even nice to me for a second. Of the two parents he was the good one. Now that he was gone my mother did not hold back. I then entered a deeper realm of torment that I think we can skip. That part of my life is something I would not repeat to the devil himself. Some things are left better unsaid and lost without a voice in time. It is enough to know she wanted me dead (said so often and tried to make it so often). Her treatment of my existence was not friendly to say the least. Despite her best efforts, I had my world inside my head to run to and I managed to keep it together without anger or bitterness for several years to come.

Skipping all that bullshit, we move to the next big change that set me on this path. The next one was the beating that left me with a husky voice. I would skip this story but there is one thing in the story I did not like to mention. I was dead (heart stopped, had to be paddled to get it to start back) three times on the table before they could stabilize my condition. One of those flat lines was for almost two minutes, almost too far gone to bring me back without brain damage. The death I was so frightened of had actually come. Yet, I had been resurrected from the grave so to speak. I did not stay dead!

I actually have no memory for those flat lines at all. The hospital staff told me about it after I was well enough to hear of what happened. I have very little memory of the attack either. That I think is a blessing. However, there was something else I had little to no memory of when I woke up in that hospital bed. I did not remember myself. Yes, the person I had been was somehow different and though I recognized my reflection, something inside me had changed. It is difficult to explain what I mean so you will just have to take my word for it. I was not me anymore, or at least not the me I had been.

I did feel it in the hospital this strange change, but it was not until I was well enough to get out of the hospital that the real proof of it showed itself. Prior to this incident, I was nervous, shy, sensitive, apologetic, gullible, forgiving, thoughtful, self-blaming, and well in a word, a mouse. After, I was cold, hard, calculating, clever, angry, uncaring about what others thought, and above all brash. It was here that the first real signs of my Goth begin to show up.

Before the attack, my favorite color was pink. I wanted to be a vet someday. After the attack my favorite color was red, and I no longer wanted to grow up at all. I wanted to go back to being dead. I was really pissed that the doctors had saved me. The fear of death was replaced with a "death wish." I was not suicidal by any means, just willing to put myself into situations that would likely end my life. I had now been dead, and it was not nearly as bad I had feared it would be. I was not in pain when dead. Hell, I did not remember anything. Life, now that was painful, unforgiving, and endless it seemed.

Now I am, and the days stretch on endlessly. Yeah, many of you wonder did they get those assholes who did that to me, sure they did. They did not serve much time and went on with their lives and I know nothing of that, nor do I care. I really was only angry that I survived and that may sound crazy but if you had been there (and maybe some of you were in your own private hells) you would understand that completely. I did survive, now I had to keep it from happening again or hasten it. Either way, the boys going down for beating me to death (literally) made me very unpopular (as if I could get anymore unpopular) with all the other kids in the school. Now, they threw things and kicked me, but no one was dumb enough to try to beat me to the point of death again.

Pain, without the hope of someone sticking up for me or the hope of it ending through death, became my world. We cannot forget my mother is still around to make sure that any part of me that is still not affected by the daily bullying is not left out. Yeah, those were bad days indeed. If it had continued, I think I would not have been the Goth Queen, I would have been either a prison inmate or a mental home lifer or dead.

That is when the next phase of what would become a Gothic lifestyle came into my life and in its own way saved me from what was likely to be a very bad end to this story. Funny, but my savior from a gruesome death was the very place of death: The Cemetery.

One day not long after getting out of the hospital, I was being chased and badly bullied by a small group of kids who were friends with the kids who were punished for hurting me. I had to walk home as most kids did those days. They saw me and began chasing me down the street pelting me with rocks and anything else they could pick up to throw. Name calling and yelling, like a pack of rabid dogs.

I ran like hell but was still weak from the injuries and still basically healing up. I was much slower than I had used to be so as I rounded a block, I saw the city Cemetery with her iron gates, and rock walls lined with pointed iron fencing. The gate was chain locked but just enough space so that I thought I could squeeze through it. Now, I still feared cemeteries but at that moment I was more afraid of falling down, out of breath, so then my attackers could have their way with me.

So, I took a deep breath and ran for it. I pushed through the gate and some of the loose iron in the gate got wrapped up in my hair. I was stuck half in and half out with my hair holding me back. I could hear the kids coming and threatening what they planned to do once they caught me. With all the strength I had left, I pushed forward, ripping quite a chunk of my hair out of my head. It was hopelessly tangled, and sacrifices had to be made. Hurt like hell let me tell you but I was in and the end it was worth it.

As the angry mob of school mates approached all they saw was the mass of blond hair and likely a bit of blood wrapped on that gate. I imagined it looked to them like a victorious Native American showing off his latest scalp. I heard them all stop and say a collective "shit!" and then they ran away. I was just on the other side of that gate to one side hiding behind the wall, out of breath and out of the will to run any further. I laughed to myself as I realized at least this time if they killed me, I was conveniently placed for a quick funeral.

Until that day, I had avoided cemeteries like the plague but now here I was panting and grateful for this most unlikely place of sanctuary. I could feel the wetness in the back of my head where the chuck had been ripped out, blood of course. My legs were cramping too. I was in no condition to run again if they were hanging out not too far away waiting for me to come out. I decided to hang out for a while, so I could recover a bit. As I sat there and the adrenaline wore off, I just sat in awe staring into the very thing that had frightened me so much since the day I got that skeleton in my Halloween bag.

I waited for what seemed like hours just staring into this very large and very old graveyard from my vantage of just inside against the rock wall. I did not venture any further still feeling apprehensive about this necessary alliance. Once I had recovered enough to run again, if need be, I pushed back through the gate and walked home without incident. The kids had scattered, and I had avoided a beating.

This lucky discovery that the bullies were also afraid of the cemetery could not have come at a better time. I was in need of a break, any break. As the next day of school began and the day ended with the same group of wild dogs after me, I made a beeline right for the cemetery. As I approached her vine covered crumbling stone walls and foreboding gate, I felt for the first time in a very long time, a sense of relief. No, more than relief. It was a sense of coming home where you are always welcome and nothing bad can hurt you. I felt an overwhelming sense of joy and excitement fill me as finally I knew where I belonged.

This time I got through the gate without issue. The same result occurred, the kids would not pass the gate and I was safe within the bosom of the death yard where no living creature dared to go. I heard them yell out, "ghoul!" For a few moments, they lingered just on the other side of the wall daring each other to go inside to "beat her creepy ass."

However, no one was brave enough to take the dare. Eventually, they gave up each leaving while hurling useless insults as they all walked away from my newfound fortress. As I listened to their voices grow more distant, I admit I wept. Not from fear or because of their insults, but because I had found something that finally did protect me. Something real, not just inside my head like the Ankh. This was something that no matter where my mother forced us to move there would always be a cemetery there.

Chapter 4: The Mask

It is 1985 the world is bursting with bigger than life exaggeration of everything. Even the hairdos are bigger than big and all around me I watch as the superficial, cliques, and fads take hold of everyone. Everyone except the small, frail, and actually pathetic thirteen-year-old me. Thirteen was certainly not my lucky number, or was it?

No, I was as close to undead as one could ever be as each day blurred into the next an endless march of abuse, moving from state to state, bullying and finding sanctuary in dank graveyards (an uneasy alliance to say the least) when the torment got to be too much. Gone were the golden and sunny days of my secret inner world of immortal beast headed Gods. I had been to the other side, and I did not find anything there but the darkness that now was crushing the very will to live from my tiny body. I no longer believed in anything. I still wore my Ankh charm, but I no longer had any faith in it. I was coming into my maturity with nothing but anger and despair to guide my actions. There was a storm on the horizon of my existence, and it was going to be one hell of a gully washer! It was fall of that year that everything began to change.

On an early autumn day, not unlike most fall days in the south, I was on one of my wild runs to the latest cemetery sanctuary, when I tripped and fell down. My attackers reached me before I even hit the ground and the beating was epic. I know what a Nike high top tastes like, let me tell you! There were two of them this time, very nasty and very large girls, juniors in fact, who really hated me because I am sure they too were being hurt at home. However, at that moment I really did not give two shits because they were using me as a hacky sack. I just wanted them to stop.

I did my best to fight back but they were too big, and my few useless punches and kicks only opened me up for the second girl to get a direct hit. I finally just rolled up into a ball and let them kick, hit, and spit on me guarding my egg of a head best I could so they did not scramble it for me. It worked because finally they were tired and out of breath and after several cruel insults and a few more good kicks for good measure they left me be there on the sidewalk in front of the cemetery destination for which I sought protection. I too was out of breath and laid there bleeding and crying like a little bitch for a bit.

Finally, I got up and crawled into the cemetery, not because I was afraid, they would come back, I knew they had had their fill, but because to be honest I could not get home in that condition. I was unsure if they had not broken a rib or two. I could barely breath.

Once inside I crawled over to the most unusual of all the graves there. It was very old with a large flat stone resting on two side stone slabs, with two large headboard and foot board stone to make it actually look like a bed. I thought this was a very weird grave but today it was coming in handy as I needed a bed.

I had kept my healthy fear of the cemetery and never stayed as dusk fell for fear of, well I was not sure of what, but I was sure as hell not going to find out. However, this day's injuries were severe, and my nose and mouth would not stop bleeding. I had a lot more to worry about then the coming dusk. I could not catch my breath, so I lay there on that gravestone bed and fell into a deep sleep.

When I woke up to the sound of rustling in the leaves (likely a mouse) I was horrified to find the sun had set, no telling how long before and it was pitch black. The world was quiet and without a single light I could barely even make out the bloody nose in front of my face. I lay there frozen in absolute terror. I was unsure if I was afraid of what supernatural thing was going to eat me for staying in a graveyard overnight, or afraid of the fact that my mother was going to make the beating of that afternoon feel like a trip the day spa. Either way I laid there with only the sounds of my racing heart pounding in my ears and the short rapid pace of my shallow breaths to remind me that this was actually happening and not some nightmare.

I tried to adjust my eyes to the murky darkness, but I only had the light of a waning moon to use as a flashlight. All around me I could make out the faint images of the dilapidated grave markers of the long-forgotten dead. I must have looked like I was awaiting the cult to come and make me the human sacrifice from some bad 1970's horror flick, laying there in the darkness with dried blood sticking and pulling at my nose and mouth. I was in all black clothing. Over the last year I had learned that the cops who regularly swept the local graveyards for teenagers up to no good would throw you out.

After being thrown out a few times, I figured out a way to keep the cops off me. I needed to look like I belonged there. I never again wore anything but the dark black of the one in mourning. I only had a couple of outfits as my mother sure as hell was not going to get me any clothes, but I did odd jobs when I could get them and second hand stores were my forte. After learning that fact and changing my fashion, the next time the cops came and every time after, I would quickly throw myself over any handy grave and wail and pretending to be lost in grief so they would stop throwing me out to the wolves waiting outside to kick my ass. It always worked and the cops would leave me be as I was pretty good at looking uncontrollably bereaved. I certainly had a lifetime of training at it. In fact, you could say I was a natural.

After what seemed like hours, I saw the light of the police car coming as it cut through the darkness of that lonesome place. "Oh shit" I thought, "I don't think the grieving bit is going to work this time."

I was now more afraid of what would happen to me if the cops brought me home to mother, (she did not like the cops, go figure) then of any ghosts, ghouls or demons waiting in that dark boneyard to gobble up little girls. In an absolute panic I rolled off that bed grave and started crawling on my belly through the damp, dank earth deeper into the graveyard. To my horror I heard the cop car pull up and the opening and closing of car doors. The two officers were getting out and coming thru the gate and they had flashlights.

"Oh shit, shit, shit!" is all I could think as I slithered/crawled faster and deeper into this very large graveyard. I did not know where I was going but surely, I would find somewhere to hide. Then I saw it dimly lit in the darkness, an open grave. The large pile of dirt and the huge grave digging machine were impressive even in the dark. I was sure that if one could not hide above, they might find a place below. So as quietly as possible I made my way to this hole in the ground listening with trepidation to the officers talk to each other about the reports of "kids screwing around with the graves after dark."

I could see the reflection of their flashlight as they were shinning them on graves behind me, and they had discovered my recent bunk as I had bled all over the place. I winced as I heard them say, "look either blood or fake blood, the little creeps. Probably sacrificing animals, the perverts! No respect! What the hell is wrong with kids anymore?"

As, the other police officer went on a long diatribe of what was wrong with my generation I finally reached the open grave and with a deep breath rolled in. It was a lot deeper than I thought it would be and I hit the bottom with a thud, and I almost let out a groan. The fear of being found kept my mouth shut. I just laid there wishing I could cover myself up with the dirt so if they looked in (why the hell would they look in, I wondered) they would not see me. They did not look in, but I could see the flashlight cutting the darkness above me like a spotlight for a movie premier as they checked the cemetery for the would be "devil worshiping, animal sacrificing loonies."

They of course did not find any of these makeup villains and finally they left. I had laid there forever it seemed and decided that I was already in big trouble so may as well stay till morning now. I was in no mood for another beating so soon and not like my mom was going to call the cops and report me missing anyway. I did not even bother crawling out of the open grave. I just laid there miserable and self-loathing. There had to be some way to end this torment.

My inner thoughts whirled like a tornado inside me as I considered my current situation. I knew that my mother would never stop till she had killed me and so there was no stopping that. I could tell on her again, but they never did anything about her. We would just run away again from the authorities. Back then they just did not take kids into custody easily, the laws were a few years from changing. Even today it is difficult to get these kind of folks as they just move away when discovered. So, that was never going to change. Now, how could I stop the bullies at school that made my hellish life more than I could bare? Bad enough I was hated, called a ghoul, and shunned by everyone, but the hitting and chasing that needed to stop. "How can I stop them?" I thought as the most recent crying jag began.

I had the right to have a crying jag that night. I was alone, in the dark, in an open grave, beaten, without a friend in the world, scared, tired, and hungry. Now how many people can relate to this? I hope none! However, here I was just crying in the graveyard until finally I was wailing for real. Had you been outside that cemetery that night you likely would have crapped your pants thinking zombies and ghosts are real. My wails were almost animal and there is no way the entire block around the area did not hear that. I felt that coming right from my soul. I finally became angry and crawled out of the grave and started kicking the dirt into the hole, cursing with every dirty word I could think of and making up a few. Then I wore out and wailed some more. It was really quite silly and quite sad but necessary. I had been strong for so long and now it was time for me to deal with this shit head on. That would require a cleansing of all the old hurts. I needed a clear head to deal with what I needed to do now.

As I finally calmed down, I laid down next to the hole and looked up into the sky. The darkness had always scared the shit out of me but tonight it held me like a mother holds a child. I was safe in the dark. I did not want the dark to be my mother. I did not want the cemetery to my home. I hated the color black, so boring! I did not want Death to be my brother either but here I was home with the family.

I wanted a real mom, color, laughter, life, friends, a real life! Instead, all I could had was this desolate, morbid, weird world were all your friends are six feet under. It was time to stop fighting the truth of my path and start to embrace it. I looked back into the hole and thought of the skeleton that would soon occupy it.

That made me laugh wildly, "Sloppy seconds, fellow, I was first in the grave. Bam, broke that shit in." I rose up my arms and made the sign of the horned God and stuck out my tongue, "rock and roll bitches The devil, she is home for dinner." I finally knew exactly what to do.

I walked home and took my beating. I got thru it easier than ever before because I had a plan which kept me from feeling her blows. After my mom wore herself out breaking a foot off in my ass, she went to bed for sleep.

I, however, did not go right to bed. First, I went into her bathroom and stole some of her make up. Not the stuff she would miss, the Halloween stuff she never used. I took the white foundation, a compact mirror and black lipstick.

The next morning after I left the house for school I stopped and put on the makeup. That morning when I walked into school the kids no longer kicked me in the hallway or hurled insults or pulled my hair. No, they did all they could to get the hell out of my way. I parted the crowd like Moses parted the red sea.

The girl I had been had died, been forced into a cemetery, and even a grave. However, I had arose from that grave everyone had put me into. So, now as the decay from death tends to do, I had progressed into a skeleton. Only, to my surprise, I had chosen to become the very thing I feared the most. It did not come for me, I had hunted it down instead.

I was not incorrect in my assumption. The kids could not believe their eyes, many just stopped and stared, mouths hanging open. I must have been one hell of a sight. Shock white-blond hair, dressed in black, black eye sockets, blacked out nose and bone white face, and neck with my mouth grinning from ear to ear with the black of an empty jaw. Not something anyone expected to see that day I can assure you. Back then there were no rules against what I had done. It was just makeup, right? Oh, but no it was not just makeup. It was my death mask.

I had come up with the plan that night. How do I keep them from beating me? I run to a place they fear to go. Why do they fear it? Because they fear death. Now how do I stop running? Well, that is easy, take death everywhere I go.

I thought of that old woman as I strolled down the hallway reveling in the terror, I could read in the students' eyes. The old lady had frightened all those kids (and me too) because of her stereotypical witch appearance. No one wanted to go near her place or person. So, the answer was all I had to do is be scary too. How? Well, all I had to do was let the ugliness from within out of my heart and wear it on my back for everyone to see it. Let me tell you, nothing was uglier and scarier than what was in my heart at that time.

Now this may seem a bit extreme but before you judge, understand this worked, immediately. They did not mess with me anymore from that day forward at any school. Sure, the first thing that happened is I got called to the counselor's office, but she could do nothing as I was not talking (that useless bag of bones where had she been all that time when I was getting beat?). Without an answer other than "this is my art my, self-expression" she had to cut me loose.

I worked now to buy the makeup needed to keep up my death mask. As the weeks rolled into months, rumors that I was a witch, a devil worshiper (I still hung out in the graveyard after all, I had learned to love it there), and a fruit loop above all ran as rampant as a flu virus through the school. The kids that had once tormented me were now genuinely afraid of me. To be brutally honest, I liked that. No, scratch that, I loved it. They made me out to be a monster and that was a part I was most happy to play.

As this little performance gained a bit of maturity, I began to blur the reality from the fake. It was not long until the monster I pretended to be was the monster I had now become, but that my beauties is yet another story of my road to Goth. So now you all see the beginning of the gothic but there is much more to the fleshing of this (excuse the pun) skeleton.

Reflect on whether you were a school bully or were you bullied at school? How did you handle it if you were one or the other?

Chapter 5: There is no Goth! Only Ghoul!

Good evening Beautiful People! Okay, so now we are about to continue on the track to the darkest world of the gothic lifestyle. Are you ready? Good, let's continue...

Definition of ghoul. 1: a legendary evil being that robs graves and feeds on corpses. 2: one suggestive of a ghoul; especially: one who shows morbid interest in things considered shocking or repulsive

I had begun to take on the appearance of what would someday be called a Goth. However, this is 1985 (almost 1986) so that word does not exist yet. Instead, to my horror, I was labeled a ghoul. I was no longer hit and kicked, but there are a lot of ways to hurt a person, and nothing can scar a soul like a sharp tongue can.

Weeks became months as I perfected my look of death. At home things were growing more violent and there was no doubt that soon something was going to have to give, or I would not survive much longer. If you could call what I was doing surviving at all. The kids at school were so freaked out by my appearance when they hurled their nasty insults, they did it from a distance which suited me just fine. However, it also further isolated me from any human contact. That was not a good thing for a budding teen who is trying to figure out her place in the world of humankind, as all teenagers do.

When I was able to get away, I would go back to my cemetery to just ponder on my situation. I also went there just to find peace and quiet with the only people who were going to be okay with my new look. The dead did not give two flips that I looked like one of them, or at least they did not complain anyway.

I had to be very careful when the cops came to sweep as with my morbid make-up, they would not buy my mourning act. To solve that problem, I bought a nice black hooded sweatshirt and a veil at a secondhand store. Now when they came in all they saw was a kid sobbing by a grave with her hood covering any view of her face. That worked just fine but I still did not stay in the graveyard after dusk set in. I was still not completely at ease in the world of the dead no matter what the kids at school seemed to think.

The next year did not bring much change in my conditions. I was getting very good with the make-up, and things continued to escalate out of control at home. My mom actually liked my new found look. It allowed for the better camouflaging of bruises after all, and she like I was tired of moving all the time. She even would buy the make-up when I could not afford it. In reality, she also like the fact that now everyone thought I was bat shit crazy. No one was going to believe me even if I said the sky was blue at that point.

In a way the very thing that had kept the kids off me at school had the unintended side-effect of also keeping me from getting much needed help. Not like a kid wearing a skull head to school is not a scream for help that should have been deafening or anything. But as I have said, this was a different time and, in those days, people did not like to get involved in family business or involved in the affairs of children when they were bullied. So, I was truly on my own. I had now become bitterly and very painfully aware of the situation I was in.

I went to school as often as possible to escape my horrid mother, and the cemetery whenever that was too much to tolerate. I would grow weary of the whispers of "did you hear she sleeps in coffins?" or "yeah a real live ghoul you know, eats dead people and everything."

Then one day while sitting in an English class I heard the three kids behind me talking about the girl of the groups granny just passing away. As the two boys tried to comfort the girl she said, "I think they will have the funeral at the city cemetery this weekend."

One of the boys said, "Oh that is terrible! That means old Ghoul there will be digging her up and having her for dinner!" The other boy started laughing.

The girl let out a gasp and said, "Oh my God! I had not thought of my poor granny having to be in there with that thing slinking around doing only God knows what to her grave!" Both boys started laughing loudly as she said that.

I winced. Now that hurt. I mean, really? Did they actually think I was digging up corpses and eating the dead? I wanted to retch just thinking of such a horror. I felt my face grow hot with indignation. Instead of turning around and asking with true emotional pain why they had to be so cruel, I just sat there seething saying nothing. The two boys laughed and made more disgusting and false statements about me. The anger inside of me was becoming a raging beast and it was growing harder and harder to keep that beast chained up.

After class the girl who just lost her grandmother rushed past me and yelled out "Ghoul!" with tears in her eyes. The boys rushed after her to try and console her finally realizing that the death of a loved one was not something to tease about even in an indirect way. I just sat there bitterly cussing myself for not thinking this little plan of looking like a dead person out a bit more before just rushing into it so quickly. It was sure not going the way I expected.

I had gym class two periods later with that same girl. She had by now alerted all her very popular and good looking girlfriends in that class of my alleged appetite for the recently deceased. I walked into an ambush in the locker room.

"Why are you such a freak?" one blond asked as she threw a sneaker at me. Happily, it missed. "No one wants you around here, why don't you go to hell where you belong?" She finished putting her hands on her hips and staring at me with pure contempt. Three more of her friends and the bereaved girl all stood in a line blocking my path from entering any further than that doorway.

I looked at her and at first thought I maybe should wait and come back later after they had dressed out and avoid this little intervention. Instead, I felt what can only be described as a flash of electricity go through me as a growl began in the back of my throat. I had finally had enough of this bullshit. I had done everything possible to let everyone know I was not one to be messed with and still they were too stupid to catch on. Time to show them why they should mind their business and let me be in my own misery.

"You had better move your thunder butt out of my way darling," I growled out while staring hard with my piercingly blue eyes, "or you will be joining her granny and I for dinner."

The girls definitely did not expect me to say that. The grieving girl let out a wail and ran to the back of the locker room uncontrollably sobbing. Two of the other girls ran after her. The one who started the whole argument just stood there looking horrified with her jaw hanging open and the last girl quickly looked from her to me nervously.

"I cannot believe you are such a disgusting freak! Why doesn't someone exterminate you for Christ's sake!" She finally spit at me breaking the silence that seemed like an eternity.

I just smiled as I said, "can't kill that which is already dead sweetheart."

Then I jumped at her letting out a vicious growl and she back up startled stepping on the girl left. That girl let out a yelp which further frightened thunder butt and the two of them quickly took off in the direction of their companions to the back of the locker room. I chuckled and felt quite proud of myself. I decided to reward my little display of courage by cutting gym class and heading out to my cemetery sanctuary. I spent that afternoon rewinding the incident in my mind and laughing out loud at how easily upset these so-called bullies actually are when you are not afraid of them. For the first time ever, I felt like a winner. Too bad I did not realize what I had just done, or where it was about to start going. There is a fine line between defending oneself and becoming a bully yourself. I was about to cross that line.

The next day I was going to my locker, when I noticed a small boy that had a locker below mine trying to hurry and grab his books forcing each one clumsily into his backpack. I noticed him but did not think much of him, at first. Until I approached and he began to struggle faster shooting frightened looks my direction. That pissed me off. I had never done a thing to him and here he is acting like a fool. I had lost total sight of the fact that I did look like a band member from Kiss before he had his coffee.

He was rushing but not fast enough. I got to the locker before he could get his last book into his backpack. As I approached, I grabbed his shoulder with one arm and with all the strength I had I pushed him backwards. He was in a crouched position, so it did not take much to send him sprawling into that crowded hallway. He tried to use his backpack to maintain balance which only caused the books to go flying everywhere and was useless to stop his short fall. He did not move completely stunned.

I was not done, I walked over and kicked one of his now freed books across the hallway and smiled with evil never taking my eyes off him as he laid there shaking afraid to move. Everyone in the area had stopped to watch the show. Some whispered and little nervous chuckles broke out from here and there, but no one came forward to stop me.

I leaned toward his prone body and still smiling said, "don't let me ever see you here again. You had better get a bigger backpack, because next time I will not be kicking books you understand me?"

He nodded obviously very frightened. Satisfied, I turned got my book and strolled off leaving this poor kid and the curious onlookers to pick up the mess I had made. I did not see this kid for the rest of the school year at the locker. He had taken me very seriously and gotten a bigger backpack avoiding the lockers.

This was a behavior that started to repeat itself daily. Anyone who looked at me oddly or make the mistake of whispering around me would get the same treatment. I attacked immediately. I would kick over their chairs, knock over desks, trip them, push them down, spit on them or in their food during lunch and take it for myself. Trips to the principal's office was becoming as routine as the beatings and worse I was taking at home.

I had a lot of experience with hurting, so I was very good at hurting others. I knew just where to strike, what to say, and how to say it to make it really stick. I do not mean to brag but I was actually very accomplished at being cruel. I was fast gaining a reputation not only as a nut job but as a violent bully. Worse than anything else, I knew better, but did not care. I justified my bad behavior as being my right. No one cared about me so why the hell should I care about them? It was the wrong thing to believe but I was no longer that sensitive, caring little girl who hated herself for making an old lady cry. Now I had matured into a full-blown monster that simply could not be reasoned with.

Then one day in August of 1986, everything began to change, for the worse. They say it is always darkest before the dawn. Well, there was a dawn coming eventually but the longest and darkest days of my short life had just begun.

It all started with a pep rally. That day I was recovering from a rather rough time at home the night before and I was in a foul humor. I hated pep rallies with all the noise and bullshit fake team spirit. I tried to cut it but got caught by a teacher monitoring the halls for the likes of me and so my escape was blocked. I walked into that crowded gym full of a sea of unfriendly faces and moaned. I saw an empty bleacher seat, but it was way at the top of the gym, and I would have to walk through that herd of bodies to get to it. I decided it was better than trying to sit with anyone. No doubt that would result in having to shove someone to the gym floor while the inevitable call to the principal's office would be made.

I stared to weave through the students as they all scrambled before me to try to avoid my person touching theirs (afraid my creepy was catching, I am sure) but halfway up my old friend the girl with the granny suddenly stood up and prevented my further climb.

"Freak," she yelled in my face. "You are not welcome here. Go somewhere else and die!" The girl stood there defiantly just begging me to do something about what she had just said.

I thought, "Oh God, not today, please not today." However, she did not budge. I tried to push past her anyway saying nothing. She put out her arms and pushed me backward. I almost lost footing and fell. Okay now, she had pissed me off.

I regained my footing. I felt that evil smile spreading across my face where every one of my teeth showed. Then before I could stop myself, I heard me say, "Your granny tasted just like chicken, UMMM UMMMM, finger licking good!"

The look of shock was undeniable (I had seen so much of that look lately) as she broke out into immediate tears and pushed past me nearly tripping over students on the seats just below us. I watched her tripping and rushing off and yelled towards her while waving, "See you, soon."

The students around me were utterly disgusted no doubt but they did nothing but look away as I began to try to climb up that bleacher mountain once more. It had become unnaturally silent in the area within ear shoot of my most cruel retort, but then a clap, then another, the several clapping hands all in unison coming from the left of me. Now that was a sound I did not expect to hear, not for me anyway.

I looked to see who it was more out of surprise than curiosity. I saw four girls and a tow-headed boy with thick glasses all dressed from head to toe in blue denim clapping just three bodies down from my little discussion with Miss granny girl. Then the tallest girl stood up clapping and the other four stood up with her. They began to cheer, clap and whistle while chanting after the girl, "run like a little bitch, you bitch!"

"Huh?" was all I could think. This was a strange thing to see but I was not too interested in their investment in the humiliation of that girl. I did not have time for such drama. I just wanted to be left to get to my damned seat without further incident. So, I ignored them and finally got to the top and sat down grateful that was over.

However, it was not over by a long shot, it had only just begun.

When you were in high school did, they have cliques? If so, were you ever a part of one? Or did you want to be a part of one? We are all human and there is a need to want to be a part of something. It is natural. Who did not want to be popular and appear to be loved by everyone?

Chapter 6: The Graveyard Queen

The pep rally that would forever be burned in my memory as the last event of a life I used to know went on for eternity. I sat on the top bleacher I had earned with a bit of bullying, wishing for an act of God (any God) to burn that gym to the ground. The noise, the cruel kids, all the lights it was pure hell on my senses. I now preferred the quiet of the darkness to all this color and life. I entertained myself by keeping a wary eye on the most recent clique that had come into my radar to keep from going mad. The five kids I had privately named the Denim Brigade.

I watched them from my perch several bleachers above. The tallest was a female with dirty blond, and tightly permed hair. The next girl slightly shorter with mousy brown hair and eyes so dark I could make them out from my vantage. The next female was slight with what appeared to be a bad attempt to have the tall female's hair, brown tightly permed hair and chubby cheeks. The last girl was buxom with black curly long hair and olive colored skin. The only male in the group was white-blond like me with the thickest glasses I had ever seen and when he had been standing I noticed he had noticeably bowed out legs, like a cowboy from an Old West film. All five were wearing the same blue denim jacket, rolled up sleeves with blue jeans, white tennis shoes and white t-shirts. They looked like rejects from a bad Bruce Springsteen concert. Of course, I really do not have a right to say anything about the way anyone dressed. However, it was funny to see all five of them dressed exactly alike.

When the hellish meeting of mindless yelling for a group of sport playing high school kids who would never go pro finally ended, I practically flew to the doors of that gym running for the hills fast as my short legs could take me. As I made my way through the mass of bodies all scrambling for their bus or track to their homes, I felt a hand reach out from behind and grab my shoulder. Now, this was not something anyone with any sense would do, had they known me.

I turned without even thinking or realizing it and plowed the body behind me yelling, "get your filthy hand off me asshole!" my fist making direct contact with a soft belly.

That belly belonged to a young boy of maybe twelve. He just looked at me eyes bugging and mouthing "why?" but nothing came out of his mouth he just gasped for air.

I stared at him radiating hate from my every pour and got ready to hit him again when suddenly the tall denim clad girl yelled, "hey, Freak, lay off him, dude! It was me not him!"

Everyone in that school knew my name, but no one ever called me by it. I was called Freak and not just because it described how they felt about me, oh no, it was now my unfortunate moniker.

I stopped my arm and fist in mid-air and tore my hateful gaze from this young boy and looked past him to see her standing there with her posse surrounding her as the entire student body struggled past us pushing and chattering. No one even noticed this would be beating about to take place as it was a Friday, and everyone just wanted to get the hell out of there. I did too so I just looked back at the kid one more time dropped my fist and turned and left them all there headed out far away from these weirdos. I did not even bother to look back because I did not give two shits what this was all about, I did not care to find out.

That weekend my mother was strangely nice to me. It was so freaking odd I should have known better but my desire to have someone love me, especially a mother, got the best of me and I let my guard down. A fatal mistake that would haunt me to this very day.

She was so super cool taking me out shopping, letting me watch the forbidden television with her, fixing me dinner, and letting me have all I wanted. Okay, we will stop there for now. You get the picture. It was an awesome weekend. When Monday rolled around, I almost did not bother with my now infamous morbid look but then my mom had one more surprise for me.

As I ate the oatmeal she had made for my breakfast (she actually made me breakfast, wow!), she dropped a brightly wrapped box in front of me. She had bought me the coolest black leather looking pants and a long black trench coat with a pair of fingerless net gloves and wrapped them up as a present. I was beyond in heaven, the most badass black outfit I had ever seen, and expensive to boot. No way I was missing this chance to wear it! So, while she smiled and I hugged her I missed her very cryptic statement, "I wanted to give you something nice enough to be buried in."

I started out the day feeling like a cool character from a comic book as I strutted around. I did catch every eye, but then again, I always did. However, this day I thought it was because they all wished they could be so cool not because I was the school ghoul.

Then it began around the middle of first period class. My stomach began to ache. Then my head began to split. I raised my hand, sure I was going to hurl, and was released to the restroom. I began walking, then running that direction for what was sure to be a photo finish at the commode. I barely made it through the door when the vomit began in force, and I mean force.

I was knocked to my knees as I retched from my very toes over and over again. In fact, I barfed until the very air inside me was coming out, and then blood. My head was swimming as the walls seemed to be breathing in and out. Weakness gripped me as my stomach cramped beyond belief. I finally stopped retching and all I could do was lean back into the wall and moan holding my stomach and praying for death.

I must have passed out because the next thing I knew a girl was standing above me staring at the unfortunate bloody mess I had made on the floor yelling "go get the teacher" to another girl that must have been outside the door where I could not see her. I suppose I had been gone long enough they figured I had cutout, so they sent these girls to confirm it.

I reach up to my aching head and found I was wet everywhere. The sweat was pouring out of me making me look like a drowned (and already dead rat). I was too weak to stand but I did try. I fell over immediately as my stomach griped me and the sensation of razor blades tore through my intestines. I fell to my face, curled up and whined like a dying dog. This pain was beyond hideous.

The teacher arrived and with her help I was walked moaning to the school nurse and put onto a couch as she tried to reach my mother. Of course, she could not be reached. I did not have a fever and I had stopped vomiting, so they continued to let me lay there moaning in agony trying to decide what to do.

I laid there for about two hours in horrid pain before out of nowhere I began to feel better. The sweating stopped and my stomach let go and the razor blades stopped slashing at my guts. My head still mildly pounded, but it was tolerable, so they finally cut me loose with a big dose of Pepto Bismol to go back to class. I had missed most of the day with this very strange attack. The nurse thought maybe I had gotten a case of food poisoning. Well, she was sort of right.

I went back to the bathroom and straightened up the mess I had become with that little drama. I noticed that when I wiped off the ruined make-up to refresh it, I had a slight yellow tinge but whatever. However, the large amount of hair that came out into my brush did cause me to pause. WTF? My investigation of this odd occurrence was interrupted by a voice behind me, "you feeling better"?

I was startled and turned to see the four girls (still in denim) from the pep rally looking at me. The tall one had been the one inquiring as to my health.

"Oh, come on," I thought miserably I was still feeling a bit queasy and in no mood for a bathroom brawl, "can't I catch a damned break today? Really?"

But what I said out loud in a smart-ass voice was, "Looks like I will live, so you can tell everyone to call off the celebration."

I then took my purse and started to walk past them to leave but they blocked my path. Looks like it was going to be a fight after all. I braced myself for the blows and decided to try for the little one and take a chunk of her to hell with me at least.

Instead of beating my ass, the tall one put out her hand as if to shake mine and said, "Hi, I am Jacinda, this is Pat and Norma and this is Gretta. We all took a vote. We think you are too damned cool and would love to have you hang with us at lunch and stuff." as she pointed to the other three girls.

I stood there dumbfounded. I struggled to understand these words she had just said, unsure if it was even English she was speaking. Finally, blinking like I had been stuck in the head, "Excuse me? What did you say?" Surely, I had misheard her. This was not happening. I wondered briefly if Rod Serling from the Twilight Zone was going to step out of one of the bathroom stalls and then it would all make sense.

"I said we think you are a cool chick! Gosh are you retarded? Man, the way you told that bitch Cindy off the other day, and you are so crazy with the makeup and shit. Now that is bad ass!" She said as the other girls all smiled and nodded in agreement.

The buxom girl named Gretta added, "You are like a Graveyard Queen or something and that is truly awesome! I love creepy stuff and baby you are like my idol!" as she looked at me with pure adoration.

Okay, so this was not a joke. Wow, what a strange few days and now what luck to have a chance to have friends, like living ones.

It was a bit too much for my cracked mind to take in so all I did was say, "Yeah, okay, so cool" as I shook her hand. Still expecting for the punchline to come any second.

Instead, the bell rung, and the girls all rushed out the door to get to class. Jacinda was the last out who then turned to say, "catch you tomorrow at lunch, we sit in the back."

I just nodded and watched them leave. When the last one was out of earshot, I finally let out my breath. I had not realized I was holding my breath most of that time. I would hang out with dead folks and lived with the devil herself, but these kids had scared the holy crap out of me. I was grateful to see them go.

Then a chill went down my spine, maybe from the weird illness or maybe it was real fear as I considered that tomorrow I would have to hang out with these people and actually interact. It had been a long time since anyone had an interaction that was not going to result in bruises or a call to the office. I started to mildly panic.

"Oh well," I thought without hope, "once they spend one lunch with me this will be over, so do not fret about it." With that thought I went back to class and the rest of the day went without further incident.

The next day, however, began exactly like the day before. I ate breakfast with my mother who was still unusually calm and went to school bruise free. Halfway through the first class another rush to the bathroom and vomiting from hell. This time I did not pass out and recovered enough to get back to class without another trip to the nurse. This time the razor blades did not stop completely either. I was pretty sick most of the day so by the time lunch arrived I was not about to even consider eating anything.

Despite that, I still staggered to the cafeteria for my date with the denim brigade. I would have been excited to finally have friends, but I assumed still it was a joke and I would get there to find no one there or worse a group of cruelly laughing teens at my stupidity of actually showing up. Either way I went if only to prove to myself that I was never going to fit in with the living.

I saw them before they saw me and was in awe that they were actually there. Then Jacinda saw my unmistakable face standing there in disbelief she stood up and motioned for me to join them pointing to the empty chair. I looked about the room and saw the other students glaring at me from their food trays, and heard whispers like, "I thought she only ate dead people" as snickers broke out from here and there. I stood straight as possible, held my head up high and kept my eyes on that empty chair as I traveled fast as I could trying to ignore the insults around me.

"Hey Freak!" Jacinda said with a smile as she chewed on a piece of whatever horrid lunch lady concoction was on her tray, "We thought you may not show up. Heard you got sick again this morning. You are not pregnant, are you?"

The group all looked at each other when she said that and then back at me and started laughing. The one called Pat (she was the Jacinda bad hair wannabe) piped up, "Uhmmm, you got to have sex to get preggers, Jacinda and unless a corpse can still man up, I doubt Freak is going to be having any pups anytime soon."

That made the whole group break into riotous laughter, well except me. I did not find that funny.

"Fuck you," I said, and got up to leave.

"Freak! Hey, chic calm down Pat was just funning you, it is okay. Come on, we know you could have anyone you wanted!" Jacinda said as she elbowed Pat. "Do not leave. We josh each other all the time, we do not mean nothing by it."

My stomach was rolling again, and I did not want to make that walk of shame back out for a bit, so I overlooked the insult and sat back down.

"Hi, I am Tom," said the bowlegged boy of the group as he extended his hand toward me, "I love your jacket. Where did you get it?" He was definitely trying to change the subject.

I just shrugged and wished I had not come to lunch. I had no idea what to do with these people or what to say. In reality, I did not even like them. Until that day I did not even know they existed.

There was an uneasy silence and then they attempted to ask me a lot of stupid questions like where was I from, where did I live, and why did I dress like I did. I did not answer them but just shrugged or glared. Let's say I was neither a seasoned conversationalist nor what may be called a "sharer."

Finally, they realized I was happy to sit there but unwilling to participate so they started to talk among themselves and let me be. I sat there listening as they gossiped about other kids, talked about their complaints of their home lives and talked of TV shows I did not watch. All in all, my first real experience with kids my age went rather painlessly. I did not have to do a thing, just hold down the chair and lurk. Now, lurking that was something at which I was really good.

I was sure as the lunch bell rang that would be the end of this little experiment but then again, a surprise as Jacinda the obvious leader of this clique said, "see you tomorrow Freak."

With that they all got up and turned in their trays still yapping to each other like this was just a natural thing. They even all waved goodbye to me as they left together, and I still sat there watching them go.

My stomach was killing me so I skipped the next class to hit the can and bark out the names of every state into the porcelain Goddess.

For the next two weeks at school, I sat in that same chair at lunch and listened the bitching and tales of the denim brigade. I did not do any talking. I had nothing to say really to be honest.

Every day, I had stomach issues that now were not just happening in the morning but showing up all through the day. They had even started to wake me up at night more than my chronic nightmares were. I was getting thinner than I already was and my clothing was starting to hang off me. Not surprising since I was never hungry much anymore. I also had to start to wear a hat as my hair was falling out at a startling rate. It was starting to thin so bad in some places I was nearly bald in spots. My make-up was hiding a yellow pallor more than bruises. My fingernails had oddly started to turn black without nail polish. It seemed like I was always fatigued, and I started falling asleep in class a lot. It seemed like somehow the life was slowly draining from me, if you could call what I had a life.

My mother had gone back to her very hateful self. So much for that respite. She was more aggressive than ever as she was very pissed at me, but for what this time she was not making real clear. All she would say is that I was stubborn and "was taking too long." I just could not do anything right at all. Her blows were more unbearable than ever. I was really thinking it may be time to try to run away, again.

Then finally only three weeks into this change from the routine came the weekend of enlightenment and my discovery of another aspect that would help cement my path to the Gothic lifestyle. I was about to learn the most painful lesson I had learned about life since my discovery of death. That you should never trust the living.

That Friday began like every day had for the last three weeks but at lunch, when I went to the lunchroom, I saw the denim brigade. Only they were no longer denim, they were all dressed from head to toe in black. Each member even Jacinda wore an ankh proudly from their necks and as I approached, I nearly tripped over my jaw which was hanging to the ground in shock.

They all smiled as I sat down still slack jawed trying to understand this strange turn of events. Gretta quickly informed me that they liked my style, so they had all voted to go "black", and that today after school they were going to come hang out with me at my cemetery...

Becoming a Gothic life styler did not happen easily or quickly. There were many twists and turns on the journey and since there was no template back then for such a thing as Goth, it had to happen naturally (or unnaturally, you could say).

Did you have a best friend or friends in middle or high school? Are you still friends with them today? If not, what happened? That will be it for me until the next chapter as the sun will shortly rise and the coffin calls.

Chapter 7: Pretty Poison

Poisoning: signs and symptoms can mimic other conditions. Some signs and symptoms of poisoning may include:

. Breath that smells like chemicals, such as gasoline or paint thinner
· Profuse sweating
· Vomiting
· Difficulty breathing
· Drowsiness/Dizziness-feeling of malaise (bad feeling all over your body)
· Hair-loss
· Yellowing/redness or burns of eyes or skin
· Intense body pain
· Confusion or other altered mental status
· Coma
· Death

I sat there still unsure I was hearing this correct and questioning my last shed of sanity as well. "Did you say you guys are coming to hang out in the cemetery with me after school? Why would you want to do that?" My mind was whirling like a top and as of the late I was not sure I had not slipped into some weird rabbit hole.

"Oh yeah! Freak, we are just dying to hang with you and see what you are up to in that old boneyard. It will be a blast! Tom will bring the music and pizza!" Gretta blurted appearing very excited as if this was a debutant party that they were all headed to after school rather than a dank and dingy graveyard.

I had been feeling even more horrid that day than the last several weeks and was in no real mood to argue. I did nothing in the cemetery but sulk and wish for things I was never going to have like a normal life. So, whatever, if they wanted to be bored out of their skulls, they had picked the perfect place for it. I simply nodded with an obvious defeat too fatigued to argue this point further. It was a free country after all.

So, the group planned on meeting me at my favorite haunt around dusk (what? dusk!) and while I wanted to complain I knew that it was useless. They did not have any idea of what kind of trouble getting caught in a cemetery after dark could bring both from the cops and quite possibly from the residents of that hallowed place. I again just nodded again in agreement while wondering how I was going to get away from the house to even be there to keep these idiots from getting caught by the law. Bringing music? Now that was sure to raise the alarm. In the end, I was out voted anyway so I just kept all of it to myself.

I noticed that during this very odd debate and discussion Tom, who was sitting next to me, kept sniffing the air and then his jacket and then his food. It was funny at first but now was becoming annoying. I was not the only one who noticed.

Jacinda shot him an angry look, "what is your damage dude?"

He looked at her seemingly apologetic and said, "don't you smell that? Like a chemical smell or something. It is driving me nuts! What is that smell!"

"Your upper lip, douche bag" said Norma laughing, "maybe try brushing your teeth sometimes."

The whole group started laughing even Tom, everyone except me. I knew that smell he was talking about. It was me. I had noticed that at times in the last few weeks I was emitting a strange chemical smell like a chemical cleaner or something. I thought maybe it was some weird hormone thing or perhaps I had sat in something and somehow absorbed it into my skin. It was not all the time but when I did catch a whiff, it was strong. It was so crazy that I had convinced myself it was in my head. Tom noticing it too made me nervous, it was indeed real. I now needed to find out the answers to his questions, where was it coming from and why. I think deep inside I already knew. I just could not face it; the possibility was too horrific even for me.

However, as lunch ended and the kids took off as usual, I had to hit the bathroom again to vomit for what seemed like the thousandth time. I watched in horror as the blood, with a yellow thick substance, poured out with my measly lunch food. I vomited so hard it came out of my nose and made it bloody yellow too. As the cramping relented and I stopped dry heaving I lay back from my latest loss of substance and thought wildly of my mom's oatmeal and the weird taste. I could taste the metal from the can that it came from, wait, oatmeal does not come in a can.

I felt the tears begin to well up as the razor blades in my guts began to rip through me as they had been doing daily for the last few weeks and I saw my mother's smile and finally heard her words, all of them. "Oh, my God! She poisoned me!"

Panic sat in. I grabbed both sides of my balding head and more hair fell to the ground which really set me into a terror. "What am I going to do? Am I dying? Oh God! Oh God!" I yelled out loud. Thankfully, no one else was in that bathroom or they would have thought someone was losing their mind, because in truth someone was, me.

I rocked back and forth crying and retching for what must have been an hour before I could get a grip on myself. Questions whirled around my head like poltergeists What to do? Who could help? Would they even believe me? What if she decides to finish the job if they do not?

Then out of nowhere, I suddenly felt a calm come over me. I reached deep inside myself and found the strength to get off that floor and made it to the sink and looked at my reflection. I was so haggard. There was a hollow eyed, balding, and yellow with streaming white face staring back. I spoke to this horrid creature staring back at me, "get a grip on yourself. Now first go to the library. You are not dead so whatever she has done surely can be undone. Second, do not eat or drink anything she gives you. Third, after you leave tonight never go back idiot. She is going to kill you if you do."

I washed that face off and reapplied my make-up thicker than ever. I could not afford to have anyone see how yellow I had become. Even the whites of my eyes were tinged yellow. Truth is, I was more ghoulish without the make-up these days. Once I had cleaned myself up, I gathered my strength and headed for the library. I grabbed every medical, anatomy and chemistry book I could find and began my research. My time was running out.

I finally determined it had to be household chemicals of a type unknown and that my yellow pallor meant my liver was in big trouble. I also determined that the damage was likely fatal from which, somehow, I found a bit of peace. Liver failure did not seem like such a bad way to go compared to how I expected to die.

By the time the final bell rung, I had decided based, on everything I had read, that I was a dead kid walking. No hope of survival. Therefore, I may as well go hang out with the closest thing I ever had to friends in the only place that had been a peaceful home. She had finally gotten her wish and I decided to go out trying to have fun and not grant her the pleasure of watching her little plan come to fruition.

I chuckled as I closed the last book and prepared to walk to the cemetery. "Well, not too many can say they went to the cemetery on foot willingly, then waiting for the ride in a box." I thought both bitterly and with a tad bit of gallows humor.

I began my walk to the bone yard and what I assumed would my new forever home but I mostly staggered. I was feeling very ill indeed. I had to stop often and just sit down wherever I was, panting and nauseous. My heart was doing acrobatics in my chest, and I often felt I could not catch my breath no matter how slow I walked. I would rest, then shake my head and chuckle as I continued on my journey.

I was taking my impending death a bit too calmly. Why I did not go for help, I will never really understand. I think deep inside I was ready to end the pain and had lost hope that life would ever be anything more than an endless parade of loneliness, hate from my mother, and despair. Maybe it was the mental changes the books had warned me my failing liver would cause. Whatever the real reason, I pulled it together one last time and with a great deal of courage I went to meet my old friend Mr. Death with a smile. At least I did have the hope that tonight I would finally have friends and dare I say a good time just hanging out and being alive, or whatever I was at this point.

I found my way the cemetery with a belly full of razors and a heady mix of terror at my predicament and excitement at having my very first guests over to my "home." It was very early yet, but the dusk would come soon enough, as it always does, and I had nothing else to do but wait. I threw up several more times that nasty yellow crap. I hid the contents under the many leaves left by lazy graveyard caretakers. No need for my guests to believe me an untidy housekeeper. I was just so tired, so I sat down cross legged in quiet repose near a fresher grave in case the cops happened by as I slipped off to the realm of the Sandman.

When I awoke the sun was setting and for once I had caught a break, no cops had come snooping. At first, I was disoriented but that passed quickly as my stomach cramped to remind me of the reality of my situation. A crisp cool breeze was blowing, and it chilled me as it licked at my body damp from unnaturally heavy sweating. Unnatural, because I felt like I was going to freeze to death!

"Oh shit, I am sweating like a hog again" I thought with disgust. I had been doing a lot of that lately.

I stood up and waited for my dizziness to pass, another thing that was happening a lot lately, while I did my best to fix my appearance. My thinning mane of hair was sticking up everywhere so I pulled the hood of my shirt over my black knit cap and tied it tight so it would not slide off. No need to have anyone see that mess. I decided to sit on a nearby bench and wait for my "friends" nearer to the gate. It was almost showtime, that is if they even showed up.

The darkness spread across the world that evening like a blanket as I waited there on the bench patiently. I thought of Anubis, who came from the land of sand and bright colors as I held my pathetic tin ankh in my fingerless gloved hand. I wondered if he would really come for me, or was there really a Heaven and Hell instead? I finally decided, there must be a Heaven because there sure was a Hell, I had seen it. That made me smile, nowhere to go from here but up, right?

Then my thoughts were broken by the sounds of laughter in the distance and several voices. It surely was my denim, errrr, dark brigade. Indeed, it was them. They were walking towards the gate, and I could just make out the contours of what I assumed was Toms' bowlegged appearance through the thick darkness. I hoped they brought some light; it was cloudy and without illumination this would be an awkward group meeting.

My question was quickly answered as I saw a flashlight come on near the barely visible image of Tom. He shined it through the gate as they all carefully walked inside, all five of them. I was off to the left of the gate, so I stood up and went to greet my guests.

I have no idea why I did not alert them to my presence, but I stood there silently till all five walked right past me not even noticing my figure in the darkness. When the last one, Pat walked by, I fell in step behind them quietly following. They were bitching about the breeze and looking for a good place to set up the battery operated boom box Tom had brought and I saw Gretta carrying a pizza box. Pizza, my stomach lurched slightly at the smell of food. I was sure I would hurl again.

They chose a group of single above ground mausoleums to park their little party and when they all started to set up Gretta turned around and saw me in the murky darkness, white pallor with hollow black eyes and silent. She let out a scream and that sent the entire group as well as Gretta running blindly in every direction. I had forgotten my physical appearance. Which may I say had I thought of that, I would have realized how unnerving that may be to see right behind you in a creepy graveyard at night.

They scattered like roaches when you turn on the kitchen light and all, but Pat fell down tripping over the sticks, broken headstones or their own feet in their wild attempts to flee the ghoul.

I realized with horror what I had accidentally done and yelled out, "hey, it is me! It is me!" I could see my final chance to be normal (normal? really?) slipping away as they continued to fall and flee leaving all their shit on the mausoleums in front of me.

Finally, Tom, who had fallen down completely, figured out that a ghoul would not say hey it is me and he yelled out, "It is Freak! Everyone cool it! Come back!" He started laughing.

I saw the shadows all stop and start to come back my direction. Tom was the first one to come into the light of the flashlights now abandoned on the ground. I could make out his smile and his high pitched but jovial laugh was unmistakable, it even made me smile a bit and chuckle. It was pretty funny. They all made their way back a bit shaken and disheveled but no serious injury from their cemetery sprint.

The girls, however, were not so easy spirited about the little unintentional scare and I got a bit of a lecture about "being cruel to cause heart attacks like that. " Whatever.

Everyone sat down and Tom set up the boom box and put in a cassette tape. I never got to listen to music, so this was quite a treat. As Tom and the girls argued over the pizza slice sizes, I was in awe of the amazing music and voice emitting from that machine. Tom noticed me slowly moving closer to the boom box, enamored with the sound of what I could only describe as the sound of my soul.

"Yeah, pretty cool band, huh? You like this music? Yeah, I figured you would. This one is "a song called Alice by a group called Sisters of Mercy. I also have some Ozzy if you are interested. That is more my speed you know. Not into this depressive stuff as much." Tom continued to blather on about how hard it was to get this on cassette, and he had to record a mixed tape from his extended play records to get any good "tunes."

I did not really hear him as I was whisked away on the wings of this voice in the darkness and somehow, I felt warm and hopeful that somewhere out there were people who did understand the feeling of being on the outside looking in. I closed my eyes (they were burning anyway) and listened with my now irregularly beating heart taking every word into myself letting it envelope me, caressing my soul like the soft hand of a lover in the night. As the song ended, I opened my eyes feeling alive for the first time in such a long time I could think of nothing but having that song play without pause until the end of time, never wanting that feeling to leave me.

However, Tom was impatient for me to hear his favorite singer, this Ozzy Osbourne person. He was excited about an album called Bark at the Moon. I listened as Tom conducted to a very catchy song named the same, but it was Waiting for Darkness that I liked better. That one made sense to me.

All this time Tom and I had gotten so wrapped up in the music box that we had forgotten the other members of this ragtag group.

"Hey Tom, what you doing dude? You got a crush or something here? You need to back off and stick to the plan man. Turn that shit off, no one wants to hear your creepy ass music." Jacinda's voice broke both Tom and I from our deep and entertaining, I must add, musical conversation.

"Wait, there is a plan? What plan?" I thought. I looked quizzically at Jacinda, but she just sat on that moss covered mausoleum glaring at me.

Tom turned off the boom box, picked it up and hauled it off into the darkness back toward the gate. I was most unhappy to see the music leaving and I felt the mood of the group had strangely changed. The pizza box laid on the ground empty and the girls were apparently sated with food so now what, entertainment? But they had just sent the music to far to be of any use. I felt a bit of fear start to make biscuits down my spine. What was happening?

All the girls were just glaring at me, and they surrounded me too as I had gotten into the middle of the group trying to get closer to the music earlier. I did not like how this was going. Tom returned and nodded at Jacinda.

"So, Freak, pony up. Where is it?" Jacinda said with a bit of hatred in her voice.

I had no idea what she was talking about, so I just shrugged and said, "Huh? Where is what?"

"Oh, come on Freak, we shared now your turn. Cough up the drugs you are doing and share. What is it Heroine, Coke, or is it Dust? That is what friends do, they share!" She said sternly as the others all nodded and looked at each other.

Drugs? Was she kidding? I did not do drugs at all, nor did I drink. That crap made people crazy, look at my mom! No way I would even consider having them around me much less do them. I suddenly realized they assumed that because I looked like a morbid nightmare, I had to be strung out on something wild.

"Oh! No, you got me wrong! I don't do drugs and I don't drink alcohol either." I tried to force a little laugh at their mistake even though in reality I was pretty offended. I could tell Jacinda was not buying it.

"You are expecting us to believe you come out here and hang out straight? No, you don't. And you are always sick and skinny, I would think it is some pretty hard-core shit but okay I will bite. It's Maryjane, right? You a stoner? I am not going to ask again, get the shit and let's get this party started. Did you really think we came out here to hang out with a psycho like you except to share your stash?" She said now starting to stand up and walk toward me.

My heart started to speed up trying to keep an irregular rhythm as real fear started to flow through me. I was far too weak and sick for a fight, and I did not have any drugs, so this was not going to go as I had hoped. I could feel my face heating up and my vision started to blur with tears.

"I swear I do not do drugs! I would give it all to you if I had them, but I do not do them!" I plead now trying to get up to run but my knees were failing me, and the dizziness kept me glued to that spot.

Jacinda jumped on me and grabbed me by my hooded collar. She was yards bigger than me and outweighed me by at least one hundred pounds (I was only about 76lbs). She picked me up like a toy and began to shake me. She screamed in my face, "Cry all you want, Freak! We all know you are a fucking liar! Give us the drugs or we will make you wish you were never born!" (Ha! she was far too late to do that!)

I felt my stomach lurch, she kept shaking me and I was oh, so dizzy. The next thing I knew the yellow horror spewed from my mouth all over her and me. She dropped me immediately and I was on my knees retching air and gasping, fearful my bladder would not hold against the force.

"You stupid fucking bitch!" Jacinda yelled at my helpless form as I violently hurled trying to breath but finding it near impossible. "Oh my God, what were we thinking you, Freak! You probably do eat dead bodies, what is this nasty shit all over me? Oh my God, this stinks! Is this rotten flesh?" She was freaking out as were her friends who now were surrounding her trying to help her wipe off the ghoulish mess I made of her.

I couldn't help it, but I started to chuckle, then I started to laugh. It was painful and between attempts to retch it was very obvious that I found her horror quite funny. It was funny. She was a stupid person, assuming that drugs are the only thing that can make a person weird. People like her and the others are just as life damaging as any drug known to humankind. The fact that I had paid her back for threatening me, albeit in a most foul way, made me laugh.

"Okay, enough of this noise" Pat said, "Let's get the hell out of here. This weirdo is not going to tell us and is probably sick because she is out drugs anyway. I want to go home this place is freaking creepy, Jacinda!" She was clutching herself and looking around.

"Yeah, screw this!" Jacinda said and then turn toward me and keeping a bit of distance she said, "I hope you die." She then swung back her foot and kicked the holy terror right out of me, making contact with my right side.

I fell over in sheer agony. Now I really could not breath. As the group left each girl came forward and kicked me wherever she could land her foot while making some derogatory statement. They left me there just barely still a bit more alive than the residents below me. Only Tom did not kick. He stopped and looked at me with what seemed to be pity, but he did not help me and left with the others.

I now was in serious trouble, the struggle to either live or die had begun before this little bad experience. Their blows had hastened my most desperate situation to a real emergency. I could not breath and the darkness was spinning around me in an unrealistic vortex. I struggled to stay conscious.

I felt like a hole had opened deep inside of me and it was pulling me into it down deeper and deeper. If I closed my eyes I would fall in and be gone forever. I listened to the night and could hear a train in the distance coming, and for the life of me I could not recall there being any railroads close to this cemetery. I was in so much pain, the razors were cutting me apart inside and my eyes felt as if they had caught fire. It seemed like I was breathing ice picks into my lungs and my heart felt like it was pounding with a hammer trying to get out of my chest.

Then a light spread across the darkness, and I thought, it must be Anubis coming for me. I felt like I was floating in the air but not really floating because there was a grip on my arms and legs holding me up. The light was so strong and then I imagined I was seeing Anubis, but he was wearing a blue shirt and had a mustache. He said, "Hold on kiddo, the ambulance is coming."

I was happy to hear that, but I told Anubis that it could not get to us because it was stuck behind the train I could hear coming. Red and blue lights sparkled like fireworks and I was so thirsty, suddenly water was pouring from the sky as I heard Sisters of Mercy sing Alice to me from the headstones. I thought I may drown in that water.

Anubis had brought all his friends and they were in white not gold clothes. I smiled at them as they all came to say hello to me, funny I though the afterlife would be brighter but only the red and blue fireworks lit up the darkness. They asked me why I was here. I knew this was a test, there is always a test to get in. I told them I died because my mother poisoned me, and I was glad they had finally come to take me to the afterlife. Anubis's friends in white shirts put a mask on my mouth and lifted me onto a slab.

One of them stabbed my arm and I was flying through the air as Anubis walked beside my floating slab telling me "Everything is going to be okay, I am here" but then the darkness came as the train finally pulled into the station.

Did you ever have friends that only hung out with you to get your drugs, or did you only hang out with others just to get drugs? What happened to make you give it up and live life without it?

Chapter 8: Born to Lose

I awoke many weeks later. The doctors had induced a coma to help heal my body from the poison that had been wrecking havoc unchecked for weeks. I have no memory of it only that Anubis had finally come and then I was back in the world of the living. A white world full of whirling machines and smiling nurses asking me stupid questions like, did I know where I was. Why hell no, I did not.

I was finally told my mother was in jail and not getting out anytime soon. She had admitted to the poisoning with questioning. That was great news! I was very happy to hear that indeed. I would never see her again (and nearly never have since). The next bit of luck was that the medication had saved my life. Also, great to hear.

However, there is no such thing as something good for free. The bad news, I was going into a foster home. The worst news was that my mom would not tell them what she used and they could not be sure of it. So, there was significant and permanent damage done to several organs including my liver while they searched for the right antidote. It was a very close call and only a few more hours would have ended my pathetic life.

Despite that, the doctors assured me that I would live a mostly normal life, as long as I never touched the hooch or any drugs ever. I had to be very careful with what I put into my body for the rest of my life. My poor old liver would not handle it well and no sense in pushing it any further. The rest of the damage was more cosmetic.

I had no hair at all not even eyelashes (the hair on my head would never grow back fully to this day). So, a kind nurse bought me my first wig and I learned to make it look pretty natural. My eyebrows never grew back either but thankfully the eyelashes did even if a bit thin and shitty. Cannot have it all.

That said, I was barely fifteen, not a good thing for a teenager to be bald and with the reputation I had I could almost feel the bullying of the future from my hospital bed, it rang so loud in my head. I also would have to deal soon with the denim brigade who by accident had saved my life.

They made so much racket that the cops were called. They had barely left when the police came by to find my dying body lying there where they had left me. I was grateful they saved me, but angry they did not mean to do so. Jacinda said she wanted me to die, and die I nearly had.

Over the recovery time, I planned in my head how to handle all of them and let me say I was not going to be giving any thank you hugs. I burned hot and cold as slowly the symptoms of the poisoning relented. It took three months. Finally, I stopped sweating and the razor blades went dull and the doctors proudly announced I was ready to be released back into the world of colors. I was really sick of the white, so I got myself ready with my plan for the battle with the kids at school and the denim brigade.

However, I never got that chance. The Guardian Ad Litem decided that the trauma from the whole town being aware of the situation surrounding my near-death experience was detrimental for my "adjustment back into society." Huh? So, I was shipped into foster care "to a sister state." Can you say sweep our fuck up for missing this very severe case of abuse/neglect under the rug? I thought you could.

Off I went on a journey into the unknown, moving yet again. Oh well, a new town, a new chance and now with mom gone I was sure it was going to be awesome this time! I had a chance to start this all over. I decided I would make my new parents love me by being the daughter of their dreams. I would be perfect and now finally I would be accepted, have friends, and live in the sun. It took a death to cure my death, who would have thought it?

I threw away my black clothes and face paint. I swore never to wear black again for the rest of my life! I also happily accepted the colorful new outfits the nurses brought to me from their own homes: donations to the teenager who smiled a lot and seemed so happy even though she was sitting in a hospital bed due to her own mother poisoning her. I was sort of adored by the staff for that very sunny disposition when I should have been angry/depressed, or so they thought.

They were wrong to expect that of course. They never met my mother. If they had, they would have seen this coming, as I did. I was full of joy that she had lost the battle I was so certain she was going to win I could not stop smiling. Every second I could breathe without being in constant fear of pain was a dream come true. Everyone was so nice to me and seemed truly happy to see me too. It was everything I had ever wanted. I even thought a couple of times maybe Anubis did come, and this was the afterlife, the same only better, just like they promised it would be.

It was with great hope that as I was discharged for my new life I willingly went to my destiny. Bye-bye darkness, cemeteries and morbid shit, I was on my way to normal town!!! Hell yeah!

A full day of driving and half a night brought me to my new home. When we arrived the caseworker and I were given the tour of the house by another caseworker that was taking over my "case" for this state. The "foster parents" were still in town buying food for me (cool, for me?). The house was single level with a slight two steps to a part that was mildly elevated. There were only two bedrooms as this foster home was called a "therapeutic foster home." A term which I was going to find out soon meant "troubled child case."

Therapeutic homes could not have but one or two foster kids at a time as these were special cases requiring much attention, but that is okay because the money is great for families that can handle such cases. The state pays a lot more for us "troubled kids" then the usual foster kids. This home had just become available and was only qualified for one at a time. So, I did not have to share a room and the parents would be all mine, yay!

As my original caseworker handed over my case files to the new one a station wagon pulled up in the driveway. A dark-haired man wearing a button up long-sleeved shirt and a thin woman in a very proper dress got out. The couple appeared to be in their late fifties, a bit older than I expected but I was not picky at all. They smiled at the workers and at me. This must be them! They all walked up and shook each other's hands. I stood there barely able to keep my excitement down. It was like I needed to pee I was so thrilled. They were so proper, not like my sloppy mom who acted the way she dressed, nasty.

The man looked at me and said, "welcome home young lady" his smile was huge!

I blushed and looked at the ground with a shy smile like a girl who had just been told she was pretty.

Then the lady asked, "So, does the house work for you? Do you like your room?" she was smiling at me too with what seemed like pride in her eyes.

"Yes, ma'am," I said very politely also smiling, but thinking, "are you kidding? A box would be okay at this point just don't send me back to that pig of a woman who birthed me."

The caseworker handed me off to this kindly looking man and woman like handing over the keys to a new car with not much more fanfare.

I did not mind as they discussed me in whispers, and I was told to wait in the living room. Then they returned and the woman said that it was late, and I should go to bed and we would talk in the morning, get to know each other. I agreed as I was beat and ready to get on with the rest of my life. The past was dead, time to go forward and hopefully, I would forget it in time.

The next morning came abruptly and early. I awoke to the lady in my face yelling for me to get up that "idle hands are the devil's playground" as she ripped the blankets from me. Now that was quite a shock, but I got up quickly and got dressed in the clothes I had arrived in as she went through the few bags I brought with me. I wanted to ask her why, but I dared not as I was so confused. That sweet lady that was all smiles last night had the face of disgust now.

She ripped all my things donated by the nurses including my wig out and threw them into the floor.

"Where are they?" She had emptied the bag and turned to me yelling in my face, "tell me right now! I will not tolerate drugs in this house, do you hear me!" Her anger was very evident.

"Drugs?" I was very confused and a bit miffed about this subject being brought up again, "No ma'am, I do not do drugs."

She stood there and put her hands on her hips clearly not believing me. "Well, we shall see about that. I know your kind! Let me make this clear, I will find them and when I do you will be very sorry you ever dared to fool with me!"

I was ready to cry, I confess. Why was she doing this? I wanted to plead my case but all I could do is nod that I understood. That satisfied her and she went back to smiling as she could tell I was very frightened. She reached down and picked up my wig and looked at it (a tangled mess now) and laughed.

"You look like a freak. When you are dressed come to breakfast." She said then threw it at me and strolled out chuckling and shutting the door behind her.

I was stunned. What just happened? What did that caseworker say to them? I had been close to crying but now the waterworks came in force. As I brushed out the wig tears streaming, I wondered what to do to fix this apparent misunderstanding. I was going to have to just wait this out was all I could come up with. In time, they would see that I was a good kid, and I would be so awesome they would love me. I also planned on punching that caseworker from my old home out if I ever saw her again. With a quiet resolve I left the room for breakfast with my new family now a bit less giddy and certainly a lot more apprehensive. Once again, things were not going the way they were supposed to go.

At the table sat the man, at the head of the table may I correct. The lady was serving the food and a chair against the back wall in the dining room sat with a bowl in front of it. The lady saw me and shot a glare then with her eyes pointed at that empty chair. I went immediately to it and sat down quietly. The man was glaring at me too. No one said a word and uncomfortable does not quiet describe how I was feeling. It was like I was a fly stuck in a web and the spider is just looking at me, but not moving but there is no doubt the end is coming.

I looked away and into the bowl, oh no, oatmeal (fuck). I felt my stomach lurch and whine. The lady sat down as I sat there terrified of that bowl now not giving two shits, about these two strange people. No way I was eating this. The lady came around and sat at the other end of the table.

"Let us bow our head to pray." The man's voice startled me from my terror gaze on that bowl of death food. "Dear Lord, please look after this home and keep your children safe from the demon in their mists. May you please forgive her of her numerous transgressions and abominations in your sight. May she feel the hell fire and beg you for your mercy. Help your son and daughter find the strength to overlook this Jezebel's past and guide her back to your fold with a hard heart to her pleas for benevolence. Remind her that the pain and pleasures of this world is temporary, and the cost of sin is eternal torment. It is your will that pain separate the chaff from the wheat. In your name we thank you for your bounty. Blessed be to God, Amen. "I remember this because it was said so often in case you wonder. He then looked up from his prayer and started eating.

As I listened to this talk with the God person, I felt the room empty of air. My knees turned to water, I could not feel my hands and my butt puckered trying to grip the seat. That was a feeling I knew all too well, horror.

"Uh oh, did he just say only pain can separate the chaff from the wheat." I thought as I tried to calm my ass down, literately. Somehow, I assumed I was chaff. Something told me this was going to make my old life seem like a ride on the tilt-o-whirl compared to the wicked roller coaster of death to which I had just graduated. I was sitting in that coaster cart at the top of the drop. and I knew I had only a few more moments to try to prepare for what was sure to be one hell of a drop.

"She wears a wig, Bob" the woman said with a hollow voice not even looking up from her plate. "Must have been very nasty drugs indeed. Her mother is in prison, so she is a born loser. I think maybe we should pass on this one."

"Settle down, Mary. God has battled Satan and won. We can surely do the same. Have faith." He said now setting his hateful eyes on me, "Eat what God has provided with his providence and be grateful."

I looked at that bowl. I couldn't eat this no matter what they try. I just got better and now I was pretty sure they may decide to "separate" me from my life like my mom tried.

I pushed the bowl away and said, "Thank you, but I am not hungry."

Within seconds of my words, the bright lights swirled before my eyes and my back teeth were rocking in the back of my throat. I felt my neck go forward with my head which seemed very heavy all the sudden. The table was getting closer as I made contact with my forehead. This man had reached out and hit me in the back of the head with his open hand and he was a big guy. I did not even bother to try to catch myself and just slid to the floor.

He jumped up sending his chair flying backwards and stood above me, "You spit on what we offer to you with a loving heart! Get out of my sight!"

The lady had rounded the corner of the table and she grabbed me by my legs and started dragging me back to my bedroom hurling insults about everything from my genetic make up to the disgust my very appearance brought to their happy home. I just let her drag me. I was so confused and scared I did not dare to make this worse.

Once she reached my room she stopped and told me to get up. I did and got ready to run. She out thought me and grabbed the back of my shirt and pulled me into the room in front of her. With her foot in my backside, she pushed me inside and slammed the door. I landed on my knees and thought, "oh, forget this noise!"

I got up and plowed through the door and the man was there waiting and he grabbed me, and I was tossed back inside. This time they used a chair to keep me inside. I pounded on the door begging to be let out. There was a small window but too small to get out of, I had already checked.

"There is a bible in the dresser. You would do well to find your comfort there, girl. You will find none from us." I heard the man say through the door.

Then I heard them leave down the hall. I pounded on that door all day. Nope, I was stuck, and this was very fucked up and let me say, I was less than happy. I finally stopped and found nothing to do. So, I got that bible out and began reading it. If I was going to survive this shit, I had better find out what was expected of me. Apparently, this was the manual.

Chapter 9: Mary had a Little Damned Lamb

As the night came, I had made it past the first chapter called Genesis, then skipped to one called Numbers where this dude begat this dude and on and on (geez a family tree, really?) and finally back to the chapter called Exodus. I paid close attention and through the night I read on about a vengeful God waiting to punish the wicked. I had plenty of time, that door was not budging and when the morning light slowly poked thru the tiny window, I was really in need of a nap and a pee.

I knew I had a lot more to learn but if I did not get to the bathroom soon there was a lot more to worry about than not getting to the next chapter. So, with much dread, I calmly knocked on the door and politely asked if I may use the restroom, please.

I heard steps coming and I almost pissed myself right there wondering if that would not just have been a wiser choice. The door came open and Mary stood there looking at me sternly down her hawkish nose with those steel grey eyes of hers.

"Did you foul up this room? I will not tolerate incontinence in this house." She was sniffing the air. (seriously?)

"No ma'am. May I please use the restroom?" I really needed to go, and she was about to get knocked down if she said no.

She did not say no but moved aside to let me thru. I expected her to smack me as I passed her. I winced and prepared for the assault, but it did not come. She let me go by without protest of any kind. She was looking at the open bible on the floor with a smugness that, to be honest, made me want to punch her out.

The bathroom was right next to my new bedroom, so I was able to get to business without losing my dignity thankfully. I could hear her in my room making racket. She was going thru my meager belongings yet again. What the hell was with her and the drug obsession? I chuckled as I imagined she maybe thought Moses had come to me in the night thru the tiny window to deliver me a big bag of coke instead of out of bondage from old Pharaoh.

When I was done with my call of mother nature, I opened the bathroom door to Mary standing there like a nightmare. She pointed down the hall and told me to get to breakfast. Oh boy, I felt as if I were a record with a scratch in it: the needle of the record player hitting me over and over forcing a repeat over and over, unable to get past the skip.

I walked into the dining room, there was Bob and, of course, that empty chair with a bowl in front of it. I thought wildly, "Just run, damn you!" but I could not get my legs to listen to my pleas.

I sat down and Bob and Mary bowed their head while he repeated the same nasty prayer word for word that I was now very offended by. I bowed my head too but mainly to look in the bowl. Corn Flakes, thank God! I almost sighed my relief out loud. I was not ready to spend another day in the room with that book, an empty stomach, and a headache.

When the prayer ended Bob and Mary began to eat in silence and I followed suit. I was a bit nervous as I was going to be for years to come eating food, I had not seen prepared, but I thought better to die of poison than to be continually dragged down a hallway by your feet every day. When everyone was finished, I was told to clean the table and wash the dishes, which I did happily and quietly. Nothing ugly was said to me. I was beginning to think I still had a shot at making this work.

Today was Saturday. After I had cleaned up all the breakfast mess, Mary came into the kitchen and calmly explained that tomorrow, I would be attending church with Bob and her. I was to keep my mouth shut and learn. I nodded that I would do that. She then told me I was a Pentecostal now, so I was very lucky to have a chance at redemption. I had to agree with her there, at least on the lucky for redemption part. As for the Pentecostal part, that was a foreign thing. Against my better judgement I made the mistake of asking, what was a Pentecostal.

Someone once said there are no stupid questions. Well, that asshole is a liar. Apparently, there is at least one and I had found it. Mary let out a loud gasp and then few into a self-righteous rage. I will not go into this little dramatic display other than to say it resulted in a call out for assistance from Bob and a quick trip (push really) back to my bedroom. I was sat on the bed told not to get up while Bob came in and preached to his congregation of two, Mary and my unfortunate ass.

"Oh shit, he is a preacher." My mind whirled as I swear my soul was taking flight trying to abandon me to my fate. I could actually feel that part of me was trying like hell to find a place to hide. This was bad, really bad. A preacher of a religion I knew nothing about, and worse, I was allegedly already damned according to Bob.

For what? Being born. Well, okay he had a point there, but really what was this other crap he is talking about. My heart started to skip again as I silently hoped that prayer worked for damned people. I prayed that I would die right there as Bob went on for another hour non-stop and I was so tired. I had not slept all night.

Miserably I also realized no one would help me. This dude is a man of God, and I am well, I am nothing at all. As I struggled to stay awake, I decided best to get with the program no matter what crazy shit was expected. If not, then I thought maybe hell would be a nicer place than Bob and Mary planned on making it for me in this house.

By the second hour of this preach-a-thon I was missing old mom as I realized a beating was quicker. Thankfully, Mary who had been standing next to me making sure I did not escape, would yelp out 'amen' ever so often. Bob's face was red by now and veins clearly visible on his forehead as he boomed out another point of his faith. Otherwise, I may have slipped off to dreamland which could only be a no-no. These people were not kidding around.

Finally, Bob felt that I was adequately answered. I was quizzed but luckily, I was afraid enough I had learned the basics quickly and without a repeat. The bible I was reading was thrown at me and I was told to keep reading and repent my sins. Then they both then left the room, and they slammed the door leaving me on the bed alone at last. I fell backward and went to sleep almost immediately. As I drifted off, I wondered if I was "locked in" again. The sound of scraping on the other side of the door told me I had been. I smiled, they feared me, how funny was that?

When I woke up it was already dark. I had slept the entire day away. I stood up to try the door, but it swung open and there was Mary again. She threw a tan dress that looked like it came off the corpse of a

19th century farm girl. It was ankle length and had a high neck with ruffles. Very plain and old fashioned is the best way to describe it.

"Go take a shower, you smell bad. Tomorrow for church you will wear this, and you will not speak unless spoken to understand?" She was glaring hard. "You slept all day so I expect you can read the bible some more tonight. When you are done get back in here and get to it. You will not need food for your spirit is the one in need of nourishment. Starve the body and feed the soul." WTF???

I nodded and took the dress as I went and did what I was told. No matter how weird this new situation was I was absolutely determined to make it work somehow.

The next day I put on that horrid dress and went to church with my new family. It was a lot like the day before, but this time Bob had a large group of very plain looking people listening instead of just me. I will not get into this too much as it is not important other than to say, I was even more scared than before. I was sure these people were nuts. That was an experience that I had not even imagined in my most horrid nightmares.

That afternoon, they made me go back to church after spending the whole day in my room having to read the bible, locked in again. After we returned, I was back in the room with the bible again. I was detecting a pattern here. I was hoping that if I learned this damned bible they would finally let me out of the room to the world I had waited all this time to live in.

I studied it hard, but I confess most of it did not make sense to me. Still, I tried hard. Finally, Mary told me to go to bed as I had school tomorrow. School? Oh yeah, I had been so caught up in this mess I forgot that at least at school I would be out of this damned room.

I had seen kids that appeared my age at church that day, but they did not even look my direction. There were a lot of teenagers there and they all acted and looked like their parents. Stern, drab, and very controlled. There was a sense of fear and poverty there I cannot explain other than to say I could smell desperation for anything to hold on to that they could to save them from this life of dust, drab, and tan.

This town where I was now a prisoner was only about 350 in population. It was once a thriving railroad town. As the end of the train era came, so did this town. Now only the false front crumbling brick buildings of a once colorful and lively town stood to even hint there had been life here once. People in this southern town were deep in poverty with work being scarce and opportunity to do better even scarcer. Most lived in single wide trailers that were scattered along the rural townscape like the broken teeth of a prize fighter. It was mostly disability checks and meager family farms that supported the last of these hard-bitten peoples. Most here were related to each other directly or indirectly. The church that Bob preached in was the pulse of this dying world and that made him king shit here. He would get up there every Sunday and promise these sad souls a better life, as long as they understood that they would have to suffer to obtain it. If you looked around for even a second, yep, you could say they were doing the suffering just fine.

I went to sleep uneasy that night trying to scare away the demons of my encounters with kids from the many schools from my past. Maybe this time would be easier because the school was so small. I decided that if I was quiet and just observed I could learn what they appreciated.

My blood ran cold as I thought, "what if they are like they are at church?" I shuddered and pulled the blanket up tight against the darkness.

The next morning, I awoke abruptly to a screaming Mary as this time she pulled me off the bed instead of my blankets. I fell to the floor still half asleep and confused.

She kicked me in the side rather hard and said, "get up sinner!" she went to kick again and awake now I moved out of the way.

Her slipper clad foot collided loudly with the sideboard of the bed. She let out a roar and yelled, "Fucking slut!" (huh?)

She realized she had cursed and quickly covered her mouth and looked above her. I looked up too wondering if maybe God was reaching down to smite her (well, I hoped that was going to happen anyway). As I was distracted, she kicked me in the face with her injured foot and I tasted blood from my now busted lip.

"Get up and get dressed! We will be late!" she smiled as the blood ran down my chin. Appearing satisfied she had paid me back she limped out and slammed the door (as she always did).

I cried a bit and put on a pretty powder blue button up shirt and a pair of blue jeans the nurses had given me in the hospital. I brushed out my blond wig and tried to stem my bloody lip with a handkerchief I also had gotten from the kindly nurses. I was very upset but today I did not have time for a pity party. This was my chance to try to fit in and make friends. If I could do that then living here would be hard, but I thought I could handle it. A kick to the face and a smack to the back of the head were far better odds than where I had last hung my hat.

I finished and went to the door. I tried the handle and it opened right up. She had not lock me in. I walked down the hallway to find Mary there. She grabbed my upper arm forcefully, dragged me out of the house, and pushed me into the station wagon. That was uncalled for, I was not going to try to run, but apparently, she thought I may. Cannot have that paycheck slipping away, now, can we?

The small farm school was only three miles from Bob and Mary's right in the heart of that decaying town. The entire building housed every grade from kindergarten to the 12th. The town had separated the K to 6th crowd from the rest of the grades by building a large wall with a single door to keep the rowdy teens from the more immature kids. At fifteen years old I would be on the north side or with the high school crowd.

Mary stopped the car and got out. I went to get out as well, but she was there on me grabbing me again by the upper arm and squeezing hard. I was pulled behind her. She power walked faster than my short legs could keep up. When I got too far behind, she would jerk me forward. I saw many kids of every age all talking and walking into the building, but this little scene caught everyone attention. They all stopped and just stared. I looked down so I did not make any eye contact as Mary towed me through the door that opened into the high school side.

Once inside I saw a long narrow hallway lined with lockers to the south and a big black wall with a single door in the center at the end of it. All along the walls above the lockers were pictures of long graduated senior classes and pictures of old dead white men from various ages in time. The smell of an old attic and mold filled my nostrils. I noticed that between every ten locker groupings was a black door on both sides, classrooms likely. This building was ancient.

Mary took me to one of these black doors and open it while she hauled me inside. It was the office. The room was very small with a large half wall that blocked off the secretary from the students. There was no glass just that half wall and the secretary looked up from her tiny desk as we came in. I was pushed rudely into one of the wooden chairs sitting off to the right of the now closed office door.

On the left side of the door a young boy of maybe fourteen with freckles, buckteeth, large ears and reddish hair sat in a chair just like mine. He stared at me. I stared back. What was he looking at? I did not look any more ridiculous than he did I thought. Neither of us took our eyes off each other in some kind of staring war.

"I have a new child to enroll Patty." Mary said as she stood looking across that half wall but blocking me from the door. Again, I was not going to run so she was wasting her time.

"Oh, you and Bob have a new one! How wonderful, Sugar!" I hear Patty say with a voice so high pitched I felt my eardrums would burst. Yikes!

"Oh no Patty not wonderful at all. You may want to warn Mr. Greene about this one. She is likely to be a problem. I would like to assure you Bob and I are doing our best to get it under control, but I would like Mr. Green to know this is a bad situation." Mary said with an air of disgust in her voice.

"Oh, you don't say Mary?" I could hear Patty get up and walking closer obviously very interested in this "bad situation."

I stopped staring at the kid and looked at Mary, I too, was interested in what exactly did she mean by "bad situation." I certainly was painfully aware of how it was bad for me!

As I saw a heavyset woman of about mid-forties in a very tight blue dress with a very red beehive hairdo, approach Mary. She looked around and at the kid in the other chair, then Patty leaned in to hear the gossip. She did not need to lean in, as Mary was happy to make sure everyone in that room heard this.

"This child was found creeping in graveyards. Bob and I were told she was digging up and eating on the corpses! She was so addicted to drugs she eventually overdosed and was found mid-meal in the cemetery near dead, Patty! Worse yet she was so delusional from the drugs she was dressing like the corpses she was digging up! The cops said when they found her near dead in the graveyard, God have mercy, they thought someone had dug up a corpse as a joke she was so bizarrely dressed! Can you believe that! Took three months to dry her out. Her mother is in prison because she was giving her the drugs she was taking.

God help us all!" Patty blurted it all out in a single breath.

All I could do is let my jaw drop as I stared in disbelief at Mary, WHAT? Patty backed away from the wall recoiling in horror her hand flew to her chest as she shot a look of sheer disgust at me.

"Oh, my glory Mary!" Patty stammered appearing unable to decide what to say or do, "You and Bob are saints to even keep this thing in your house for a night much less till they find another placement. You are going to send her away, right? Oh, we cannot have that here, Mary." Patty was still backing away.

I stood up, I had had enough of these lies, "I did not do any of that! You are a liar!" I yelled at Mary. (okay, yeah, I did dress like a corpse she had me there)

Mary turned to me and smacked me in the face open handed hard as she could. I grabbed my now smarting cheek as she pushed me back into my seat and I fell back with a thud.

"You, shut up!" Mary yelled in my face as I felt the sting really set in. "You do not speak unless spoken to first! Sit there and keep your foul mouth shut!" She was baring her teeth at me like a snarling dog.

I looked to see what the boy was doing. He had a look like someone had just seen his very first boob.

His mouth hung open and his eyes were wide as he stared at me. I could see a smile spread across his face and evil in his dull eyes. My gut told me he could hardly wait to get out of there to impress all his friends with what he though was one hell of a story to tell about this "new kid." My gut was to be trusted on this one unfortunately.

I looked down at that wooden floor in absolute misery. Mary had just shot my only chance to fit into this tiny new world before I even made it the first classroom. As Patty and Mary continued to speak of my abominable acts, fact that I had to wear a wig (really?) and falsified drug history, I nursed my now very red and angry cheek. What could I do? No one was going to believe me now, and all I could do is hope that the kids here had a great sense of humor. Otherwise, this was going to be a very dreadful school year.

Patty released "Opie" the redheaded kid as she and Mary continued to gossip about me. As he went out the door he took one long last look at me and laughed as he left. Oh, I was so screwed now. He was off to spread the "news." Damn.

Then finally satisfied she had completely destroyed my reputation (did I even have one of those) forever, Mary turned to me and said, "if you run, they will find you. When they do they have nasty jails for sinners like you and the others in that place will not be as kind to a monster like you there. Do you understand me?" She was smiling in what she thought was a victory.

I nodded yes, but to be honest I was already planning my escape, fuck her.

Then she turned to Patty, and as if she had not already humiliated me enough said, "Patty, can I use your restroom and wash my hands? I don't want to catch any creeping crude from this creature."

Patty agreed and they both washed their hands.

When you were in school did anyone ever start a nasty rumor about you that was completely or mostly untrue? If so, how did you handle it?

Chapter 10: Rearranging Deck Chairs on the Titanic

It is me yet again here to tickle your terror bone with a tale of woe and sorrow; I mean to enlighten you about the path to my Gothic lifestyle. Now a quick warning: this chapter has an ending that is a nasty subject. If you are easily upset or dealing with serious depression, I would ask you to skip this one. No need to add any darkness if you are already dealing with a great deal of your own. You have been warned.

After Mary left, Patty told me to follow her as she led me like a calf to the slaughter to the awaiting student body. She kept a kept a baleful eye that I did not get too close as she continued down to the very end of that hallway. Patty was afraid I may run up, touch her then she would catch the cemetery herpes I suppose. The bell for first period had already rung so the classrooms were full. The teacher's voices echoed thru that ancient wooden hallway as they lectured about various subjects.

I looked at the floor and followed at a distance I hoped would be safe for Patty, as I felt great sorrow overtake me. Well, now what? No way that Opie kid was going to keep that juicy tidbit of gossip under wraps. I wondered how long I had before the chants of Ghoul haunted me in every nook and corner of this shitty little schoolhouse. Maybe till lunch hour? (Ha! Who was I kidding?)

Patty stopped at a door and directed me inside making sure to move away so I did not accidentally brush upon her chubby body. I walked in without argument and the teacher inside, a woman of at least sixty with white hair and a dress at least as old as she was, pointed me to an empty desk just to the left but in the front row. I did not look up to see the staring eyes on me but sat down grateful for a quick escape.

To my absolute disbelief Patty then began to speak to this teacher about what she had heard from Mary. Now to be fair, Patty was sure to keep my confidence by sharing with the teacher only, she did whisper after all. She whispered loudly! If I could make out most of what she was saying, so could the rest of at least the front row. I swear I could feel their eyes burning right into me like cattle irons fresh from a campfire. I could simply not take another minute of this bullshit. I stood up took one look at that rag tag classroom full of rural backwater teenagers, as they glared in obvious abhorrence back, and started for the door.

"Sit down now!" Patty yelled barely able to tear herself away from sharing her ill gained gossip. "Where do you think you are going?"

I looked right at her and answered truthfully, "To hell apparently. See you there." Smiling I broke into a mild jog then a full-fledged run right out that door and down that hallway and out the door to the sunlight I had missed so much.

I had no idea where I was running but, damn it, I was getting out of here. This was a dead end no doubt. I heard Patty yelling at me fading in the distance as she had tried to follow me out the door, but I was younger and faster. She could not catch me. I ran with every ounce of speed I could muster heading right for the old single lane road that led to the school. It seemed like the right thing to do at the time.

I slowed to a jog as the school began to disappear into the distance behind me. I had no idea where I was at all. This was not my old town, and I was very confused as to which direction I was even heading. It just felt so good to be free and in the fresh air away from the dust, despair, and hateful glares of those people. I admit I was very happy for the first time in a long time. Even though I was most certainly lost.

It was not very long till my great joy was overshadowed by the sounds of a car coming and to my absolute horror it was Mary and Bob's station wagon.

"Oh shit!" I yelled as I tore off down that road fast as I could running for my very life.

I could not just get off the road as there were huge ditches on each side apparently this place flooded often. The road engineers had solved it by digging deep drain ditches on each side. All I had to do was get far enough ahead to find a place to jump them without breaking a leg. However, Mary was in a car. I could not outrun a car.

She gunned that old box of bolts and caught up without any problem. Once she was right behind me, she slowed down without stopping the car. Mary just kept pace with me never trying to pass. I was at a fevered pitch of desperation now. I thought maybe I still had a chance as true I could not outrun the car, but I could outrun Mary.

I could see the ditch on one side growing narrow just ahead so with all I had left I pushed myself harder headed for that and bracing for a jump. However, I saw a police car coming from the other direction cutting me off from that targeted location. Mary behind me, police in front, no time to wait for that narrow spot, I jumped right there. I made it but was stunned for a second as I landed painfully on my knees.

The cop car stopped as did the station wagon and all the occupants got out, but I did not stick around to say howdy. No, I got my ass up and took off running into the thick tree cover without looking back.

I ran wildly often being sent sprawling as I tripped over fallen branches through a canvas of heavily forested land. I could hear the police officers behind me yelling to each other of my location. They were gaining on me. There was no way I could push much harder, and I had already been sprinting awhile. My lungs were on fire and my legs felt they were full of molasses.

The more fatigued I was getting the more I tripped and fell. Each fall hurt my knees making it harder to keep up my speed. I was skinned all to hell already from the jump. I had torn my clothes to tatters ripping through countless briars and thickets. The very landscape itself appeared to be against me as I was battered by low hanging branches, thorns, and vines.

My chances were looking better that I had escaped (to where I have no idea) until I discovered the joys of old barbed wire fences hidden by years of overgrowth. I hit the old fence at a full speed. Screams of sheer agony ripped out of my mouth as the barbs dug into my ankles and waist I was sent into a spin and flipped onto my head hopelessly tangled. The pain was hideous, but I struggled to free myself ignoring the ripping of flesh. It did no good I was trapped. All I could do is struggle uselessly as I watched the two police offers approach me, both winded but with a look of confidence that I was not going anywhere. My bid for freedom was lost.

It took both cops thirty minutes to free me of the barbs. I was then handcuffed and led back to the waiting arms of Mary. She of course pretended to be concerned and then, lucky for me, made sure to explain why I would do such a thing. I had to sit in that station wagon in handcuffs as Mary rattled out the lies about me, she had already spread all over the school yard. I just closed my eyes and wondered why I was such a loser.

Of course, the cops ate that shit up and told Mary to keep me "on a leash" and away from decent citizens. She assured them that with the help of God Almighty she and Bob would help me to see the errors of my ways. She had that right. I could clearly see the errors. For starters, I had been born. The rest was downhill from there.

After a lot of bullshit that I will not repeat here, I was uncuffed and released into Mary's loving hands. The cops joked that she could have a pair for home use if I got out of control and she joked that was not such a bad idea. Now, at this point, I sincerely wondered if I had been a very awful person in another life. This was too unreal to be true. This had to be karma for something I had done somewhere in time.

Mary got into the car, and we headed back to the house. School was over for me until "I learned my place" so, she and Bob would be handling my lessons for a while, I was told. Oh boy, that did not sound good, and I felt my stomach lurch. This was bad, really bad. Mary went on about what a sinner I was but by now the future bruises, scraps and cuts from barbed wire were screaming loud enough to drown out her voice.

On the way back I stared out the window and watched the world flash by the car truly miserable. Then I saw it. The familiar stone wall of a cemetery. As we drove past, I marveled at the large black wrought iron gates with a definite old school gothic era flair. I could not see inside it well but for backwater people they sure knew how to build a cemetery, I thought. It was very large from the size of the wall which seemed to go on forever. I felt a sense of calm as we drove past it. I wanted to push the feeling away. I did not want to be that anymore, but there it was silent, inviting, and peacefully calling to me. I listened and could hear "Alice" playing in my mind. Even in my darkest moment it brought me a bit of comfort. With all my will I pushed the idea out of my mind, no more cemeteries, damn it. I was not a ghoul, no matter how much Mary wanted everyone to believe it!

We arrived back home before what would likely have been third period at school had I not decided to cut out like a startled colt. Bob was waiting in the living room sitting in his old beat- up armchair glaring at me with a look only the devil could have withstood. He said nothing as he glared, and Mary guided me by my aching upper arm up the two steps to the upper level. I was taken to the bathroom and told to clean up and change clothes. The door was slammed. I heard her just outside it, standing there waiting. I looked around and for a moment looked for anything that would open a vein and end my pathetic life.

There was nothing sharper than toilet paper and no mirror. Nothing in the medicine cabinets. I guess they already had other "druggies" in their home and expected this. Maybe I could slip in the shower and break my neck I thought.

"Wait, what the hell is wrong with me?" I wondered as I stripped for the shower noting a very battered body beneath the rags that used to be my clothes, "I do not want to be dead!"

There had to be another way. I would get another chance to run no doubt. They could not watch me forever and this time I would plan it. With resolve to work this future escape plan out I took my shower and washed off the evidence of my recent failure.

When I was done and opened the door Mary grabbed me harshly and tossed me in the bedroom. Bob was there holding a leather strap. You can use your imagination here because there is just so much I care to share. Let's just say I had a personal tour of the torments of hell. That day I re-discovered a dimension of human depravity that I had not so quickly forgotten since my mother and I had said goodbye.

For the next several weeks I was not let out of the room. I was thrown food from time to time and allowed to have bathroom breaks. Daily I got to take my tour of hell with good old Preacher Bob as he found new and horrific ways to make me repent for sins. When I was not begging for redemption at the end of whatever implement Bob fancied, I was expected to read the bible. Most days, I was in too much pain to even read my mind. I would just cry and stare at that blasted book wishing I could meet God and spit in his apathetic face. Where was this God now? If this was designed to get me to come to God, it was backfiring. All I found in my search for forgiveness was hatred for all things that called themselves righteous.

Then three weeks into my terror I was pacing with anxiety over when Bob may come for our "crack" at the bible study when I noticed a strange dip in the carpet just under the window. Maybe a hole? Could I fit through it? I dug under that carpet watching with apprehension for any sign that door may open. I found the weak spot just under that dingy brown shag, but it was not a hole, it was a journal. It was pink and only slightly larger than my hand. On the front in written in a pretty hand was "Michelle."

I was fascinated. I opened it and the first lines said, "If you find this, I am probably dead."

I shut it fast. My sense was this would answer my questions. I needed to hide it and investigate when I was sure to not be caught. So, I stashed it into the mattress coils just in time as I heard Bob coming down the hall.

I got thru that nasty situation thinking of my stashed treasure and as soon as the coast was clear and I had recovered best as I was going to, I went and got Michelle's journal.

She told me she had been the "problem child" there before me. As she recalled her time with Mary and Bob, she revealed a dark secret about them. Bob had been molesting her and Mary knew. Mary was angry as apparently Bob always molested the teenage girls of this foster home. Mary was jealous but instead of telling or leaving Bob she would torture the girls out of jealousy. By the time I finished this journal I was colder than when I had been poisoned. Apparently, the molestation began with what Michelle called "strap sessions" where he beat down the girls' willpower.

Michelle had written this journal as a warning to any kid in this home to run if they could because "no one will believe you. They tell everyone you are a drug addict and make up lies."

Michelle ended the journal by saying she was going to kill herself. Her last entry was to her mother. She told her mother she loved her. Michelle then apologized to her mom for being a bad daughter and getting hooked on drugs. It ended there. I dropped the journal in tears.

"Oh, fuck me," I moaned, "What am I going to do?" I wept for Michelle, for myself and for other any other kids these two monsters had destroyed.

I had not been molested yet just tortured thus far, so for that I was lucky (lucky?). I was about to lose my mind at the thought of that nasty bastard. There had to be a way out of this mess. How? All night I lay there and then suddenly with the daybreak an idea came to me. I knew what to do. It just might work.

I waited by the door patiently till I heard Mary coming with my food. When she went to open the door, I grabbed her arm. She yelled and tried to pull away.

"Mary please, will you hear my confession? Please, I do not want to go to hell. I want to be saved." I forced tears and did my very best to look sincere.

Her initial hard stance softened immediately. It was working. She walked into the room shutting the door behind her. I fell to my knees and threw myself at her feet and began to plead for forgiveness for my sins.

"Get up you fool, I am not God!" She said surprised by my display of remorse. "Let me go get Bob," she started to leave. Oh, hell no!

"No please Mary! I never had a mother, I used drugs to fill the hole in my heart but now I want to fill it with God and make you proud. Please let me prove myself to you! I will do anything. No more trouble I promise! I swear it on my damned soul!" I was full on crying now and I could tell it was working.

Mary looked at me with a bit of pity in her eyes, "Okay child get up and let's go eat at the table but anymore trouble and you will never leave this room again."

She walked off and I quickly got up and followed hiding my smile. I was going to get out of this situation and not even God could stop me this time.

Should have seen the look on good old Bob's face when I walked out there and sat down at the table. He shot a confused look at Mary, and she told him I was ready to repent. He looked at me and I kept my head down. Inside I was recoiling in horror at this monster but outside I played it meek and remorseful.

I ate my breakfast, cleared the table and washed the dishes without being told and without looking up once. I sniffed pretending to cry quietly. When Mary came to check I said prayers in whispers loud enough for her to hear me. I was quite the actress. I had read that bible and thanks to many painful lessons I knew enough to sound damned qualified for redemption.

When I was sure Mary was busy, I snatched a handful of Tylenol tablets from her purse that was sitting unguarded on the kitchen counter. I had seen her put the bottle in there several times. You see I had a poor functioning liver thanks to my mother's little trick, and I was told I could never have Tylenol, or my liver would fail.

While I was snatching the pills, I saw she also had some other stuff such as Actifed, Sudafed and pills without names on the bottles. I snatched a bunch of those too. I barely got the entire bunch into my pockets before Mary came back and sent me to my room.

Apparently, my was belief was correct. My act would not let me off the hook from Bob's "lessons." Bob's plans had not changed. All I could do is hope that today was just a beating, and it was not too late to enact my plan before it progressed to a place I would not recover from.

That day was no different than the last several weeks with Bob's behavior. However, I was about to leave and this time I would not be worried about which direction I needed to run. I knew right where I was headed.

When Bob was finished, and I was left alone I got the water that Mary always left so I did not die of dehydration and started my escape. I started with the Tylenol. Then, began on the next group of colorful freedom pills. I took so many they started to dissolve in my throat, and I was foaming at the mouth, but I kept taking them. Now drooling and foaming my stomach screaming out in anger I got the last one down. I leaned back against the window and re-hid Michelle's journal where I found it.

Then I relaxed, as the drool poured down my face, resisting the urge to vomit. "Oh, no you don't." I said aloud to no one, "this time I am going where they cannot hurt me anymore and this time, they will not be able to bring me back."

I silently thanked Michelle for showing me the way as the walls began to breath in and out. The sun seemed to be setting but it is only mid-morning. Everything begin to spin, and I was so sleepy, but the nausea kept waking me up. I wanted to vomit but I would not allow it. My heart was racing, and the room got so cold I began to shiver. Then my drooling finally stopped, as my mouth dried up like a desert in a thirty-year drought. I could feel my lips cracking open and now breathing was getting harder. Ah, there she is, the train is coming! All aboard!

The darkness folded around me like a long-lost friend as I thought I saw the terrified (or terrifying) face of Mary just as my vision closed down. My memory fades to blackness.

If you are so inclined to know how a Goth Queen was born from what seems an impossible situation, I will continue so share in the coming chapters. Here is the marker for ground zero of the Goth I became. I know that seems like an odd event to cause such a change, but it is what it is.

A quick note: I do not condone this ultimate and irreversible choice. Suicide is a serious social ill and should never be taken lightly. It is also very personal for those of us who felt pushed to the point of such a horrible fate. I have paid for this stupidity in ways I cannot count and still do, to this day. Do me a great honor and do not attempt to shame me for this moment of extreme weakness.

Chapter 11: Dark Redeemer

"Make the best use of what is in your power and take the rest as it happens."
-Epictetus

The darkness would not let me go from her peaceful embrace easily. Spotty memories of faces above me hovering and voices from the void speaking in hushed whispers. I hear an alarm clock, but the beeping alarm has a strange rhythm, beep beep, beep beep, beep beep. Damn someone shut that fucking thing up!

I open my eyes to glaring light and a doctor staring at me. Where am I? In a blurry vision I see Mary in the corner sitting in a chair. "Oh shit! I did not die!" I think drowsily, "how?" I am groggy, this must be hell that I was told I was going to.

I try to get up and leave but my arms are tied to something, the bed. I am restrained. This is not hell, (well that is relative) it is the hospital. I am still very confused and drowsy from sedation medication pumping into an IV in my arm.

My very calm mind tries to piece together how I am still here and obviously very alive. "Oh, I saw Mary before I got on the train. She called for help, shit! They will not even let me die for fuck's sake!" I think while sleepily looking at Mary in the chair looking at me. I so hate her.

Then a new woman appears as the doctor leaves apparently satisfied I am awake. She is someone I have never seen before but is in a dress suit. Maybe mid-thirties and dark hair pulled up severely in a bun. This lady is holding a note pad and is looking sternly at Mary. Mary looks nervously at this lady.

"Huh, Mary is afraid of this lady. Who is she?" I think calmly as the lady walks over to me.

She introduces herself as my new caseworker and I can call her Sandy. Sandy tells me that she is here to ask me why I tried to kill myself. Of course, Mary is sitting right there, so I just stare at her. Sandy then tells me that they are looking for a new placement for me and I will be leaving Bob and Mary's home soon, as they apparently cannot handle my case. I have caused enough trouble she says in a stern retelling of what a pain in the ass I am to the agency.

I had already assumed Mary had already told lies, so I did not bother to contradict the Preacher Wife or this obvious tool of the system. I refused to speak at all no matter how pissy she got. Sandy was agitated but finally said she would be back tomorrow when I was more alert, and we could talk then.

Sandy walks over to Mary, "We will find another child soon as we can. There is always too many needing placement and not enough placements. I will do my best to get a better match. The department thanks you and your husband for all your kindness offering these wayward kids a place to stay. I will, however, have to have an answer about this suicide attempt officially from this kid. It is just formality." Sandy dryly said.

"Why? Bob and I already told you what happened Sandy." Mary retorted sounding on edge.

"Well, since the last child in your care just committed suicide this year the state makes us follow up close. It should not be a problem. Look, Mary, we have known each other for years. There is only so much you can do with these kids. You can lead the horse to water, but you cannot make them drink. Some cannot be saved. I want to apologize for the red tape in advance, Mary. It is nothing personal. No matter what the kid says it will all go smooth, and we will get you a new placement as soon as possible." Sandy reached out and shook Mary's hand and with a quick look at me says, "see you tomorrow kiddo." Sandy walked out of the room.

I was now alone with Mary. I was on a lot of medication but already the horror of hearing Michelle had indeed died like this was sinking in. It also was sinking in that I was getting out but to where? Something worse likely (worse? yikes) and some other poor kid would be in my place. Michelle had done that to me by taking her life and opening a slot. Now I was going to do it to someone else. Bob would get a fresh child to hurt in a cycle that would never end. Then I would be shipped off to a new horrific family or group home. Oh, this was bad!

I shook my head fighting tears. "Oh, why didn't I die damn it!" I thought the horror I had awaken to was worse than death could ever be. I could not stand the thought of another's blood on my hands, much less the idea of having to fight another battle with new abusers or worse.

Mary just sat there glaring at me with what I imagined was victory. She hated me and the feeling was mutual. She was the real monster here. Mary let Bob do this and kept his secrets. Even worse discredited, tortured, and victimized his victims. She stood up and approached me seeming to want to say something, but she did not get the chance, the doctor came back into the room. His appearance saved me from her onslaught of verbal abuse.

A very heavy-set man with a portly face and balding head of about fifty introduced himself. He asked me how I was feeling, and I shrugged as my response. I did not think any of them deserved me to bother with harassing my scared up vocal cords with wasted words. Not that anyone gave a shit what I said anyway.

He then asked Mary to leave the room. She protested but he insisted she leave as he needed to talk to the patient privately. So, shooting a threatening look that seemed to say, "better keep it shut missy" she left the room. Now just me and Doctor Potbelly were alone.

I immediately meant to unload my burden about my discovery of Bob's obsessions hoping this man could help in pure desperation. However, the doctor's next statements sent me into a private hell that I still must endure this day.

"You are not a very lucky lady," (no kidding) he said looking down at the floor, "I understand that earlier this year you were poisoned by some very nasty chemicals. You must have been warned by the last physician that there were some things you should never do, right?" He looked up right into my eyes.

I nodded, now a bit concerned, "what is this shit all about?" He had my attention as I now can tell something is wrong here.

"We pumped your stomach but most of what you took was already in the system by that time. You had to be resuscitated and it was really close. We thought we had lost you." He then drew in a big breath. (uh oh)

We did our best for you, but the damage is not reversible. You have destroyed your upper GI system, and severely damaged your pancreas, as well as your liver at a genetic level." He was looking at me with pity. "This is really bad if you are not understanding what I am saying to you."

Oh, I understood what he said, but my real question was, "am I going to die? Is that what you are trying to say?" I asked while thinking, "careful what you wish for."

He nodded. Then went on to tell me that indeed I was going to die from this but eventually not today. The kicker was that no one could be sure how long I had. A year, twenty years, or twenty minutes? Any could be correct. One thing he did know is that I would die young and slow.

I sat there with tears in my eyes as he told me the dirty details of what I had done to myself. He explained in grave detail how my intestines would have difficulty absorbing nutrients, and my immune system was in shambles. Without a properly functioning liver my cholesterol would be out of control, and I would not be able to handle protein, oil, fats or vitamin D. Basically, I now had heart disease, high cholesterol, and a cancerous immune system with no upper gut.

At only fifteen years old I faced stroke, heart attack, cancer, slow starvation, and even pancreatic hemorrhage at any time. Eating would forever be painful, and sometimes useless. I could not go out into the sun or my skin would burn rapidly with no ability to process the vitamins I needed so badly from it.

"You have thrown your life down the toilet, kiddo." he said sighing. "There is no cure, but we can put you on medications to treat some of the conditions. Sadly, they will not hold off what you started forever. All I can say is, I hope that now you see that no matter how bad it may have seemed, it could be so much worse. Life is worth fighting for. Too bad you will learn this too late little lady. You have my sympathy." With that he got up, shook his head, "what a pity and so young." He turned and left me there to deal with this heavy shit alone.

I laid there staring at the ceiling in disbelief. I was dying horridly and painfully slow. In my frantic impulsive effort to escape a moment of pain I had become the ghoul everyone had accused me of, not alive and not dead! I had no reason to plan for a future now as I did not have one. I could have a few months or a few decades but no reason to assume either. I wanted to cry, scream, and wail, but I could not.

Inside I was empty. I had so wanted to find a real life and instead of having faith in myself to find a way I had found a type of death. I wanted to blame Mary, Bob, my mom, God, Michelle, hell, everyone! However, I was empty because they did not make me take those pills. I let them win by finishing their job with my own hands. Wow, what a brilliant move. Bravo!

Mary had not come right back. I assumed she had caught Doc Potbelly and was grilling him about what I may or may not have said to him. Oh, did I hate her. It was then that it started to dawn on me that now I had nothing left to lose. The doctor told me it would be slow and painful. So, if I fight and I am beaten or even killed better than what I had coming right?

A new strength began to fill me as I realized my position of power. I had nothing to lose and nothing to gain! Sure, this was a real hell but if I looked at it the right way, I was unstoppable!

Now a plan began in my mind. I had to stop Bob and Mary from condemning another child to mine and Michelle's fate. Well, I once heard it said that when you have nothing to lose, then you are already a winner. Finally, I had found a way to stop being the loser in every game. All I had to do was go all in.

When Mary came back in, she found me sitting up and smiling an evil smile at her. This seemed to throw her off balance.

"Are you stupid, girl. Did you not understand what that doctor just told you? That is nothing to smile about." She stood there defiant. "You will be in hellish torment for your sin till you die alone and begging for release." That made her smile back at me.

Even with the knowledge of my terrible condition it was not enough for her, she was ready to hurt me some more. Too bad for Mary that was no longer possible. No one could ever hurt me like I could, she was just a novice. I had proven myself the Master.

"You had better sit-down, Mary. Or I will call back that doctor and tell him a secret about Bob and you. I do not think he will ignore it like others will. You see he has to take my confession by law, and he will. So, do I call the doctor back and tell him a story or do you sit down and listen to me for a change." I kept smiling.

Mary was observably shaken. She did not know I knew about Bob, and she was trying to figure out how I knew.

"Oh no, darling, Bob did not touch me like that, yet. I know that is what you are thinking. Oh no, you see Michelle told me. She left evidence and I found it darling. I have hidden it where you will never find it. No one ever need find it if you are willing to listen to what I have to offer you. Otherwise, I will tell the doctor, and Michelle will provide the evidence." Ah, this was fun! I was almost giddy making this bitch squirm!

"What do you want? Drugs? Money? What?" She barked while sitting down looking as if someone had kicked the wind from her.

"Oh yeah, you would think that wouldn't you." I said still smiling. I found it somewhat humorous that even when under a thumb some assholes cannot help but stay assholes. "No, I will offer you a deal that will benefit us both and stop Bob from touching anyone else again."

Mary's hard glare melted to shame. She evidently loved this creep, and his molestation of these kids was a real humiliation for her. She looked back at me, and I could see her eyes were filling with tears.

"Bob is sick." She said as a tear rolled down her cheek.

I was not moved. "Yeah, I agree with that. Now, you call that Sandy up and tell her that you can handle my case and I will tell them I was on drugs, and this was not your fault. I will tell them how much I," I had to pause to say it, "love you and Bob and want to try again. I will be staying." I finished.

"What? Why would you do that? You would damage your credibility to stay? How is this going to stop Bob!" She seemed bewildered but then again, she was not very bright.

"Well, for starters no new girl will be placed. Second, I will not be there for Bob to get to. I will leave and only return when the caseworker comes to check on me. He cannot touch me if I am not there to be touched. You will give me enough money every month to survive on my own and I will stay out of trouble, so no one need be the wiser. You get to keep most of the money they pay you to take care of me, no new kid comes to replace me, you never have to see me and best of all I don't have to look at your fucking faces but when the caseworker calls. Everyone wins." I said feeling very satisfied that this plan could work.

"What about school and where will you go? How would I even find you?" She said obviously considering my proposal seriously.

"I will attend school no problem. I am already enrolled. I will live in a cemetery that is not heavily used, surely there is one around here." Mary shot a look at me with that, and I glared her to silence, "I do not give two shits what you think. That one I saw on the road the day I ran away, is it a busy cemetery?"

She shook her head no and said it was mostly abandoned as it was filled a long time ago. Hardly anyone went there anymore so it was perfect. Her shoulders fell in what I assumed was defeat.

"If you are going to do this, I need to know what I am going to tell people with you slinking around like a ghoul in the graveyard. It will hurt Bob's and my reputations. What if you get sick? You are going to need medication for the rest of your useless life." She sighed.

"You will pick up my meds and I will take them. I told you I will need money every month for food or whatever. You will mind your business about my business. As for your reputation darling, fuck with me on this and I will make sure that your reputations will even be known in the prisons you are both sent to.

You know how they feel about child rapists there now don't you?" I gave this bitch no quarter.

She nodded in agreement. We spent the next hour haggling about how much money and what I would tell Sandy and how she would handle Bob. Eventually, I tired of her being in my sight, so I told her to get out. She did as I told her and left. She appeared finally satisfied with our secret deal. I was tired and I needed my rest.

I would not be in a nice bed for a long time now, but like it or not, I did not really have the evidence against Bob I was claiming I had. I was damned grateful Mary had bought my bluff. I knew that if I tried to tell they would sweep it under the rug. Sure, I would get out, but some other poor girl would suffer. By staying in the placement, I blocked that. If I stayed in that house Bob would get me for sure. So, I had solved it even if it meant I got the short end of the stick. The town was small, ignorant, and superstitious. No one would mess with a Ghoulish Huckleberry Finn since the people there really were very closed knit. If I stayed away from them, they would keep their distance too. No one here wanted attention from the outside world.

Reality is that it didn't matter anymore now, did it? I was dead anyway. The cemetery was safe, and secluded. It is also where I belonged now more than ever.

The next day Sandy came to speak with me. As promised, I told her I had managed to sneak some drugs into my room and when I ran out then I was going through the DTs. I told her the horrid bruises and cuts on my body were self-induced as I had been throwing major fits in my room hearing voices from the side-effects of the shit I had been taking. All this while poor, loving Bob and Mary had been trying to help me. The dumb bitch bought it hook, line and sinker because it was easier to believe me a monster than the upstanding Preacher and his wife.

Sandy signed off on my continued placement and closed the case without even bothering to order counseling or psychological intervention (Sandy is an idiot). She left my hospital room and now my side of the bargain was done.

The next day I was released and ordered "bed rest." Mary checked me out and pulled the car around to pick me up as I was wheeled to that station wagon. I wondered if she would try to crawfish me on her end of the deal. I resolved if she tried, she would be very sorry for it.

Once in the car I told her to take me to the nearest town that has a secondhand store of worth. She did it no argument. So, I now knew she was going to follow through. I imagine she tore up that room looking for evidence, but I knew she had not found Michelle buried under the rug. Had she, things would not be going so smoothly I knew that.

Mary and I finally had the good old-fashioned mother, daughter shopping trip I had always dreamed of. I selected several outfits of new clothing all of it in my old friend the color black. I also bought a fresh batch of white, grey, and black make up, blankets, a cassette tape player, a few cassettes including my precious Sisters of Mercy, a handheld mirror, and a lucky find a black and silver ankh. I also bought sundries and a backpack for all my possessions in the world. The Freak was back.

Mary was observably in disagreement, but I did not care, she was my prisoner now so she would have to just deal with it. We agreed that she would give me a house key so that on Sundays when they were at church, I could have the house to shower and wash my clothes. Bob would not be around so the coast would be clear. I reminded her that bad things would happen to both of us if she did not keep her promise and she of course reminded me too. The two of us trapped in hell by one damned idiot, how funny was that?

Our last stop was to the drug store to pick a months' worth of medications that would buy me time on this earth to consider what a bone head I truly am. I watched as the druggist stared in disbelief that he was filling out these "old people" prescriptions for a teenager.

As usual Mary could not help herself but to fill him in on my "mistake." I just glared at him as he shook his head and shoved the medications at me. He said he hoped I had learned my lesson. Oh, had I ever (jerk). Everyone seems to be so judgmental, but I did not see them there that day. If they knew so much I sure as hell wish they had told me about it before I learned, it the hard way.

Mary drove us back to town and I watched out the window wondering about all the other people in their cars, was it like this for them? I supposed it no longer mattered. This was the way it was for me and there was a lot left to handle before I started asking about the trials of others. I would have to deal with school next week as I had been given a week off. That would give me time to get settled into my new routine and home hopefully.

When we arrived finally at the city cemetery gate, I had seen that day I made my crazy run for freedom, Mary pulled up as close as possible to the gate. She was afraid someone was watching from the thick woods that surrounded the place on every side, I guess.

"You are going to play the hypocrite to the end, aren't you? Nobody is here and nobody gives a shit, Mary." I said chuckling as I got out of the car and started grabbing my new things.

She came flying around that car in a rage and grabbed my shirt by the back spinning me around.

"You are a sinner" but she was cut off as I hauled back and slapped her hard in the face.

"Get your fucking sick hands off me! You are the sinner!!" I yelled as she recoiled backward shocked. "Don't you ever touch me again hear me darling, or I will kill you, and eat your corpse!" I began laughing at my little joke as I walked to the gate. It easily opened as if it had been waiting for me all this time.

I slammed it hard behind me as Mary had done so many times in the last few weeks of my previous life. This was my house, and she was not welcome here. I heard what I would like to believe was the sound of Mary sniffing back tears as her car started and she left me there to my fate.

I was not even sixteen and I was on my own. As I entered what will be my home for several years to come for the first time, I look around and realize I had always been on my own. I had spent years hoping someone would save me when only I could save me. When I needed to be strong, I had failed. There was no taking back this nightmare I had created for myself. That was a lesson I should have learned before taking my damned life. Now, I would have to find a way to cope without a support system, a roof over my head, good health, or even apparently much of a future. It was time to grow up and fight for whatever I could salvage from this mess I had made of everything.

The graveyard was beautiful and very large but also dark. It was completely tree covered from lack of care so almost no light entered this desolate place. Most of the headstones were unreadable, broken or missing, but a few newer ones still stood proud and tall. I found what had been the community out house, so I did have a privy thank goodness. I already knew from previous experience as a youngster that the old southern cemeteries did have public bathrooms, you just had to find them. I had guessed this one correctly. On rainy nights I would be grateful for the shelter of that outhouse.

I toured the grounds and found plenty of old benches under years of undergrowth and with some work I freed a few for my coming slumbers. The place was a freaking mess all in all. I decided soon as I was rested to clean the place up. I could tell no one had been here in a long time, at least a year or two based on the unchecked growth. This was a very lucky find indeed. I might get away with this I thought happily as I laid down on one of my cleared benches to rest. I could not eat much with my dietary restrictions, but I did purchase a few items including bags of Doritos. I had not really eaten at the hospital but now I felt hungry.

To my absolute horror I had my first encounter with the repercussions of what I had done to myself. I spent hours not only vomiting but in terrible pain unable to get off the ground wishing for death. The pain and vomiting lasted for six hours well into the night. I could not get up to even seek help I was so sick. All I could do is crawl and moan holding my screaming upper abdomen. The razor blades of old had returned. It was with great sorrow that I realized I was condemned to replay that horrible poisoning at any time with little to no warning. I prayed for death, but as usual no death came. As soon as I recovered, I did two things, I threw out all the chips I had left and made a note that I would have to be very careful eating in front of people from now on.

I had a lot to learn about this thing about my new weaknesses and I had very little time to learn it. If I did not return to the land of the living by showing up at school the next week, my plans would fail. No way I was going to let that happened after all I had sacrificed to make it this far. I would be ready to face the next big test of my resolve. I would need to take back my power while carving out some kind of life for myself, or what was left of me.

So, this is the stopping point for this chapter on this crazy ride. Quite a change of pace in this high-speed chase. No worries we have sharp curves and uneven lanes still ahead of us in the journey to becoming Goth Queen! Have you ever had to make a choice that hurt you but helped another? Did you accomplish what you intended?

Chapter 12: Dance Macabre

Back again I see, well bite me and call me Dracula, I am surprised! So, are we ready to dig into the past and see what tidbits are buried below the surface? Great! Then grab your shovel, spades, and lanterns because it looks like this is going to be a dark night tonight. Follow me, I know just where the body is hidden...errrr...were to start our haunt...errr...hunt.

"Life asked death, 'Why do people love me but hate you?' Death responded, 'Because you are a beautiful lie, and I am a painful truth."
-Unknown

I was really hoping the week would pass quickly without a single rainy night. It was nearly Christmas and the nights had become viciously cold making my existence so uncomfortable I knew I was not dead yet. I certainly was starting to re-think this little plan of mine.

I spent the day picking up the garbage, clearing the overgrowth and trying to repair what I could of the headstones of my new home. I stayed very busy. This place was a real mess. It was not the city cemetery even though I had mistakenly thought so. No, this was a private ancient one who's families had lived in this town when it was a thriving place. When the town turned to dust, most of these residents' families had blown to the four winds seeking fortune elsewhere. So, this place once visited and cared for was now like me, lost and mostly forgotten.

As I looked after the final resting spots of those who could no longer look after themselves, I would read the inscriptions on their markers. It seemed sad to me that, despite the fact that many had lived into adulthood, this is all that remained of their deeds and voices. Sad, but a fact. Death is the great equalizer, and the evidence was now my only distraction from my own private little hell. The headstones, big, small, and shattered all sat silent. It did not matter if they had been important people or the town drunk, they were all the same now. Cold, lonely, and rotting away.

I will not lie, I cried a lot that week. I hated cemeteries. I had never truly understood why but now it was dawning on me. The sight of my unavoidable future, everyone's unavoidable future, was not something I wanted to dwell on. How could one live with nothing but death all around? Mortality is what all of us try to keep at bay by staying busy living. However, as a newly homeless, underaged kid, I also knew that it was the only place I was safe from worse fates. Abandoned houses could contain drug addicts, drifters or worse. No one wanted to be in the cemetery, and I was not an exception.

Yet, here I was stuck trying to make the best of a bad situation hoping to someday, soon, improve my lot. I tried hard to ignore the death all around me and told myself lies that this was just temporary. Still, from time-to-time reality would reach out its greasy hand to shake me out of my childhood fantasy.

I think I knew deep inside that I was not going anywhere, anytime soon. I did not have anyone to ask for assistance, anyone to run to, and no money to get there even if I did. I was just as stuck in this place as were the other inhabitants six feet below my feet. Funny how all my life I had known that it is easy to get into the cemetery, but no one ever gets out once they enter. I had tried for years to escape this fate.

Now here I am stuck living in a cemetery, sourly surveying the shambles of my pathetic existence with nowhere to return to when the dreaded dusk comes. Nothing could be done now to undo what had always been a probability. It was time to stop fighting myself and embrace what I had become. That was going to be harder to do than I ever imagined but without any other legitimate options I had no choice. If I did not learn to truly have confidence in myself, then I would not be able to wait for the death I had been promised.

On the third day of my new life, Mary came to visit. She brought food (that had been approved by the doctor), extra blankets and fresh water. Now, she did not give a shit, other than to make sure I had not died and to make sure that I did not die. How would she explain that one if it happened? I know this because that is what she actually said.

She did attempt for a few moments to convince me that I could come back with her and that it would be different this time. Sure, it would. This time they would tie me up so I could not get away at all. I knew better than that bullshit. I only shot her a go to hell look and made sure I kept her at a distance. I did not trust her not to try to kidnap me to drag me back by force.

"Forget it, Mary. I am never going back with Bob and you. Now you had better be on your way. I do not need a car out front to let the whole neighborhood know I am home," I said looking over the stuff she had brought but keeping a watchful eye on her.

She suddenly looked startled and looked around wildly, "are you mad? No one lives around here! You do not have neighbors. This is not your home! You live with Bob and I!"

Now that made me laugh, hard. I do not know why but I could not stop laughing and the more I thought on it the more maniacal my laughter. That really upset Mary. In fact, it downright scared her. She turned and ran from the cemetery jumped in the station wagon and peeled out headed out fast as she could. I just walked to the gate and waved smiling big, while laughing as she sped away.

I had just learned a powerful lesson. Crazy scares people. Being scary has always kept people the fuck off me. A plan of action for my return to school began to form in my mind. I had been fretting about it since I learned I would have to go back, but this could work. If they fear me, I may be able to survive this after all. I only had to go for one week before the Christmas break would begin. Whatever I was going to do to freak them all out it would have to be big and loud. So big they did not forget over the two weeks they had off for vacation.

I spent the rest of the week learning all my weaknesses, cleaning up the cemetery and perfecting my new look. I had decided to reinvent the old skull face look of Freak from before and do something more subtle but effective. This school was small enough showing up in a skull face may call attention of another school counselor or other well-meaning but useless idiot.

So, I worked on smoothly creating a death white pallor but instead of hollowing out my nose and mouth I only hollowed out my eyes to the brow bridge and blackened my lips. I did not black out my nose as before and only lightly contoured my very sharp cheek bones using grey instead of black. The look was more corpse than skeletal. It took a few days of work, but I did believe I had created a look that could be easily maintained through a busy school day.

By the end of the week, I had accomplished a full reinvigorating of the cemetery, a walking corpse look, and memorized all my cassette tapes by heart.

The music of Sisters of Mercy, The Damned, Joy Division, and Bauhaus had kept me company in the atrocious darkness every night. I was still afraid of the dark. Phobic of the darkness is a more accurate a statement. Trying to keep my mind from snapping in panic every damned night was beyond unbearable. It was draining trying to deal with baggage from my old life. I also discovered new baggage such as nightmares, sleepwalking, exaggerated startle reflex over every little sound louder than a mouse fart, and paranoia that something bad was about to happen. Nice, I was showing signs of Post-Traumatic Stress Disorder. It really did seem so overwhelming but, somehow I was getting it together and readying myself for the battle that was coming.

The Monday I was expected to be back in school finally arrived and I was up with the dawn having spent a fitful night of bad dreams and anxiety over the darkness. However, I was not tired. I had my adrenaline to keep me alert. I quickly prepared my new look, stashed my things in case anyone happened by to snoop around and took off out the gate headed towards the first of many walks to that blasted schoolhouse.

The walk was only a little more than thirty minutes. I kept to the same road that not so long ago I had made a break for freedom. This time I would not need to jump the drainage ditch, I hoped. I did have an old beat-up watch and Mary said I would have to be there by 7:45 am to get my books and class schedule before the bell at 8 am. I was a bit early just in case. No need to get there late and have to walk through that sea of disapproving faces if I could avoid it.

As I entered the school yard, I saw the station wagon parked in the driveway. Mary was sitting in the car, and I thought, "seriously?" as I also noted all the students going into the building. Everyone had stopped and jaws dropped all around me.

She saw me and jumped out power walking fast as she could my direction. Oh, hell no, I was not sticking around for this show, so I quickly sprinted into the door she had taken me into before and right to the office. I rushed through the office door and closed it behind me loudly, an accident actually. It was not as heavy as the cemetery gate, and I had misjudged how hard I needed to push to shut it.

Patty had her back to me digging into her typewriter for a correction tape and the loud bang made her jump. She turned startled and grabbing her chest but as our eyes met, I swear she nearly passed out of shock. She fell back slightly into the desk and her eyes widened as did her mouth.

"Uh yeah, Patty, right? I need a class schedule please, Mary already checked me in so it should be around somewhere. " I said without emotion.

Patty just stood there, mouth like a gaping guppy appearing in a trance. It was then Mary made it to the office. She plowed through the door and tried to grab my arm. I saw that coming so I stepped out of her gripping distance and shot her a nasty look.

"Oh, Patty. So, Bob and I decided that she is ready for school again, so could you get her all set up?" Mary said seeming to be unable to decide what to do.

She obviously did not approve of my look but did not want to cause a scene in front of Patty. I had made it very clear I would cause one if she got in my way. So, she was stuck. I could tell it was eating her up inside.

Patty finally broke free of her trance and began to look for this schedule of mine. She was very shaken. Several times she dropped the folders off her desk as she went about searching for it. I noticed she did her best to keep from making eye contact. It was hard not to laugh as I thought of what Patty was thinking at that very moment. However, with Mary standing right there it dashed my open display of amusement. Mary could ruin a wet dream trust me.

Patty finally found the stupid thing and as she reached out to hand it to Mary, I snatched it from her sausage fingers. "Thanks" I said as I turned to leave the office, my schedule now in hand.

"Wait! Don't you need Patty or someone to show you where to go?" Mary asked appearing to care. Always the actress.

I saw the full-on relief in Patty's eyes when I said, "No need. What are there ten classrooms in this school? I can count to ten Mary." I smiled at her and left them both to do their gossip without my having to hear it this time.

I entered the hall and as I closed the door became aware that every head and pair of eyes in the crowded hallway was on me. Bet this was a first for them, but not for me. This was familiar territory, so I just kept my eyes forward as I began my walk pass them all to the door of my first class. Everyone moved aside to let me pass. The crowd went silent. You could hear a pin drop as no one could believe what they were seeing. I could see the typical dress for this group of teenagers that appeared to be decade behind the rest of the world at the very least.

Boot cut jeans, big belt buckles, t-shirts, and cowboy boots, every face ache covered. The hair of the females long and straight and the boys short cropped. Every kid looked like a rodeo performer reject. I was standing out even worse than before. I felt like an Oreo cookie on a plate of corn bread. I may have overdone it a bit I thought, but too late now.

As I entered that classroom, I allowed my mind wondered about what Patty and Mary were saying now. I smiled as I thought of old Mary trying to come up with an excuse for my morbid appearance to try to salvage her and Bob's upstanding reputation. Good luck with that.

I saw the desk I had been directed to before, and that the room was empty. Finally, a bit of luck. I made a quick dash for it and sat my ass down. This would be tough but at least I had a place to defend myself.

The bell rung soon before I had even a chance to look over the room for an escape route just in case. The door came open and kids of all sizes and genders started to pour in each one yapping to another. Their chatter stopped as each one saw me sitting there watching them like something right from a horror flick. Some of the girls even gasped and tried to back out of the room but the push of students behind them forced them inside. Each kid kept their eyes on me as they found their seats.

I saw several shoot looks of confusion to each other once they sat down. Likely, they thought this was either a joke or a guest speaker. What the fuck I would be talking about beats me, but I heard at least two whispers to that effect. The room was filling fast and as the last desk claimed its occupant the student in the desk behind me pulled her desk back further from mine. The boy in the desk to my right followed suit.

I chuckled to myself over that, "good" I thought, "keep your distance fuckers." My plan seemed to be working.

The teacher of a very advanced age finally came through the door last and closed it behind her as the final bell rung. She didn't even look at me. Immediately she began her lecture about equations staying far away from my desk, not even acknowledging my existence which seemed to further confuse the class. I heard whispers all around me of the kids wondering what was going on.

I smiled. I knew exactly what was going on. This was the fine hand of Mary through Patty working here. This teacher Mrs. Philips had been warned. This was better than I had hoped. Now surely the teacher thinks I am crazy or whatever shit Mary had spun to save herself. While I should have been offended, this solution worked for me at the time. None of the typical stand up and introduce yourself to the class bullshit was going to happen. I was happy to be spared that.

Mrs. Philips while still lecturing and ignoring me, went to her desk in the front and grabbed an Algebra book from it. Without even looking at me or pausing her discussion she dropped it on my desk already open to the page being discussed. The only way I was going to get through this very uncomfortable situation was to focus on something else, anything else. I took the book and spent the hour doing my best to block out the whispering behind me while I learned about exponents and polynomials.

When the bell for the end of class rang everyone got up and dashed for the door. I pulled out my schedule to see what door my next prize would be behind. I saw Patty fight to get into the room through the onslaught of exiting students. She and Mrs. Philips stood there in hushed whispers shooting looks at me from time to time. Gee, wonder what or rather who, they were discussing. I did not care. They could think whatever they wanted to think. Yes, it was pretty uncomfortable having all the eyes on me. Yes, the things they were saying hurt my feelings, but in truth, it was very cold and lonely in that cemetery. Any warmth and any human contact, even this negative contact, was better than going back to the nothingness that waited for me at the end of the day.

I got up and headed for the door and noticed both women stepped as far away as they could to let me pass, even though there was plenty of room. I do not know to this day what came over me but as I walked past it struck me as shitty of them. Before I could stop myself, I false jumped at them and hissed.

They both let out a yelp and jumped back into the chalkboard startled. That was funny. Laughing I strolled out the door feeling both mildly vindicated and surprised at myself. The students in the busy hall tried to avoid me as I wandered looking for the door of my next class. I found it pretty quick.

I walked through the door and a woman in her late thirties very thin with almost cropped to the skull hair pointed me to an empty desk at the back without saying a word. I sat down quickly and wondered what that little outburst was about back there. Was I asking to get detention? Maybe, at least I would be warm for a bit longer and maybe I could just live at the school. The kids all piled in and the same thing (except Patty coming in at the end of class) happened as in the class before. This teacher did the same thing dropping a book on my desk but never saying anything to me directly. It was weird to be sure, but that was okay. I was used to weird, so I just accepted it with relief.

Everything would have gone great that day had it not been for lunch break. I was getting what I wanted until then, well mostly. The whispers, chuckles and stares I could have lived without. However, that is the sacrifice I would have to make to be sure no one got too close to hurt me anymore. I simply could not take any more pain of any kind from anyone.

When the lunch bell rung, I realized I had not planned on forty-five minutes of "free ranging" students. I could not go to the lunchroom as I could not eat the food with my ravaged gut. Sitting in a crowded cafeteria with the entire high school body was not a nightmare I was willing to have without more experience of what to expect from this group. To my relief, as I looked over the schedule, I saw that there was a "ground" with park benches. It was an area to sit outside the cafeteria for those students who were finished with eating early. This looked like the break I needed.

I watched as the students exited the building through a pair of double doors opposite of the single door wall that separated the lower grades. When the last kid went through, I followed and once outside saw the "grounds" just outside a small outbuilding. The students were all heading into that outbuilding, so I assumed this was the cafeteria. I went right for the benches and sat down grateful to be free of that noise.

It was very cold, but I was used to the cold. I had bought a long black jacket on my little trip with Mary, but it offered only a bit of warmth in this deep winter freeze. So, grabbing both arms and hugging myself tightly against the cold I put my head down on my arms. It seemed like a good idea to grab a few minutes of sleep. It had been many long nights, so this little nap was welcomed.

My slumber was rudely interrupted by a sharp poke to my shoulder. Groggy and forgetting for a second where I was, I looked up at a very large girl at least twice my size in both weight and height standing above me. These country kids were big people it seemed to me.

She had long brown curly hair and was dressed in a typical t-shirt with jeans and a fleece jacket. I noticed to my surprise she had a lit cigarette in her hand. She was taking a long drag as she stood there surveying me with what appeared to be a bit of amusement in her eyes.

"Didn't anyone tell you Halloween is in October?" she said smiling at her statement, appearing to find it witty.

I looked at her and decided to ignore her and put my head back down. I immediately felt another poke into my shoulder. Damn, she was persistent.

I looked back up at her and saw a crowd of students had started to gather. Several boys and a few girls. One of the girls with reddish brown hair closest to her said, "Get her, Kelly!" and all the onlookers started laughing.

Kelly smiled at that and took a long drag and blew it at me, "you are one creepy bitch, but you don't scare me. You are sitting at my bench. Get your nasty ass up and do everyone a favor and slime back to whatever coffin you crawled out of." She and the crowd really laughed at that one.

"Fuck off." I said and started to lay my head back down a third time, but Kelly tried to reach out and poke me again.

I snapped. I caught her hand with my left hand in mid-air rising from my seat with speed I did not know I had, I punched her in the sternum with my right fist. She fell to the ground her air rushing out of her lungs with a loud groan. Without even thinking I began to kick the shit out of Kelly making connection with her body anywhere I could. I used every ounce of strength I had refusing to relent even as she began to scream and cry.

The crowd was stunned as they stood there paralyzed watching me kick Kelly within an inch of unconsciousness. I suddenly realized what I was doing, but I was so blinded by my rage I could not stop myself. It was feeling so good to hurt this girl. I wanted to kick her until she died.

Perhaps I would have done so had a male teacher not come out of the lunchroom and spotted this little situation. He ran up and pulled me off Kelly who was now begging for me to stop while crying loudly. The teacher grabbed my arms from behind and held me tightly in a "bear hug" like hold. It took him a bit to restrain me as I wanted nothing more than to return to killing this girl, but finally I quit struggling against his stronger hold.

Once I was spent, he told a couple of the students to help Kelly to the school nurse. They quickly helped her up as she sobbed blood pouring from her mouth and nose which were covered in shoe marks.

"Break it up all of you. Show is over." He said as he began to haul me by my upper arm to the principal's office.

Every student had by now heard of the fight and so as we entered the building, I could see everyone gathering around and this time the whispers were hushed and nervous. I started smiling, then laughing and then howling. This even startled the teacher as he immediately released my arm and pointed towards the office door. His look was a mix of concern and confusion. I could only imagine what he was thinking but I really did not care. He could kiss my ass too. They all could. I would not tolerate being touched, damn them.

As I walked into the office of my own free will it began to dawn on me that this little temper tantrum I had just had may have compromised my deal with Mary. I stopped laughing at that thought. This was serious and what the hell was wrong with me? Acting like an asshole, by kicking the shit out of other students was not part of the plan to keep a low profile. Finally, the gravity of my moment of impulsiveness sunk in and I felt the cold of fear course through my veins.

Lucky for me I caught a break for a change. In the office was Patty but no principal. He was out on early vacation and would not be back till the end of the break. So, Patty was the acting principal in his place. Funny how the very rumor that Mary had started and had sunk my chances at this school would be the very thing to save my bacon now. Patty thought I was just a very troubled child. She did not want to cause more grieving for the poor kindly, Preacher and his wife by having to suspend me over acting a fool. Patty gave me a week of after school detention and shut the case with a warning that next time I would not get off so easy.

Truthfully, I think she was afraid of me. That suited me just fine. I was released back to class and when I entered the classroom this time no one made eye contact and the whispers had ceased. In fact, everyone avoided me the rest of the week. If I went into the restroom every girl already in there hauled ass out like the place was on fire. I did not see this Kelly person at all the rest of that week but apparently kicking her ass had scared the whole student body into deciding I was not to be messed with. I had caught a break and I needed that break badly.

However, it did bother me about my joyful feelings while hurting that girl. I feared something inside me was changing. This changed was not something that I was pleased about. In all my life I had never been a violent person, not even when I had a brief stint as a bully. It had all been in my defense for the majority of cases. Now, I could feel a desire starting to grow to hurt others just because I felt like it. My fear that I would become like my mother or like Mary started to consume my thoughts. No way, I would let that happen, right?

As for the detention, I was grateful to have at least a few more hours of warmth before having to return to the blasted cemetery. The week was over in a flash. While the other students went home to enjoy their Christmas trees, colorful wrappings, and family dinners, I returned to the lonely, cemetery where the only color were shades of grey and the darkest black. I had never had a Christmas, so I did not miss the trappings, but I had at least had a roof over my head during past Christmas holidays.

This year, I would be very sorry that it would be a white Christmas as Mother Nature sent me a cruel gift under my trees. The snow began the very afternoon that school let out for the vacation.

Chapter 13: The Evil That One Does Lives on Forever

"Abandon All Hope Ye Who Enter Here."
- **Dante's Divine Comedy**

The day was dark even though the sun would not set for a few hours as the first snowflakes swirled around my face just as I began my trek to my graveyard home. I pulled my coat tight, but the cold was like the razor blades of my gut cutting through and stealing my very breath. Until now it had not actually gotten below freezing, though it had been colder than death. For the first time I really realized that being out in the elements had dangers I had not considered. One of them was exposure and the other frost bite or freezing to death.

I hastened my pace in an effort to get home before the darkness truly arrived. My next big problem was how to stay warm. I considered what I was going to do to avoid becoming a human popsicle. I thought of the outhouse that I planned on using in the rain and remembered it had a wooden floor and no real door. It would serve to keep me dry but not against the snow with freezing temperatures. All I could do is get home and figure out what to do now.

I arrived in record time and headed right to my stashed cache of items hidden in the outhouse. All was still there undiscovered. With anxiety I dug into my stuff and with great relief found a box of matches in the box Mary had brought the week before. She must have thought of this situation. I had been too inexperienced to realize that weather is not controlled, it is moody. I dashed out in the now whitening landscape to collect as much burnable items like stick, leaves and even branches before the snow made them too wet to burn.

This outhouse was truly a find for a homeless graveyard teen. It was larger than most outhouses of its time being about the size of a storage shed. It was my assumption that at one time it housed not only those who had a call of nature while paying their respects but also as a "tool" shed for the items required to attend the grounds. The privy bench was like any other outhouse with a bench and a single hole cut into it for the comfort of its occupant to sit while reading the latest Sears Catalog or whatever they read in the day. It was not a two-seater but had a long bench on both sides of the "business seat." I have no idea why there was so much bench, but I was very grateful to have seating when not in need of such services.

The only real issue with this outhouse was they did not dig a hole into the earth below the privy hole. That means all the people who had required the privacy of this old building sewage had been discarded on the earth level with the floor. Despite many years of abandonment, the building had a smell not much better than a chicken house. It literally smelled of ancient shit.

The building was old and starting to show serious signs of termite damage and rot, but it had a good solid tin roof. The roof looked newer than the building so I thought it may have been a more recent edition. It had a door, but the door was barely hanging on with a rusty hinge. I was very careful not to be rough with it. The wood used was obviously an afterthought as it was thin and too short at the top and bottom leaving a lot of space. But it was at least something.

After I had almost filled every inch that I could of the outhouse with the "fuel" I went out into the weather again to try to collect stones (some of it cracked headstones) to build a fire pit. The snow was falling hard and fast now, and a strong wind had begun. I could no longer feel my fingers and they were stiff almost unusable. Somehow, I managed to get the stones into a circle and went back and grabbed some sticks and leaves from my "storage area." I had read a lot of books and had seen stuff about building fires, so I tried to replicate what I had seen in photos. To my horror the fire would not start though. The snow was falling so fast and my being a novice at building one allowed for the snow to keep putting it out. All I was getting was a lot of smoke. Smoke was bad. Not only did it not warm me, but it might be seen by some passing car. That is all I needed is someone to call the cops to say they saw the cemetery burning down.

I was so cold and my hands useless. Frantically I ran to the outhouse truly terrified I was going to end like this. Frozen to death in an outhouse in the graveyard. Oh well, not like anyone would be that surprised, least of all me.

I huddled in the corner that was not filled with "fuel" covering with every blanket I could find. I was still freezing and getting sleepy. There was no doubt what that meant, I was in big trouble. Then to make matters worse I began to cry like a baby. Now I would get wetter than I already was from the snow that I had been working in for an hour. Misery is not even the word for the way I felt. Being that cold really hurts. Sobbing like a baby at what I thought was my pathetic end I stared at the floor trying to accept my fate. It was then that I noticed something I had missed.

Just near the door was a hole in the floor with obvious rot around it in a circle. Perhaps it had a leak in the roof once and this was the water damage remains. Whatever the reason, a sudden idea came to my mind. Without a single second more I came out of the blankets and began to tear up the wooden floor starting from the hole. The wood gave way with little effort. I did not throw the wood out but added it to my stash of gathered branches. It did not take long to have most of the floor ripped up all the way to the privy bench. I did not hesitate but ran outside and grabbed my stones and hauled them back inside the outhouse.

Once the stones were in a circle as before I again attempted to build a fire and with some effort got one started. Small at first but then I was able to get it raging to just the right size. It's lifesaving heat began to fill the air as I warmed the blood back into my fingers and toes. Even with the shitty door shut too much hot air was escaping outside and it was only mildly helping the dangerously low temps in my outhouse. So, I sacrificed a blanket. I began ripping out old nails pounded in all over the place but that held nothing (makeshift tool holders of old maybe?) and using a rock nailed the blanket over the door. I was not worried about being smoked out as there were enough holes in the walls to keep me from dying of smoke inhalation even when I covered the biggest offender, the door.

It did not take long for the deadly cold to beat a retreat to just an uncomfortable painful cold as my fire did its job. Another disaster averted. I wanted to sleep but did not dare. If I fell asleep and the fire got out of control or worse went out (yeah, burning to death at that point seemed like heaven) I may not wake up again. So, I listened to the snowstorm rage outside and tried to keep myself busy playing a game with myself. I sat there making up stories, speaking out loud to no one about what I would do to Patty, Mary, Bob, my mom and others if murder were legal. That made the first of many unpleasant nights in the wild tolerable.

The next morning the graveyard seemed even more hushed than ever I had heard before. I went outside to find it was freezing, and white as far as the eye could see. Three inches of horrid white death had fallen overnight, and the blue skies of morning would have made it a gloriously beautiful sight. But only if you were looking at it from your freaking bay window sipping on a cup of cocoa. For me it was a white nightmare of freezing wet feet and hands. My future fuel sources were covered in snow. Damn, it was the south! This was not something I had expected. It snowed here only when hell froze over, and it seemed that the evidence was there. Hell froze over that year.

As a young city kid, I realized I had a lot to learn. I decided I had better hit the library, if I survived until school let back in, and learn how to live in the elements. The urge to damn myself for not thinking of this the whole week kept nipping at my conscious. I tried to keep those inner voices of laying blame at bay while I did my best to seek out wood sources that were not too wet.

I constantly had to return long enough to the outhouse to not lose a couple of toes to frost bite. It was truly a hideous day. I had never been so cold not even when I had died taking those pills. It seemed to settle in my bones making them feel as if they would shatter below my skin.

The only thing worse than that cold was the fatigue. I could not sleep and watch the fire too. In such close quarters I knew what the risks were, so there I was with nothing to do for distraction and so tired I felt I could sleep a week. So, when I heard the car pulling up, I nearly ran running to whomever was coming to beg hoping the car had a heater in it.

Well, whomever is who had come to visit. As I flew out of that outhouse near dusk of the second night after the snowfall, I saw to my utter disgust Mary's station wagon. I almost went back inside the outhouse before I remembered she could corner me there. No, I would have to stand my ground shivering as she hurled her stupid insults. I think I had a tiny hope she had at least brought me some hot soup as any heat would have been welcomed even from her. I tried not to smile as I imagined it would be chicken noodle, with a secret ingredient. The flavor is in the arsenic darlin. I shook the smile off my face wondering what the hell was happening to my mind. That was not funny, damn it, but it came right back and again my smile spread.

There was no time to question my mental health as Mary was getting out of the car and indeed had a big box. She saw me and motioned for me to help her by opening the gate. I stood there and contemplated how funny it would be if I opened it into her face to send her sprawling headfirst into the snow. However, I erased the thought and opened the gate. No reason to have whatever was in the box spoiled right?

She walked in with a box full of more blankets, a long black duster of wool (wow, lucky find), and yes, soup lol. I took the box and immediately grabbed that soup and sucked it down like a starving dog hits its food bowl. Its warming life caressed the inside of my mouth like a ray of hope but when it hit my gut the razor blades began their work. I immediately felt sick and thought wildly, maybe she had poisoned me.

I threw the empty container at Mary, "what the fuck do you want now!" I yelled at her sure she had just come to watch me die slow of her little trick.

She looked surprised not expecting my hostility apparently, "I just came to help. Is that anyway to act when I just brought you a Christmas gift? You are truly unappreciative of generosity!" Mary finished appearing to pout.

I was not believing this shit, "Generosity? Fucking Generosity? You have to be kidding me! Judas Priest woman! I am living in a fucking cemetery because of you! Just get the fuck away from me and leave me alone!" I was really yelling now and laughing too. I could not believe her lack of shame. I started to stomp and pace almost ready to blow and break Mary like one of my branches for a fire.

My behavior which was pretty obviously indicating serious agitation had frightened her, "I did not put you here! You put you here! I want you to come home!" She yelled while backing up, and what is that do I see, tears?

Now this was so confusing. "Tears? Really? She is crying because she is scared." I thought to myself. "Mary is soulless, she is not crying for me or what she has done, she is crying because someone may find out what she has done."

"Cry if you like and you should! One day I will see you and Bob dead! In fact, if I do not live, I will do one more thing before I die. I will sell my soul to the Devil, Mary! Do you know what I will buy with it? A ticket! To see you both burn in hell." I shouted laughing hard now and crazy almost with anger. I was starting to scare myself I was so angry.

Mary then fell to her knees in the snow. She covered her face and began to weep hard. I was stunned not sure what to do. Another of her famous acting jobs? I became paranoid that she was trying to distract me so someone maybe Bob, could sneak up behind me and drag me back to the hell they called home. Either Mary was one hell of an actor, or this was a trick. She has no heart. Looking around me and backing up, I was no longer laughing. Suddenly I swore I could hear footsteps in the snow coming from every direction. I had to get out of here and fast, but where? There is nowhere left to go. I back up wildly watching all around finally backed into the walled barrier. I surely had lost my mind.

"Stop crying and leave me alone." I yelled at Mary's kneeling form desperate to get her gone and stop this weird undertow that was in my mind. I could not get my grounding, and nothing seemed real.

Mary looked up at me and with real tears in her eyes she said, "I can't leave you here to die. I already did this once and now I see that God is punishing me for that sin. I was wrong to not try to repent. Now, please you have to help me repent! I don't want to go to hell! Please just listen to me." She was indeed pleading with me.

What did she mean already once, Michelle? I was curious to know but also very sure this was a trick. I was used to being tricked and, damn me, I was not going to play the fool again. I told her to leave again just as angry as before. She did not budge.

"You do not understand. Please hear me. You are not here by accident. Your mother is my daughter that I gave up a long time ago so I could be with Bob." She was sobbing hard, "They brought you here because I asked for you. I never told Bob about your mother. He does not know. Only the caseworker knew. I thought I could help you, but I saw you were a monster. Bob started to lust for you like the other girls. He could sense the sin inside of you. Please let me help you find God and leave this life of sin before it is too late." Mary said while sobbing.

Now that stopped me dead. What? Huh? I now also fell to my knees in the snow. This had struck me dumb knocking me off my feet. What could I say? It was like a storm cloud of shit just rained from the sky right onto my wig clad head. The woman who had tried to kill me from birth had a mother. I had been taken from that beast mother and thrown right to the very She Bitch that created her in the first place. This was just too fucking much. How could I have missed this? This cannot be true? Can it? I felt like I could not breath as I listened in horror to Mary continue her dark confession.

"I was weak and when Bob started with you, I wanted to hurt you but then you almost died. I felt you had been punished enough, and I wanted you gone but then you helped me help Bob so there must be some good in you! I talked to the case worker and closed our home forever to anymore foster children and accepted you as a relative placement. Bob does not know it, but our home is closed now. I gave your mother to my mother and father, and she was in a loving and Godly home. Because she was born of sin, she started using drugs. Then she had you breaking my mother's heart running off like that. Now I can clearly see I must undo what sins have been done. I thought a few days out here would make you see the errors of your ways, but you are full of demons. Please come home now and let me help you find the path to God and save your soul." She finished and stood up looking at me with pleading eyes.

I stuttered out, truly blow away by what I was hearing, "you brought me here? You knew that Bob might try to fuck me! You stole me from a chance at a real life so you could clear your ugly soul of your sin! Your sin, Mary, not mine, not my mom's. You selfish piece of shit! Get out of my cemetery and never come back!" I was growling now and ready to kill this woman with my bare hands.

However, my head was light as air and my knees like lead, gluing me to the spot. I thought I may have passed out right there. I blinked but it was like I could not clear my vision. Gravity was pulling me to embrace the snow-covered earth as my stomach gurgled and churned finally pushing up the soup in one horrible gush. I helplessly vomited until, I swear, I could taste the very inside of my wasted guts. Mary stood and watched as I expelled my "Christmas Dinner."

She had dried her tears with a handkerchief appearing to recompose herself as I slid into a mess before her. Now, I was the one crying as she looked on with no sympathy. The bitch had turned the tables on me again! What could I do? Every turn, I found a brick wall. A rat running a maze with no escape and nowhere to hide.

"Please come home. You will die out here." Mary said calmly but sternly, "I am not going to argue this anymore. I can make you come home you know. I now have the legal authority. You are not going anywhere but home, hell, or jail. Make up your mind." She looked at her watch appearing impatient.

"I chose hell, Mary" I sobbed out. "No leave!" I was not ever going back even if it meant I would die of exposure freezing to death in that very spot.

Mary snorted. "I will be back. Another few days of this cold we shall see about that. You are sick, too young, and this country is hard even for those with homes. If you change your mind before I come back, you know where to go. You are welcome home anytime you are ready. If you live, that is." She turned and left peeling out as she did in the snow almost fish tailing into one of those ditches.

I continued to sob in that spot trying like hell to wrap my mind around this information for some time after Mary left. It felt like my brain would explode with the screaming inside of it. Mary had blocked me from a possibly loving home, she is ground zero for my very existence as my mother's mother, and worse still, I had actually designed my own trap by helping her block Bob. She now had legal rights to haul me back by cop. My world had been cold, lonely, and scary but now it was desolate. Only the creeping death of the cold was breaking through the numbing effects of shock at Mary's revelations. I got up and walked almost blindly to the outhouse and set to working on my fire. This was going to require some time to truly accept and now a new plan would need to be worked out.

That night was one of the longest, coldest, and darkest nights yet and I had a long history of those already. Only my beloved music kept me company as I floated away on the dark and understanding cords of sounds only a wounded soul could truly feel. Despite my best efforts I fell asleep, and the fire went out.

Mother Nature as unkind as she can be, must have understood and taken a bit of pity for me. That night a warm front moved in, and the temperature began to rise. I awoke to a morning of melting snow that rapidly exposed my companions head stones and my decaying mental health.

Did you ever learn a secret about your life/family/another while growing up that was earth shattering for you? If so, then what did you do? Now if you never learned one that is okay, but please be ready for the next leg of our journey. I cannot thank all of you enough for joining me in this open discussion about becoming the Goth Queen.

Chapter 14: The March Madness of Spring Fever

"Insanity is often the logic of an accurate mind over tasked."
-Oliver Wendell Homes, Sr.

The warmth of the new day helped my frozen body thaw. The pins and needles, however, were not felt in my fingers and toes as normally they are. It was felt in my mind. The secret of my destruction echoed in my head louder than thunder during a spring storm. I could not deal with the simple fact that I had not only created my own hell by trying to kill myself, but now I find I had also dug my own grave by helping the monster Mary gain all she had ever desired. A chance to start over, a chance at redemption, a chance to really make me pay for sins of which I had not even committed in my wildest dreams. All this was soon to be hers. I no longer had the leverage to keep her from taking possession of my sorry remains and dragging me back to the hell she called home. Mary had the law on her side.

The voice inside my head began to torment me beyond imagination with taunts crueller than Mary or my mother ever had. It was so deafening I could not even bring myself to get up and leave the outhouse. They were right I was a loser and a fool. I just laid there without the will to face another day listening to my self-berating. I did not bother to eat or drink the water Mary had brought me.

Day turned to darkness and day again while I lay there replaying my past. In my mind's eye I was forced to watch it all over again like a low budget horror flick. I wondered if I was either the unluckiest or the dumbest person on earth to ever live. Fool was my middle name, how had I missed so many clues, not just over this latest disaster but so many times. So many paths I had taken only to lead back to the same place over and over again.

The dark seeds of self-loathing internal hatred took root in my very soul. I had been fighting all this time to only find my lot worse than I could have ever imagined. Maybe I was waiting for death to send me up for parole on an early release program, but until my parole date I was going to suffer more than I thought I could stand. As I gave into my deepest inner demons, I suddenly became aware that they were not just in my head anymore. Some of them were becoming flesh and blood maybe more so than I was anymore.

To my absolute horror I watched as shadows began to breath and speak from the corners of that outhouse. The buzzing of cicada rose with the shadows despite it being the heart of a cold winter. I could hear them calling me names, hurling insults, and offering dark advice that I did not want to hear.

"Freak!" one would shriek. "Die, Sinner," would hiss another. "We are coming for you," whispered another.

The shadows awoke me from my catatonic stupor, and I knew I had to get out. I had to get out to where I had no idea, but they were going to get me if I stayed here. Without any idea where I was going, I pulled myself off the floor and tore from the outhouse. I broke into a wild run right out the cemetery gate running with all my energy sure that "they" were coming.

Fear and terror ran down my spine making my skin prickle everywhere as I ran away from the cemetery in a blind panic. I looked behind me and saw the shadows keeping pace without any difficulty. I pushed myself harder. I had to lose them, or all would be lost as they dragged me to hell, I was sure of it.

Finally, out of breath and collapsing from stress I fell to my knees then just rolled over onto my back in the middle of the road. Fuck this. I could not run anymore. I was ready let the demons do their worst. My heart was pounding as I tried to steady my nerves for what I was sure my end. Laying there staring into the darkening sky I started to come to my senses. Shadows do not breath, and they cannot talk. I sat up and looked. Nothing, just woods, and fields, no demons. Shaking my head and wondering if maybe I had cracked a gasket I stood up.

I still felt anxious. Like I was being watched by slit eyes from the woods. "Leave me alone," I yelled into the air to no one. Then before I could stop myself, I began to yell like a madwoman standing there in the middle of that old country road. "AHHHHHHHHHHHHHHHHHHHHHH!"

I yelled unintelligibly till I was hoarse. Frustration, anger, fury – there is not a word strong enough for how I felt. Finally spent, tired, and out of breath I sat down on my ass and briefly considered waiting for a car to hit me right on that spot.

The dark was swiftly coming, and it was cold still. So, after my insane bitch fit and some rest I got up and began the long walk back to my outhouse in the graveyard. Throwing a fit and acting like a nut was not going to solve my very serious problem, that much was very clear. However, I suppose I deserved that one. Heading back, I did my best to keep my thoughts of insecurity and shame out of my mind's eye. Right now, I needed to focus on digging my ass out of this latest hole I had fallen into. I promised myself we would revisit who was at fault once I had a plan of escape or failed for good. Either way, self-punishment would have to wait for now.

Talking to myself had become a bit of a bad habit. In the early days of my self-imposed solitary existence, I did not do it. This behavior had only become common for me since coming to live in the cemetery. At first, I felt pretty silly doing it but now I was always chattering away to no one at all. I suppose it was just to hear the sound of a human voice at first. Then it was to keep me entertained in the long hours of nothing to do but sit.

On this day, I kept saying things that were pissing me off or were even absurd. With no one there to bounce my ideas and thoughts off it seemed that I was unraveling at the seams a bit. I suppose loneliness does that to anyone in time. It was beginning to dawn on me my mind might be a bit off kilter.

My fear that I was slowly going insane now appeared very grounded in reality. I had the insight that something was going very wrong with my mind, that I was not thinking clearly anymore. I just did not have the power to stop it. Like most situations I had already encountered, this was an unavoidable outcome.

Human beings are social animals. We need each other to work out our problems, comfort our troubles and to keep our crazy ideas off each other instead of them bouncing us right into outer space. Being cast out of society always leads to a level of insanity by natural law. Even though I had chosen to avoid social interaction purposely I was not above this law. With the addition of my horrific living conditions and the stress of Mary's tormenting me with promises of worse conditions still to come, there was no doubt a break down in my senses was coming as sure as the

Spring would arrive. The only question was how long I had until I shattered completely.

I made it back to the cemetery just as the last light of the day faded. I felt sick and weak. At first, I thought it was the wild running and acting a fool, but as I settled into my outhouse the chills began. Oh no, I had come down sick with something other than madness or the residual from my suicide attempt. Within an hour my aching joints, chills and head splitting headache, informed me this was the dreaded flu without a doubt. I actually was grateful for a bit. I could blame the weird visions and behavior of earlier that day on the onset of illness instead of believing I had lost my mind.

Then the reality sunk in, I was in big trouble. The flu is always a dangerous thing to have even in the best of circumstances. In a stressed environment, it can be deadly. Snow, secrets, insanity now the flu. Death certainly was looking like a handsome gentleman indeed as my fever began to rise and the real misery began to take its hold. Despite the knowledge that I really needed help I decided to stay and fight it all alone. Live or die, I would not go back to Mary and Bob. Now it was up to whoever was calling the shots, be it God, Anubis or some other deity I had never heard of. I was determined to stand my ground.

As the fever rose and my illness grew in strength finding little to no resistance from my malfunctioned immune system, I no longer was truly coherent enough to even get fuel for my meager fires. By the second day, I could not get up at all. Weakness had overtaken me with intense fatigue and delirium following close behind. There was now no doubt in my mind (when not delirious) I was finally going to die. Death would come in a cemetery, which somehow to me, seemed a very fitting end to this story.

On day three I was barely conscious at all. However, Mary kept her promise to come back and offer me another chance at coming back with her. She found me deathly ill and too weak to fight her. This time with much effort she managed to walk, drag me to the waiting station wagon, and off we went straight to the emergency room. I now was well past the flu and entering the deadly world of pneumonia.

I could not fight the emergency room attendants as they hoisted my fevered body onto their gurney and hauled me to a hospital room. Bags of antibiotics and fluids forced were into the carotid artery in my neck by IV. The veins in my arms were too collapsed due to dehydration. They tried to ask a million questions that I seriously could not understand. Everyone seemed very fast and excited making me feel even more hopeless. Too much light, too much noise and all I wanted to do was sleep. I could not even get enough energy or interest to worry about Mary who was there watching appearing worried. Yeah, worried

I would die likely, and she would have to put a new spin on what actually happened there.

I heard the doctor asking her what happened. Mary told him that I had been sick for at least three days (she was mostly right there) and that my condition had only gotten foul that morning. Until that time she had thought it just a normal winter bug. The doctor appeared to buy the bullshit, and I did not bother to contradict her. I no longer cared. I just wanted to be left alone to sleep. At least I was finally warm.

Several days passed as I slept, was medicated with various lifesaving medications, and healed from my latest brush with the boatman. Again, I did not get on the ferry and cross the river to a destiny I had been sure was only a stone's throw away. Not one of the hospital staff discovered my illness was due to exposure and poor treatment. Amazingly, no one even questioned my very poor condition upon arrival. Of course, they didn't. I was already well known for my failed attempt to kill myself earlier. No one thought much of it, assuming that most of my illness was due to a poor immune defense and a high school bug.

My youth did me great service as I began to bounce back and regain my usual health once more within the next five days. I had spent my Christmas in the hospital. School had already started back. It became clear that I was going to soon be released back into the cold, cruel world I had created very shortly. I was not looking forward to it as I prepared to run, if need be, from the awaiting claws of Mary. I was weak as a newborn kitten and the thought of the squalor of the outhouse was not very welcoming. However, the idea of more "bible study" did nothing for my interests either. Oh decisions, decisions, whatever is a girl to do?

I did not speak to a single nurse, doctor, or nurse's aide. When they came to see or help me, I would just glare at them. I had no intention of bothering with them. I was not there to have a tea party after all. Asking me how I was feeling seemed like a joke to me, and I was in no mood for laughing. I was in the hospital with a monster, Mary, hanging around watching me. How the hell was I supposed to feel?

The day of my release I overheard the doctor talking to Mary outside my door about his concerns about my mental health. That perked up my ears immediately.

"I think she may need to see a psychiatrist. She just tried to take her own life not that long ago and she is not on any kind of medication for depression? Did you follow up with a counselor at least?" I heard bits and pieces of his hushed conversation with her funneling into my hospital room.

I stopped listening at that point. I knew Mary had this one without my assistance. She was just as good, if not better than my mother, at covering up her messes. A psychiatrist or counselor was not going to happen. As far as I saw it not like I needed one anyway. How was medication going to fix my problems? Talking to some idiot about them was not going to make them go away either. No, this was something I would have to handle on my own. As I had always done. My plan to escape Mary's clutches had already been conceived and was about to be birthed as soon as she checked me out of the hospital. It was a nice little vacation, but it was time to get back the dirty business of reality.

As I was wheeled to the curb for the waiting station wagon, I had flashbacks to the last time I was being picked up like this. My gut rumbled at me with the thought as if to say, "stupid bitch, thanks a lot." I chuckled at the thought.

This seemed to interest the nurse pushing the wheelchair a bit. I had not said a word the whole stay. Likely, this tiny emotional display perked her curiosity about their odd patient. She asked me what I was laughing about. I stopped giggling and went silent. She sighed loudly, obviously she did not like me not sharing my private joke.

Then as we stood there in an awkward silence (for her lol) she said, "looks like rain, huh?"

None of these people mattered to me. Useless as the tits on a boar hog the whole lot of them. Patch me up to send me for more wear and tear. All she would do is want to engage me in some superficial bullshit conversation about the hospital food or whatnot. Those small talk sessions were meant to make her feel better, not me. Later she would brag to all her co-workers she got me to speak, maybe even add some shit to the retelling of the tale to spice it up. Nope not today darlin. Now she would have nothing to yap about around the old water cooler later. Well, fuck her.

Mary finally pulled up and I was stuffed into the car with not much fanfare. As we pulled out, I sat there smiling. Mary had been right the whole time. I was full of demons. Maybe it was the pneumonia, maybe I was going mad, maybe it was the bad moon I had been born under. Whatever the reason, I had become devoid of any thoughts other than making sure no one got what they wanted out of me. Mary was not going to get away with having the redemption she believes she deserved.

My goal was to be a thorn in Mary's ass. To be exact, I was now ready to embrace my role as the devil she had told me I was. Hell was coming and I was going to take Mary on a personal tour.

"You can drop me off at the cemetery Mary, and I will be needing some fresh supplies tomorrow, water, matches and a bit of food. Make sure it is canned. I won't be eating any of your cooking anymore so don't bother," I said still smiling as I waited for her to protest as I knew she would.

"You cannot be serious! Are you insane! You almost died! You cannot go back there. Surely even you are not so stupid you can understand that!" She said almost running off the road in sheer surprise that I had not learned my lesson.

"You will take me to the cemetery, Mary, if you know what is good for you. You will also bring what I asked for or so help me, Mary, I will make you sorry you ever squirted my demonic mother from your womb. I do not think you want to mess with me on this darling. I have had enough of your shit," I said calmly now staring at her smiling, knowingly.

Mary may have the legal rights to force me home, but not even Bob's whip could force me to not use every ounce of my intelligence to fuck her world in ways she had not considered.

"I will call the police do you hear me? They will help me restrain you, and once I have you home Bob will make you sorry for your sins," Mary retorted snorting. "No one is going to believe you no matter what you say. It will be best if you just accept the Lord in your heart and come home."

I was really smiling now. Mary had said exactly what I expected her to say, so predictable. "Oh, yeah, Bob. Hmmm, well you are right. Bob can make me sorry for my sins that is true. However, I can make you sorry for yours darling. Bob is not such a bad looking man. You know I have been thinking Bob and I could get along just fine in fact. I think even better than fine. I really am starting to enjoy his whip. You know what you are right, let's go home Mary. We can be one big happy family. You can have your Lord and I can have Bob, hahahaha!" I started laughing wildly and making more grotesque references to how Bob and I could be "friends" in the biblical sense.

Mary's face drained of blood, and she went paler than my own face after a good make-up job. She had not considered that at all. She had assumed I would fight Bob off to protect my precious dignity. What dignity? I have been living in a shithouse on the edge of a boneyard. I was walking around resembling a ghoul on purpose. I could not even eat a bag of chips without throwing up like a drunk. I think it is safe to say I was none too concerned about anything as silly as dignity.

I could see anger start to flash in her eyes as she listened to my continued taunts about how much I would enjoy sleeping in Bob's bed as I would slowly replace her with my seductive abilities. "Shut up, you slut," she yelled, "you stay away from Bob."

I really started laughing hard and making obscene gestures dancing around in the passenger's seat while singing a dirty ditty about "Bob and me sitting a tree." The chant words changed to reflect a very foul union, nothing like the one I remembered from my sorry childhood. This was really fun, and I could have done it all day. Seeing the anger and jealousy in Mary's face was better than a warm bed or roof over my head could ever be. My demons were laughing along with me. From every corner of the station, I could hear them laughing.

The cemetery gate stood silent and waiting for me to come home as we pulled into the short drive. "Get out, get out, get out," Mary started yelling and hitting her steering wheel with each yell. "Go where you belong, you fucking monster. I hope you die out here. May the devil have you," she was turning red yelling so loudly with tears of anger beginning at the corners of her eyes.

I was still chuckling but shut up the whole routine about Bob and my fantasy love affair as I got out of the car. She had had enough for now and I would still need those supplies. This was so easy. I knew her weaknesses as she had assumed she knew mine. Well, Mary did not know me at all. There was no future for me, so avoidance of pain was my only goal in whatever life I had left. Attacking her right where it hurt was not such a complex solution, if only I had thought of it earlier, I may not have been in the spot I was now condemned to. It no longer mattered though, as I had finally discovered the way to keep Mary from ever wanting me "home" again.

"Don't forget my supplies tomorrow, Mary. Wouldn't want to force me to make a visit home to ask old Bob for a few crackers and a blanket now, would we?" I said as I closed the door and headed to the gate.

I heard the motor reeving and turned just as Mary lurched the car at my body. I just stood there smiling at her as she slammed the breaks on just short of cutting me down. I did not even flinch. I could see her behind the wheel inside gritting her teeth angrier than a wet hen wanting me to die. Now that was worth a dying for!

I lifted my arms in the sign of the crucifixion and said in merriment, "I am ready to die for your sins, Mary!" I looked to the sky, "Forgive her not for she knows what she does, oh Lord!" then broke into maniacal laughter that even was even creeping me the fuck out.

She let out a scream of rage and threw the station wagon in reverse. With the pedal to the floor, she threw dirt and rocks pelting me with them as she sped off down the road leaving me there laughing.

I stood there as she disappeared in the distance and yelled loudly her direction while waving, "Bye mom, see you tomorrow" as I really fell into a laughing fit.

It took a bit to stop laughing and my side was killing me from the strength of it. I pushed open the gate with force and walked into my cemetery like I owned it. "I am home everyone! Did you miss me? Oh, that's okay, no one missed you either I see!" as I started that damned laughter again. Everything I said was cracking me up these days, or just cracking up is more like it.

I went to the outhouse and set up for my lonely night with only my Sisters and my demons to talk to. There was no doubt that this path I had chosen would be hard, long and fraught with danger. No matter what was coming I was finally ready to face it with my cunning and inner demons to rely on. I accepted that the normal life I wanted was not in the cards for me. I settled in for the night ahead no longer afraid of the darkness. I could hear the scrapings and sounds of the creatures in the night and started laughing again. They were not to be feared, they just wanted to live in peace like I did. What is so frightening about that?

The whole situation seemed so absurd that one had to laugh in order not to cry. I had just pissed off the Preacher's wife so I could live in a shitbox surrounded by corpses and rats in an effort to avoid beatings and molestation. As the rock and a hard place crushed me in the center I had initially liquefied. Now the pressure was creating something new. A dark diamond able to cut glass was replacing my broken heart. I did not know how long I would have left above ground but that night I made peace with myself and with death. I also swore to myself that until the day came for Anubis to punch my train ticket, I would find a way to keep anyone else from joining me in this wasteland of despair. My journey toward Goth Queen sovereign of the lost had finally begun. I was still a long way from where I needed to be, and school was coming the next day. I slipped off to my usual nightmares of things that cannot be changed but this time without a shred of fear left inside me.

Okay my beauties, have you ever done something that was so out of your comfort zone that it surprised you? If so, how did it go? Where you happy with the results?

Chapter 15: She has Graveyard Eyes

"It never ceases to amaze me: we all love ourselves more than other people, but care more about their opinion than our own."
– Marcus Aurelius

The morning came on like so many more in the future would. The sun slowly rising chasing away all the shadows as it grew in strength as I watched them flee looking for places to hide in the shrinking darkness. I knew Mary would be back today, so I decided to hold off returning to school one more day. My doctors note had given me a few more days off but I had decided holding off too long only would make the return harder. Best to just go back right away. I was feeling better and ready to deal with school.

The law had just recently changed and quitting school was no longer an option. Getting full time work also was not, for now. I had no way to get to a job if I could find one to start. My next big problem would be the strengthening child labor laws that prevented me from even gaining part-time work with the poor to nonexistent GPA I had. For now, I was stuck in a horrific loop of poverty, dependence, and homelessness. Okay I did have a home, of sorts but it did seem to me that trying to obtain one with running water and a heater would be a goal I would hopefully get to shoot for sooner than later.

I had nothing to do in my cemetery hell. Each hour would drag as I listened to my tape cassettes for the millionth time. Finally, the batteries drained it dead.

I walked around the grounds and re-read each stone that was legible and asked the occupant questions. Once in a while, one would even seem to answer back. I was unsure if I was hearing them actually responding, or if the response was in my head. When I did hear the answers, I felt something between fear and confusion. I felt I should be afraid but was confused at why I was not. This day I did the usual and to my complete surprise I heard a lot of responses when in the past it was only once in a while.

I also noticed many of my "roommates" were quite clever with witty responses. I often would be sent running back to the outhouse to write something one of them said because it was so cool. These people had lived whole lives so I am not sure why I would be surprised they were so wise. They certainly knew more than I did so it made sense that talking with them may help me to understand not only who I really am but where to go now. I did ask some of them, who I assumed were the smarter residents, a few deep questions but often I got only the sound of the winter breeze and rustling leaves in response. It appeared they were as superficial as everyone else I had ever met. By noon I was losing my temper with them. No one wanted to talk about anything of any worth.

I began to stomp on them and yell obscenities at their markers. If I had died and had all that information, I would not be discussing stupid shit like making tea! As I became angrier, they began to taunt me. I then realized they were playing a game with me and that made me even angrier. I covered my ears and tried to drown them out. My cassette player gone, I had nothing else to ease all noise they were making. My head was splitting with all of them speaking at once now in gibberish or languages I could not understand.

Holding my ears, muttering while pacing in the middle of the graveyard is how Mary found me sometime after noon. I did not hear the station wagon pull up because of my little slip off into crazy town population.

"What are you doing? Who are you talking to?" Mary's voice snapped me out of my bizarre overload. "I brought your supplies." She said while looking towards the outhouse suspiciously.

I stood there stunned. Was this real? I could not be sure. I took down my hand from my ears slowly. The many voices of the dead had silenced. I was relieved. Maybe I had fallen asleep and that was just a nightmare. I did sleepwalk after all. Mary was never a welcomed sight but today I was almost grateful she had come by. Mostly because I needed supplies, but also because I was afraid of what was happening to my mind. Lie as I might, make excuses all I like, I am starting to go batty.

I recover quickly, "Did you bring everything I asked for?" I asked immediately pulling myself together. I cannot let Mary see this weakness. She will likely find a way to use it against me.

Mary stares at me like she is examining a new type of bug. I could sense she was trying to place this thing she knows is me but is also not me too. She lowers her gaze and gets closer to my person really looking hard with abhorrence and curiosity.

"Are you sleeping with boys for money or hiding a man out here?" She asks while glancing again at the outhouse. Jeez of course she would think that, wouldn't she?

"Yeah, Mary. I have the whole high school football team stashed in the outhouse and before you got here it was one hell of a touchdown." I spit at her, angered at her opinion of me. "Hey, stick around a bit. We are about to go into overtime. You can even handle the ball if you want, Mary." I let her name drag as I said it sarcastically.

"You are so crude! Demon! Sinner!" she said taking a posture of indignation at my silly statement. "Why did I ever think you could be saved?"

"Beats me, Mary. I mean Bob beats me, Mary." I said in a sing song voice that did not seem to be my own. That made me start laughing again this strange play on words. I did not think it that clever or funny, but the horrid river of insane giggles had me and was not about to let go.

Mary backed away immediately, "You are crazy." She then turned and walked off two paces where a box laid on the ground I had not noticed before.

Mary reached inside it and took out the bible I had been forced to read that had been in that infernal room. She opened it and began to recite passages at me about coming to reason or some shit. I was no longer listening as I saw a large shadow rising behind her. One of the demons that haunted me at night was growing larger as my eyes widened in horror. Mary kept reading as if she did not even know it was there, now large enough to block out the light darkening the entire graveyard.

The breeze that was lazily blowing suddenly carried the sounds of a thousand cicada rising from the ground. I knew that sound, it was the voices of the dead. Hissing, like a tire letting out air, joined in. Chaos broke out all around me as my vision shattered into pieces of colored glass. I was lifting up, floating away with those shards losing my ability to control this situation. I felt the warmth of the sunlight for but a second until suddenly I came crashing back to earth right to my knees in such force as to knock the wind right out of me. I could not catch my breath as it felt I may smother. What was happening? My mind grasped wildly at an answer to this confusion of senses, these things that could not be. Finally, it dawned on me, Mary must be doing it. She has found some way to mess with my mind and now while I was distracted, she must have hit me or something that is why I cannot breathe.

Mary it is always Mary! I look at her still reading that damned bible. Something must be done about her I decide. She looks up at me and looks startled. She had better be, I am going to enjoy listening to her whispering from below very shortly, if only I can catch my breath.

"Dear Lord! What are you doing? What is wrong with you? Why are you looking at me like that?" She screams at me. "Get up you sinner!"

That is enough of Mary. I find the strength to get off my damned knees and start running for her. I am going to shut her up once and for all. I am dead I have nothing to lose. Mary screeches and throws the bible at me. It hits me dead in the face and stuns me. It made a direct hit. I feel the hot pain then numbness as it collides with my nose knocking me slightly backwards. My eyes start to water as I grab my nose grateful it is still there. I was sure it has been shoved into the back of my skull. The station wagon is starting. Mary has made it to the car as I recover from the bible smack.

"Oh no you don't!" I think as I run for the station wagon. It is backing up as I run through the gate full speed completely filled with rage.

I can see a very frightened Mary inside trying to back up and yelling something from inside the car. I jump and land on the hood of the station wagon. Grabbing the windshield wiper with my left hand while balancing my body like a lion attacking a jeep on African Safari, I smile wildly through the glass at a very terrified Mary.

The giggling rises from my chest as I growl out, "I will show you, Sinner." With my bare right fist, I begin to pound on the glass trying to break Mary's face through it. Animal sounds erupt through my giggling and attempts to break the windshield.

Mary hits the brake and I almost fall off, but I regain my balance quickly and double my efforts to break the windshield. She speeds forward. This time I am not able to maintain, and I am thrown from the hood to the ground hard. Inertia forces my body in a roll. I am almost unable to stop before I fall off into one of the drainage ditches. Dust and rocks pelt me as Mary speeds off down the road leaving me there giggling like a fruit loop on my back looking up into the endless sky. I have something in my left hand. The giggling becomes howls of laughter as I realize it is Mary's windshield wiper.

Slowly the infernal laughter stops as I lay there realizing what just happened. I was going to kill Mary. What is wrong with me? Yes, she did deserve to die, but what am I thinking? Going to prison is certainly not going to make my situation better. I sit up and throw the wiper into the ditch. Standing painfully, I realize my nose is bleeding. Dust and dirt are all over my clothing. I needed a shower and a washing machine. I had neither. Slapping as much debris as possible off my long black wool jacket and pants I walked back into the graveyard shutting the gate behind me. Apprehension filled me as I waited for the whispers, or shadows to grow but everything was quiet and peaceful like normal. I waited at the gate to see if this was a trick to lure me in further but after a bit of time decided all was back to normal, whatever that is.

The box had been overturned in Mary's mad dash for the car. I went to it and saw all the supplies and more I had asked for and money too. Only twenty dollars. Not enough to even find a bus station. It was useless in the graveyard. Cannot eat it and cannot warm up with it so I threw it back into the box. I found fresh batteries and breathed a sigh of relief. At least I would have something else to listen to besides my busted thoughts again.

The bible laid open just off from the box. I went and picked it up while rubbing my nose. I really hated this thing and started to pitch it with the wiper. As I walked to the gate ready to chuck it hard, I changed my mind. I had read this far, what else did I have to do anyway? So, despite my inner self screaming at me to throw this reminder of pain away I took it and threw it into the box with the other supplies. I headed to the outhouse and used the music to keep my ailing mind busy for the rest of the day and night.

I was doing my best not to think of what I knew deep inside. Over the last weeks I had learned to endure the ravages of the physical pain I had caused, the elements, and even my enemies. I was at a complete loss at what to do with the new problems now plaguing an already troubled existence. All I could do is hope whatever crazy shit was going on in my head would pass like any other illness. I also thought maybe I would find a solution like I had done with everything else. Until then, I decided to stay busy as possible and not try to kill Mary again.

I could barely wait for the sun to rise so I could head to school the next morning. It was pure gut instinct that another day alone in my cemetery may send me over the edge forever. So, almost too early I fixed my corpse make-up, brushed out my wig, and did my very best to make my dirty clothing look presentable. It was a Wednesday, so I was stuck wearing these clothes until Sunday wash day. Oh, well.

The walk to school was uneventful and no shadows or demons appeared to have followed me from the cemetery. I had always hated school but today I was grateful to have a place with life to run to, any place.

I was spotted by a few loudmouth students before I even got to the school yard and I heard people yelling, "Oh my God! It has come back from the dead!"

"Ha!" I thought, "I am never coming back from the dead at all so fooled all of you." I winced at the truthfulness of that thought.

Doing my best to ignore them I went into the schoolhouse as several of them made derogatory comments or snickered. That was fine. At least, I knew it was real and not some deranged story made up in the mind of a lonely teenager who was losing it. For the first time in my life, I was actually glad to see things returning to what was normal for me. I even felt relieved when I went to my first class and the kids around my desk moved theirs away. It seemed like all would be okay. Nothing weird here. Well, except me. Everything was exactly the way I had left it before the Christmas break.

By lunch time I actually was starting to feel, dare I say, happy? Happy as I was ever going to be. The students hated me, scattering in every direction whenever I happened in their area. It used to hurt my feelings. Maybe deep inside it still did, but for now I needed to know I was still in control somewhere in my dark world. Their disgust and fear kept me in power over them. No one would hurt me if they feared me. Best of all, the words I heard all made sense with the reality I had come to take for granted. Only when it was unraveling did I truly appreciate what it means to be able to be grounded in reality.

I went out after the students marched off to the cafeteria for their food that at some time may have resembled something eatable. No lunch for me, as usual, so I quickly went to the bench table I had been at the last time I had been to school. This time I doubted Kelly would bother me as I stole a few moments of peaceful sleep. I laid my head down in my arms on the table and closed my eyes hoping that my inner voice would shut up long enough to let me slip off quickly.

Half asleep, I heard taunting. Lifting my head quickly, truly expecting a crowd of hillbilly vigilantes to be surrounding my table ready to burn me at the stake. However, there was no one around me at all. It must have been one of my nightmares. I started to put my head back down when I noticed a crowd of teens standing around just two picnic tables from mine. The tall unmistakable form of Kelly was standing in the center of them. That caught my attention.

It was where all the taunting was coming from as I could hear them saying awful things.

"Little slut," said a girl's voice. "You are an ugly whore, Stephanie." said another girl's voice. All of them began to laugh.

Well, it was not me they were bothering for a change, so I decided to ignore it and enjoy the break. This was the problem of some other poor slob. None of my business. Not often I was not the center of the bullying from sheeple after all.

"Looks like Kelly is trying to regain her reputation as a bully after having her ass kicked by a corpse." I chuckled at that thought and put my head down again.

The taunting got louder, and more kids voices joined in. I did my best to ignore it. Then I heard it, sobbing. I tried to talk myself into just closing my eyes and ears to this. Really, I owed nothing to anyone and if they are picking on someone else, so what? However, I could not take it. They were hurting someone, and I know what that feels like. I would be no better than they were if I did nothing.

With a groan, and my mind still trying to say stay out of it, my feet listened to my dark heart and stood me up to walk over to see what all the hub bub was about. As I approached the excited crowd of insult throwers, I spied a small blond headed, pretty girl sitting on the bench in front of them with tears streaming. Well, this was apparently the Stephanie they are picking on. She saw me coming up behind the others.

My delusional mind heard her say, "help me." In reality, if she actually said that she likely meant she needed help to get away from me.

I walked up behind Kelly and poked her hard in the shoulder. She turned angrily. I watched as the anger melted to fear when she realized it was me again. The other students also noticed me now and every head turned from Stephanie to the corpse.

I smiled and waved pleasantly. "Hi." I said very civilly. I think I was hoping they would just stop picking on Stephanie if I gave them a target and that would be the end of it. As usual, I was wrong.

"What the fuck! You again! Christ! You stink! Do you ever shower after you crawl out of your crypt creepy?" Kelly said trying to hide her obvious fear while covering her nose and waving the air. That distraction did not help. I could see it in her eyes. I have to give her credit she was standing her ground. Too bad for her.

My smile never wavered as I replied in a matter-of-fact tone, "Only when your mom is out of town and your dad and I can get some alone time." Now that shocked me.

"What did I just say? Who is running this show? Where the hell did that just come from!" I thought inside my head but outside I stood there calm, cool, and collected still smiling.

All of the students with looks of utter confusion looked at Kelly to see her response. Kelly stammered and looked as if she may cry. She did not know what to say. If she called me a name, I may punch her again, if she did not retort she would look a fool. I could hear her thinking, "What do I do? I have to do something!"

"Watch out she is going to go for your stomach." I heard a voice say behind me. But there is no one behind me.

As Kelly took that lunge for my breadbasket I had already been warned by that voice from nowhere. I stepped out of the way almost in slow motion. She expected to make contact, so she had put all her force in that jab into thin air. This threw her forward as I caught her in the throat with my arm. I pulled her close to me and used my entire body to exert extreme pressure on her neck. I began to crush the life out of her. I was giggling again.

"Just cannot leave people alone, can you darling," I said giggling believing I could feel the blood flow damning up in her arteries. Her face was cherry red, and she began to wildly claw at my arms trying to reach my face.

A smaller girl from the pack came forward and kicked the shit out of me making contact with my thigh but I held tight. She attempted to break me off Kelly again by grabbing my arms. I held tight and now we used Kelly as a human tug of war rope. Kelly was gasping and turning blue as I continued to hold tight refusing to let her breath.

"Help me, damn it!" the smaller girl yelled to the others and two more, a small boy and a medium sized girl, came forward. They grabbed my arms too and that was too much force for me to hold on to my prize. They wrested Kelly from my grip. I fell backwards and Kelly fell forward right into the kids who had freed her. I landed on my ass panting but laughing like a hyena.

Kelly was coughing and crying. She tried to get up and come at me again, but the other students held on to her saying, "she is not worth it, let it go Kelly!"

Kelly started to get her color back as I sat there laughing but defiantly refusing to get up. I did think of plowing her again, but I was comfortable, so I did not bother. She was still coughing but at last I could see she was done with this scuffle. She stopped struggling against her friends and they released her. She walked over to me but kept a safe distance.

"Psycho! Fucking Psycho! Go back to the graveyard!" She yelled at me hoarsely (hehehe) and then looking back to her friends, "let's go. I need to wipe this nasty rot off me before I start looking like this creep!" Kelly stormed off and all her little sheep followed each asking if she was okay.

I crossed my right leg over my left and leaned back on my arms looking into the sky just laughing and enjoying the moment. "See you tomorrow, Kelly. Same time, same place. Next time I will kill you." I said aloud to the clouds above me.

"Uhm, thank you." A soft voice startled me out of my discussion with the heavens. I had forgotten about the girl I had started the fight over. She was still sitting there looking at me. "No one has ever helped me before. My name is Stephanie. What is your name?" She said with drying tears in big pretty, hopeful eyes.

I just looked at her the laughing stopped. She was not much taller than me but unlike me was very pretty with long blond hair and big blue eyes. Stephanie was dressed the way most poor kids of the day dressed. Her clothing was in need of repair; torn jeans and wrinkled flower shirt that was a decade out of style or more. She was looking at me and started to smile sweetly.

I got up immediately, quite irritated at her for having dared to speak to me in the first place. Why I was not sure and that pissed me off even more. I do not like to not understand my feelings and this girl needed to stop being nice before I kicked her ass too.

"I would like to know your name. We could maybe hang out sometime?" She said in that same friendly voice with not even a hint of disgust at what she was offering to me.

I looked at her and snarled, "Fuck you is my name." I turned and stormed off in the same direction as Kelly back to the schoolhouse.

As I walked in the double doors, I could see Stephanie's' sweet hopeful look in my mind. I also could see that hope dashed like a baby seal's head by a poacher's club as I had said those hateful words to her. I felt as if I should care but damn it, I had saved her ass and risked mine. Yet, that was not enough for her? No, she wanted to repay me with adding her bullshit to my already toppling one. I decided as I headed to my next class, no more getting involved. If my problems were not enough for me, then I obviously should get a hobby other than bully killing. I am not the savior of the world I kept saying to myself all through class.

I kept waiting for a call to the office as I fully expected to get called up for attacking Kelly. How stupid could I be? Each time I heard someone shift in their seat I would apprehensively look to see the door of the class open with Patty motioning me to follow her to my doom. Each time it was a false alarm. Kelly had not tattled. Probably afraid this Stephanie would have a tale of her own, I thought. Still, I awaited my impending execution I was sure was only seconds away.

By the end of the day, I had worked myself into a full-on frenzy of anger at myself for having felt mercy for that girl. My skin felt like it was going to jump right off my body and my head was tingling with imaginary bugs. Even the walls seemed to be narrowing and a feeling of being trapped was washing over my senses. When the final bell finally rang, I was in a full-on panic, and I knocked down half the class running from that room and out of the school at high speed. I had to get out of there! I could not take this shit anymore!!

Did you have a friend in life that you met in a strange way? If so, how did you meet and are you still friends?

Chapter 16: Mirror Mirror on the Wall,
Who is the Most Cracked of Us All

I ran over more students in the hallway and practically knocked Patty out by slamming through the door to the outside. She was apparently about to open the door from outside when I pushed it open with force. Patty yelled and fell down, but I did not stop to help her up or apologize. I kept up full speed on the road to my cemetery home.

I kept up my pace with the bug feeling now crawling down from my head to my spine. Then it spread further. It felt I was crawling with things I could not see with my eyes. I smacked my head trying to smack the crawlies and rubbed my arms hard, but the things kept crawling. prickly skin rose everywhere as the sensation of cold cut through me that did not come from the winter day. The road was heaving suddenly as I realized I was having another of these strange confusion moments.

I stopped running and stood there hoping that the rushing blood in my ears would drown out any weird noises or sounds that I was sure would begin any moment. Panting I stood there still feeling crawly and cold but the road steadied. Slowly, as I got my breath the other odd sensations ceased as well. The only noises I was hearing were those of the woodland creatures and breeze in the fallen leaves. It had stopped again. I sighed with relief and walked the rest of the way to the cemetery.

When I got to the gates, I had gone back to mulling over my behavior at school again dropping my many questions about these bizarre moments of unreality. As I arrived, I went to open the gate, my heart nearly stopped as I heard a woman's scream rip through the silent bone yard. The iron in my hand (I was still holding the gate) wiggled like it was alive. I let it go and it slammed shut. Fright glued me to my spot as I watched through the gate as the headstones began shattering one after another. Then I saw the outhouse catch fire. In terror at losing my "home" I almost went inside without thinking but another female scream sent me running like hell down the road again as I had the day before.

"Fuck! Fuck! Fuck!" I yelled. "What am I going to do?" as I started to cry. My shelter is burning down, and I am running down the road like a loon.

I ran until I could run no more and finally slowed to a walk. I did not know where to go. The night would find me without a roof over my head vulnerable to the elements. I began to look for a new shelter, anything an old barn, or a culvert.

I walked for over an hour, but nothing was alongside the road but trees and fields. The rare home was observably occupied with many signs of life. This was looking very bad. The sun would set in only two more hours, and I had found nothing. In the distance, I saw a narrow bridge coming up ahead.

Since I had started my journey, I had not seen a single car but just in case, as I approached this bridge, I made sure I did not hear any coming in the distance. Satisfied that it was safe to cross I began across. It was an old bridge with cement blockers to keep the cars from slipping off the edges It was not a long bridge at all. In a car you would not even notice it. Walking over it I looked over the sides to see a large water body below. That caused me to pause. A creek? A river? A lake? I was unsure so I looked over both sides. It was narrow body of water but large and I could not see where it ended from this vantage on either side. As I examined it from the bridge, I noticed a small foot path from the road that seemed to lead to a slide down the raised sides of the road. Likely fishermen made this path to get closer to the water.

I started down the path but then realized fishermen could be down there now, so abandoned my curiosity about this path quickly. It was steep anyway and I did not need to get any dirtier than I already was. I walked back onto the bridge and looked down.

The horrid giggling began again as I imagined I could take a bath in the lake with Kelly's dad long as her mom was out of town. That was not funny, but I could not stop laughing at the thought. Soon, I stood there on the edge of the bridge staring into the water below thinking that one way or another I had to stop this laughing. I am not sure what was coming over me. I was not myself and half the time lately it seemed I was doing things against my own will. But how could that be? Am I not the one in control here?

"Who am I!" I yelled out laughing. "Who the hell am I?"

The breeze picked up and answered, "You are a sinner," as it played with the hair of my wig.

"I am not a sinner! I am not my mother! I am not Mary! You hear me!" I yelled out still laughing. I ripped off my wig and threw it to the road and took off my wool duster.

In a trace I took a step up on the concrete barrier. I balanced on it still laughing and looking below at the water.

My mind was whirling as I stood there unable to get a grip on my thoughts. Each was like a greased-up piglet, I would grab it, but it slipped by with a just a squeal.

I lifted my arms to the sky and took a ballet pose I saw once in a book. "Once upon a time far away in a castle lived a beautiful fairy princess." I said out loud really laughing.

This was a story Marie had told me so many years ago now. She would tell it because she was going to live there one day or so she said.

"Outside this castle there was a moat. An evil dragon guarded the moat. Then the handsome prince, let's call him death, he came to claim the princess for his own." I yelled in merriment still posing.

"He killed the dragon with a sword that was dipped in poison. He killed the princess with his kiss." I finished the story laughing and took a bow to no one. Now my laughter turned to tears as I looked below. This had to end. I cannot do this anymore.

I let my body fall forward headfirst into the water below.

I am falling. I do not care. Any second I will feel the quick pain of a broken neck. I will be free of all this pain. Instead, I felt the pressure of water, as I did the most awesome swan dive into the lake below. The wind left my lungs and water hit my face as I sank.

The water was deep. I kept sinking deeper and deeper but no bottom yet. Finally, I felt my feet hit the ground. I could not see anything in the murky water. I floated there a moment thinking that a drowning would work just as well as a broken neck.

However, my lungs screaming for air and my lower brain betrayed my intent. I pushed off the bottom with my feet. In an almost animal desperation, I fight to the surface of the water. I make it and gulp in the life saving air angry at myself for my weakness. I was not a good swimmer. My dad before he had run off taught me enough. I was able to get to the bank with some struggle and close calls.

On the bank I crawled out and laid there truly spent. Not just physically but emotionally and mentally. I looked up into the darkening sky and said out loud, "Well, great form Bob but I am afraid she had a bit of an error there at the end of that dive. I would have to say I give her a six." I began to laugh as I made Bob's voice, "Oh, Mary. This Olympic Suicide jumper is not the best our team has to offer but she gave a good effort. I will go easy and give her two more sixes to match yours."

I really started to laugh at that wildly but then I began to cry at the same time. Completely cracking up I stood up doing both. My head felt like it was splitting. I began yelling with all my might until finally falling back down on my knees at the bank where I had just crawled out of the lake. The bridge was not high enough and the lake deeper than I had hoped. I would not die today.

Holding my bald scarred up head, I cried and laughed on my knees feeling so defeated I thought I may just stay there and let the elements finish me off. Then I heard them, the cicada began the chirp of my coming break with reality. I looked up horrified, as I snapped out of my emotional meltdown, or did I?

I watched the lake turn to white and static, not unlike I had seen on the TV once when I was little, and the stations shut down. Behind me the trees began to shade into shadows melting into walls as I stood in my old room at Mary's and Bob's house. I see a girl on a hospital gurney with cracked lips staring at me, she is alive but barely staring at me with rage. She looks like me.

I try to back up, but I feel something kick the back of my head. I turn and see a girl hanging from a hook in the ceiling that used to hold an old lamp wire off the ground so you would not trip over it. This girl is hanging by a pair of nylons and struggling against them trying to free herself as she is slowly strangling. In horror I watch as she turns blue, and her eyes bulge out, but I cannot help her. I am so scared. What is happening? No words will come from my mouth.

I turn back to see me in the gurney she is still staring at me dying and accusing me with her eyes but then I see Mary. She is so skinny I can see her skeleton under her skin and her eyes have sunken in as she stands over the me in gurney. She is petting that me's head and talking to her. I want to look away, but I cannot. I am being drawn to the me on the gurney. I want to tell her I am sorry so she will stop looking at me that way. Then the hissing sound begins as I fall face forward as if something tripped me. I feel I am being dragged down the hallway but not toward the room. I am dragged on my face out of the room and away, far away from the room. The static is everywhere as it settles back into the lake.

The trees reform and I am back on the bank like nothing had just happened.

Slowly the brown and grey of reality falls back into place leaving me back to my senses. I blink and look around. There is no laughter this time. I am not even sure how much time has passed. I am still wet, and the sun has not set yet. So, maybe only a short time and not days I hope to myself.

"What the hell just happened? Where am I?" I yell into the woods. "Someone please tell me what the hell is happening! Is this even real?" I yell again. Only the chirps of birds settling in for the night answer me back.

Desperate for an answer I stare at the lake water again, trying to get the static to come back. I felt like my answer is here, I am just missing it. This is happening for a reason I am sure of it. However, staring hard and trying to focus I cannot see anything other than minnows breaking the surface of the water. No static, no cicadas this time. Just peaceful water with rising fog as the dusk settles in.

"Shit!" I yell frustrated. I would have to come back another time. I am wet, it is cold, and the cemetery is a long walk away. I realize at this point that maybe the outhouse did not burn down.

"Nope, I am bat shit crazy that much is pretty clear." I say as I am climbing up the foot path I had found earlier, only up this time. "So, no way I can ever trust a damn thing I see from here on out. Well, good news is that at some point you will not even know who you are so there is that to look forward to," I chuckled at that but just a quick nervous one.

This was no laughing matter. If I am crazy, then I cannot be trusted to look after myself. If Mary finds out she will get the law to come get me. This fact was not lost to me as I grabbed my tossed wig and put back on my jacket. I was freezing cold. At least, my clothing had gotten a wash.

I walked back and got home in the dark. I opened the gate to find no shattered head markers. The outhouse had not burned down either as I had suspected. I chuckled at that. I wished it would burn down, otherwise why that hallucination?

Once safely inside my hovel home I lit my fire and put on my headphones to play my Sisters in case any voices decided to interrupt my thoughts tonight. The music from the tape player seemed to keep me level.

"Ah, then this may be a useful tool if it is true." I say to myself as I consider that fact. The music seemed to short circuit the strange loss of reality. I was unsure why, but I did note that not one of these delusions happened while listening to the tape player. Grateful that I had maybe found a way to combat my insanity. I saw the tape player as almost magical, and I needed some magic right now. I began to think I should test that to be sure.

I went outside the outhouse into the dark cemetery and could make out the grey and white markers just barely in the darkness. I sat down cross legged in the center of my fellow roomies. I closed my eyes for a second and thought of what I had seen today in that weird vision.

My heart began to speed up as I could see my eyes burning through me from that hospital gurney. I was angry with me no doubt. I tried to keep my breathing calm taking deep breaths, but I could feel the stress rising. Oh no, the cicadas were chirping! I opened my eyes and turned up the music to deafening levels to drown out those evil creatures. It worked I could not hear them anymore. Waiting for some time, nothing happened. No static, no shadows, no demons. Just the dark as always.

Sitting there blowing out my eardrums in the middle of a cemetery in the dark, after just jumping off a bridge an hour earlier, I decided I was not crazy after all. With a satisfied smile I went back into the outhouse and turned down the music and listened. It had worked. No cicadas.

Tomorrow I would have to find a place to use my twenty dollars to get batteries for my magic box and maybe some more music too. I would also have to see if I could hide the small earphones from any teachers' eyes if I needed it at school. I could not take the chance that this could come on anywhere at any time.

I worked on effectively hiding the small machine in my shirt and setting the headset by breaking off the metal that held the earphones together. I wrapped the wire under the back of my long wig hair and with some work got the earphones to stay close enough to the ears to hear the music. This could work.

I had found my weapon against the world of the unreal. Dare I say my cure. That would remain to be seen. As I drifted off to sleep that night a nagging question kept popping into my very unstable brain, "how can I see me if I am me? I was in two places at one time? How?"

The next morning, I got my money from the box stuffing it in a pocket. As usual, I then ate one of my canned horrid meals. After struggling in pain for my usual forty-five minutes I got made up for the day and, with my new weapon against madness, I happily headed to school. Yesterday, was just a bad day I had decided. Today would be better, I was sure of it.

I did not even flinch as the students pulled their usual insults and whispers of indignation when I arrived. All seemed as it had been. I did not even have to use the madness murdering machine hidden in my shirt under my coat. I was really starting to feel better about everything. That is until lunch hour approached.

It had not escaped my attention that I had already had two lunch fiascos and was not really ready for a third. Despite my trying to will lunch time to not come, it did, right on time.

As usual, I went out after everyone else and found the picnic benches empty of students. This time, no nap I decided. Instead, I got out my madness machine and listened to music. If Kelly came today, I would be watching for her.

I sighed with resignation as I saw a girl come out of the cafeteria headed towards me and the picnic tables. I really hoped she would leave me alone.

However, it was not Kelly, not yet anyway. It was this Stephanie person. She saw me and smiled that sweet smile. I looked the other way ignoring her smile and stopped watching her.

Instead, I closed my eyes and listened to my music. I let the Sisters sing to me of a dark world that seemed to understand cemetery kids. When I opened my eyes, Stephanie was sitting across from me still smiling sweetly, shall I even hazard adoringly?

I jumped startled almost out of my skin. "Leave!" I yelled at her angry that she had scared me.

She did not budge nor stop smiling. She then said, "hey, look I am really glad you helped me out yesterday. That Kelly is a real bitch, and all. You know a lot of the kids here think that you are a weirdo, but I think you are nice. I don't mind the make-up. I love Halloween myself." She finished appearing to expect that to soften my response. Well, she was wrong.

I was livid now, "I said fucking leave! Are you deaf? What the fuck do I care if you like Halloween or fucking Valentine's Day? I do not like Kelly. I beat her ass because I felt like it. I did not help you! I was helping me! So, now you think what we are girlfriends here? Fuck off!" I snorted at her.

She still smiled and even giggled at that (huh?), "no not girlfriends silly. I just am trying to get to know you better is all. I would like to be friends is all." She started twirling her pretty blond hair.

I was blown away. This girl was crazier than me. I stood up to leave no way I was sticking around this, I had enough of my own demons. "Fuck off," I yelled at her.

However, before I could walk away, I saw Kelly and the crew coming from the cafeteria looking right at us. Even from that far off I could see her smiling evilly at me.

"Damn it can I not just have one day of peace?" I thought almost groaning aloud.

I held steady watching them. Yeah, there was no doubt they were headed right for Stephanie and me. I pulled down my earphones. My instinct was there was about to be trouble.

Stephanie stood up noticing I had not left but was staring at something. She then looked and saw them coming too. Stephanie gasped.

I heard behind me, "they have decided to gang up." I turned startled but no one was there. Stephanie saw me look behind me, so she did too.

"What are you looking at?" She looked scared.

I looked right into her eyes, "they are going to gang up and try to beat us up. You better get ready to fight," my tone was cold as death. This was bad. I knew the voice was right.

She teared up and nodded. "I don't know how to fight." She almost whispered back. I nodded, I understood, and I walked over to her side to stand beside her.

This was going to be a bad one. Kelly had brought six other students with her both boys and girls. All big. Stephanie and I were very small slight females, there was no way we were going to win this. I removed my magic mad box from my shirt and took off my coat. I heard Stephanie whimper a bit as she watched me prepare for battle.

"They will try to separate us so when it starts, keep your back to mine no matter what and aim for the stomach or throat, okay?" I said to her quietly, looking for an indication she understood. "It will be okay, keep your head covered." Pity for her washed over me.

She nodded with tears streaming but she got closer to me as the group finally reached our table.

Did you ever have a fight while in school? If so, what happened? Did you win or lose?

Chapter 17: Infamy, the Fight for Survival

Has everyone taken their medication, brought coffee and loud music to get through the voices...errrr...rantings...errrr...ravings...words of a story about the making of a Goth Queen? Great! So, start running and I will be stalking...errrr...right behind you!

Kelly stood there smiling defiantly with her six goons spreading out like your fingers when you try to fit on your gloves. They blocked me and Stephanie from any hope of escape. They should not have bothered. I was ready to stand my ground and so was Stephanie even though she was scared as hell. We both knew running only would prolong the inevitable show down. I felt Stephanie's warmth as she moved in closer almost standing on me.

Then I almost pissed myself as I felt her reach out and quickly grasp my hand with hers and squeeze. She dropped the hand embrace quickly. Even my dumb ass understood this kind gesture.

She was saying "we are in this together, come what may, live or die." at least, that is what I heard her say with her clasping.

It threw off my resolve of 'every kid for herself' as I felt a new feeling wash over me. No. I would not let them hurt this kind soul. In my dark heart I suddenly knew I would die for her. Only over such a small offer of kindness? Why?

In my dark world, it was a shot heard round my soul. No one had ever stood beside me in any situation. Now facing complete loss, this girl was ready to suffer with me. It was now all I could hear or see, blinding me to the impending pain about to be dished out on my body.

Compassion was this new feeling but would have to be examined in depth another time. For now, I had a job to do and for the first time ever, I knew what that was. Protect innocent Stephanie. I faced Kelly and started smiling myself.

"Well, well look at what we have here. A creep and a whore. Both smell like shit, so makes sense," Kelly mocked still smiling and pointing at us. She was so sure she had us.

"Fuck off, Kelly. We all know it is you that you smell darling. Remember to wipe front to back. Didn't your momma teach you proper hygiene," I said laughing, mocking her back.

Kelly was suddenly scared. I could see it. She expected us to be afraid and Stephanie quite visibly was. She expected begging and pleading. In a way, she was getting it, just not as she expected. I was just begging her to shut me up.

"Wow, your mouth is nasty as the rest of you is creepy.," he said trying to sound tough and still smiling but that was starting to fade a bit.

A boy standing next to Kelly with an oddly shaped head and bad haircut then breaks in, "Are we going to beat these bitches' asses or what?" He was apparently getting antsy.

"Amy!" Kelly said looking briefly at a brunette girl (the smallest of them) standing just to the left of me, "Go watch the door for Coach Crouch."

Amy nodded and took off running back to the cafeteria door. The epic battle was about to begin. To my dismay I saw fog rising from the ground all around me. The darkness started to bleed out of the shade slowly covering the ground coming toward this little scene about to be played out.

"Oh, shit," I thought to myself, "Not now, please not now!" This was no time to fly off to never-never land, Goth damn it!

The cicadas began to sing their song of disaster as I saw Kelly's fist coming for my face.

She was too slow. I grabbed her fist quickly before it made contact. She was startled and tried to wrestle it away. Steadying myself against her heavy body struggling I took her fist and bit the pointer finger at the ring section. Screams of pain erupted from her mouth as I bit harder now tasting blood. I continued the pressure.

At first her goons were surprised and stood there but her screams of agony woke them up. Two boys came to assist Kelly and I could not see the other three. I thought of poor Stephanie as these two grabbed me and started the same old wrestling me off of Kelly as the day before.

As their strength got to be too much, I bit harder and felt her finger snap as Kelly wailed out. I broke it. She would not be pointing at anyone else for a while, I thought as my body was hauled backwards and Kelly was freed.

Unfortunately for me, my turn. The two boys held me and one of the other girls I could not see came from nowhere and began to plow my wide-open middle and head as the other two held tight. No matter my struggling I could not break free.

As I took the blows, I caught sight of Kelly on her knees crying and wailing. She was out of the fray. One of the boys (odd head) was there trying to help her stop the bleeding.

Then as I got a good solid punch to face as it was forced to the side, I could see poor Stephanie being pummeled on the ground by a large girl who was sitting on her. Poor Stephanie. I was in a bit of a jam so I could do nothing but watch and take my beating. I closed my eyes as I took a blow to the chest.

Then I heard it, "Now! Now!" I opened my eyes ignoring the pain and saw the girl hitting me grab my hair. She went to pull and off came the wig.

She was stunned, as was my captors. With all the strength I had, I wrested free as they all stared in disbelief at the wig in the girl's hand. Finally free of their grip, fast as lightening I turned and kicked both boys in their manhood. This sent them writhing to the ground. Then I turned to the girl who had dropped the wig with terror and decked her right in the nose. Before she could even recover, I tripped her and jumped on top as she landed and grabbed her throat squeezing hard.

Stephanie was crying and bleeding. The girl on top of her had stopped hitting her knowing Steph was done. She got off her and came for me as I continued to strangle the girl in my grasp who was now clawing up my hands and arms fighting for life. I intended to kill her no doubt.

I saw the big girl coming but did not care. I only squeezed tighter laughing like a hyena. The girl came up and hit me in the back of the head sending colors splitting through my vision like fireworks on a summer night. I fell off the girl to the ground stunned. She then kicked me in the stomach. All the wind left me. Now both myself and the girl I had been strangling were gasping like fish out of water laying side by side.

I watched as that big girl came at me to play soccer with my body again. I closed my eyes, so I did not have to see it coming. I was helpless to stop it. Nothing came. I opened my eyes to see why. Out of nowhere had come Stephanie! She jumped on the girls back grabbing her hair and pulling her to the ground. The girl was grabbing wildly trying to get a hold on the very battered Stephanie. She was too fast and kept her hold riding the girl's back like a bucking bronco in a rodeo.

I got up with all my will and kicked the shit out of the coughing crying girl laying on the ground next to me. I had to make sure she stayed down. I then joined Stephanie still wheezing and trying to breath. Stephanie held on to the big girls back, as the girl bent forward trying like hell to knock her off. I walked over to the struggling girls. Before the big girl could lift up to a standing position, I planted a foot right into her face. Blood went everywhere as her lips burst and she gurgled. Stephanie fell off her back to the ground and the girl went to her knees. Stephanie and I smiled at each other. She did not get up but rested on the ground. I stood looking at her and the wriggling big girl next to her trying to suck in any air of worth. Both of us looked like hamburger meat, bloody and bruised.

Then I felt a hand grab my shoulder. Startled from our smile of victory (sort of) I turned and punched the person right in the face. I had mistakenly thought one of the boys had recovered from their "ball game" and he was looking for revenge.

However, I had just hit Coach Crouch right in the face. Oops. He stood there holding his mouth now bleeding from a busted lip with a look of surprise. I did not have any classes with him but knew who he was. Amy had gone for help when she saw the battle was going badly, she became a tattle tale. He had come to break up the fight, a bit too late. I looked down to his other hand. He was holding my ratted wig.

He held it out to me, "I think this is yours." I took it and affixed it back on my head best I could give the condition of it.

He looked at the hand he had been holding his mouth with. He began rubbing the blood all over them between his fingers. "This is to stop now," he said loudly while surveying the battlefield.

I looked around too at that point. Stephanie on the ground sitting next to a crying big moose of a girl. Kelly sobbing as odd-shaped boy had put a paper towel around her finger and was helping her up. Two boys standing up rubbing their crotches. One girl out cold next to me on the ground. What a mess. Over what? Bullying. I shook my head went to the picnic table grabbed my coat and madness box as started for the school.

"Where do you think you are going young lady?" yelled Coach Crouch from behind me.

I did not stop or turn around but said back, "to the office to be expelled. I already know where it is." I went through the double doors headed for the office damning myself for this stupidity.

What had I been thinking? None of this would have happened if I had just minded my business in the first place. Now it was time to pay for my mistake. The graveyard hell and beating I just took would be a blessing after Mary got a hold of me. I assumed she could have authority to do whatever she liked at this point. I had just thrown my freedom away. Surely, I would be strapped to a bed, and have the bible literally shoved up my ass for sure. No one would stop her as I would surely be turned over by the cops.

Patty was on the school landline gossiping and eating from a Tupperware bowl when I came inside the office. The look on her face told me I looked worse than the dead I normally looked like. Her eyes widened and she told whoever was on the line she would have to call back and hung up immediately. I sat down in the chair Mary had me in weeks before and waited for my turn to be called into the principal's office without saying shit to Patty.

"What has happened? Why are you bleeding?" Patty had walked to the half wall and was staring at me. I did not respond only shrugged.

"Fuck you. Gossiping asshole," I thought. She would have to wait for the rumors like everyone else far as I was concerned.

She did not have to wait long. The door opened and in spilled the whole group of fighters, even Stephanie. Only Amy was not among the broken teenagers. She had pretended to be innocent of it all. Coach Crouch was with them. We shot looks of hate at each other, me sitting in the chair the others all standing. Stephanie pushed past them and stood next to my chair and shot her own look of hate at them. She had chosen her side even in this time of defeat. Had to respect that.

Coach Crouch asked Patty where the principal was eating lunch. He was told the teacher lounge. So, the coach informed the whole herd of us that we were to follow him. We were going to go answer for our crimes and receive our sentences after the principal had heard our defenses. Everyone of Kelly's crew and Kelly followed right behind the coach. Stephanie and I waited and took up the back of the group. The teachers' lounge was a very small building next to the cafeteria, so we had a bit of a walk.

Stephanie walked next to me, "we will not get expelled, you'll see." She whispered to me. I just shrugged back. She had caused me enough trouble.

"Look they started this. We defended ourselves! What could we do?" she tried to reason to both herself and me, I think.

I glared at her, "shut the fuck up and by the way stay the fuck away from me!" I said softly but then raised my voice at the end of my demand.

The coach looked back and shot us both a warning look. All of us continued our journey to the lounge in silence.

When we arrived the principal, an aging man of around mid- fifties with comb in black dyed hair, wearing an old-fashioned grey suit was finishing his lunch. He was sitting at a table with the ancient teacher from my first period class. As he saw our rag tag group coming up behind the coach, I could tell he was not a happy camper. Principal Greene had one of those resting bitch faces and today this bitch face was really bitchy as he listened to a description of what Coach Crouch had witnessed.

Turned out the coach had seen more than I had thought. Just as Stephanie predicted, she and I were not held as the cause of the fight but the defenders of our skins. Actually, and accurately, I may add, he told the principle that Kelly had been caught bullying me before, and Stephanie on several occasions. To the

Coach this was something that was a long time coming or so he said. He told the Mr. Greene that Kelly had been warned by him several times to knock off her shit as one day these kids she picked on would rise-up and beat her ass. He said today she finally got hers.

I admit, I was stunned as I listened. I saw Kelly holding her hand still looking at the ground sniffing in a feigned display of shame. That was bullshit. She was not sorry for anything other than that broken finger.

Yes, I was very surprised to hear what the Coach said but I was floored by the sentence handed out by Mr. Greene. After he listened carefully to the coach's story: Kelly was expelled for good. The other five participants were suspended for a month. Stephanie and I were given detention also for a month after school.

Mr. Greene told Stephanie and I to leave. We could go wash up but then go back to class immediately. We were also warned to report to detention after school or our guardians would be called, wait, did he say guardians? Like both of us had guardians and not my guardians and Stephanie's parents. Now I was curious.

Stephanie and I both hauled ass out of there. We did not have to be told twice. She and I went to the bathroom and started washing up first in silence.

Apparently, she was still hurt I told her to stay away from me.

Then she could take the silence no more, "Told you," she said in a sing song voice.

I smiled at her, "yeah, you did." I went back to fixing my morbid mix of white make up and blood to its usual corpse morbid look. I was trying to brush out a tangle when I saw Stephanie come up behind me watching me in the mirror. She had a sad look on her face.

"I am sorry you are bald. Cancer? My mom died of cancer; you know." She said tearing up a bit.

Ah, so there was my answer. Mom was dead and Stephanie has a guardian.

I looked at her coldly, "Poison. My mother wanted me to die, and I made that wish come true." I tossed my brush into my purse and stormed off to class leaving Stephanie standing there with a confused look on her face.

I was tired of this dumb compassion feeling already. No more trouble, damn it. Far as I was concerned this was over. I had enough close calls already this week. I just wanted some peace and quiet. So, I ignored what I had felt for Stephanie before the fight telling myself I had done my job. Kelly would never hurt her again after all. Kelly was now gone forever thanks to that fight. So, my job was over, and I could go back to the real problems in my hellish existence as I struggled for solutions to things beyond my control.

As I walked into the class all eyes looked up from their books. I went and sat in my desk in the back quickly to avoid the staring. I sat down and to my surprise everyone was turned in their seats smiling at me. Some were giving me a thumbs up and others were nodding making silent clapping gestures.

"What the hell is this happy bullshit?" I thought totally confused as I stared back in disbelief. "Yeah, I am gone. Oh boy, I have slipped my wig." I was sure of it.

The teacher told the class to pay attention, and everyone turned around. I had already hidden my mad box in my shirt while cleaning up and fixed the earphones. Now I turned on the player sure I was having another of my now infamous slips into unreality.

When the bell finally rang to signal the next class, I got up to get to my next. Students in the hallway did not part like usually to let me by without being accidentally touched by any part of my creepy self. No. They all went by trying to touch me, pat me on the back or high five saying things like, "way to go creepy," and "bad ass!"

I dodged their attempts almost ready to freak the fuck out. What was going on? They were actually happy to see me and somehow, I had become the high school hero.

"What the fuck is wrong with everybody!" I thought as I ran like hell to the next class to get away from the noise. I could not deal with this. These kids are going to bring the cicadas, I could just feel it coming. I sat down at my desk grateful to be out of the hallway and blasted my mad box loud as possible trying to calm down. I watched as the class members entered the room all of them smiling at me. A pretty brunette with dimples in her smile came to my desk as I just sat glaring coldly at her. She quickly put a grape blow pop on my desk with a note. She gave a thumbs up. I did not touch it as I watched her then go to her own desk in the front.

I left it go as class began but finally could not take it anymore. Maybe the note had an answer to these weird behaviors. I opened it and saw a crude but carefully drawn flower inside. Under the flower it said, "Thank you, love Crystal," and nothing more. Well, that did not help. So, I wadded it up and dropped it and the blow pop on the floor. I couldn't eat the damned thing anyway. Useless as the note it came with.

I only had to dodge the students one more time and I was the most grateful student in history of horrid high school to hear the final bell ring. At last, the peace of an empty school with its wonderful running water, heater and real bathroom. I was ready for the quiet and luxury of detention.

I walked to the door where detention students were assigned and opened it feeling pretty relieved as the last noisy student left the building. I sat down in the first seat near the door ready for a nice rest. The door opened again and in stepped Stephanie. Shit, I forgot about her again. She smiled at me. I shifted uncomfortably in my seat. She appeared to be wanting to try to talk again. Stephanie was like a rat, difficult to keep out of your outhouse.

She came right to the desk next to me in the front and sat down. "Oh my God! We are like popular!" she squealed at me smiling proudly. "Haven't you heard! You did this! We are so friends forever now!" she finished.

I just groaned and put my head on my desk. Could this day get any worse? I really should learn never to ask that, because it always does. A fact that somehow, I already knew, was in the works of my shitty journey I seemed to be on whether I liked it or not. Stephanie was still happily chattering about our newfound rise to the top of the high school food chain as I heard the door open again.

I looked up to see a very angry Mary, and behind her a police officer stood looking right at me.

Have you ever been arrested? If so, what happened.

Chapter 18: Arrested Development

Now I will not lie this is **the hardest part** of my story to Goth Queen I have had to write and likely the most devastating and most life impacting of all things I've ever had to encounter in my life. I write tonight for the first time since this began with a large amount of trepidation. Nothing I have told you thus far has bothered me (and while hard to believe, it is truth) but this part of my story is something very hard to talk about. **So, with that in mind I will ask all of you to be understanding, empathetic and if nothing else, kind.**

What is contained in this part of my story is something I have never discussed or admitted to publicly nor to most people even in my personal life, ever. I have decided this part of the story is important for you to know. It is maybe the most important part of my own story that may be helpful to help you also understand the trials you may be handed down in your own journey. I do understand that this is something few if any of you will ever have to face as I present it here, but **devastation comes in many forms**. How I handled mine is what made me who I am. How you handle yours makes you who you are. While mine may be a different type of devastation from yours **(none worse or better as pain is pain, there is no measure for it!)**, this is what makes all the same in many ways. We live through it and deal as we can.

Now with that in mind, all kidding aside, if you are ready to walk down through one of the darkest of paths one can be cursed to walk, you start, and I will be right behind you.

"You are not your illness. You have an individual story to tell. You have a name, a personality. Staying yourself is part of the battle."
-Julian Seifter

Mary motions for me to come to her and the police officer. I look desperately to Stephanie and see her suddenly silent. The color has drained out of her face from fear. She looks at me and shrugs appearing not to know what to say. I feel my stomach curl up like a fist as my body goes numb with pure terror. I am doomed.

I find myself standing up, but I am not sure why as I did not want to stand up. Slowly my body walks to the door despite my inner voice screaming at me to stop now. My field of vision has narrowed, and the dark is closing in. I hope I will faint, but I do not.

As I get to Mary and the officer, I am told to follow them out of the school. Mary takes the lead as I am followed by the cop. In my mind I can see myself as a calf being led to slaughter. Questions begin to circle my head like a swarm of angry hornets, 'what is going on,' 'has Mary called my bluff,' 'where are we going?" No one is telling me anything. They walk in silence with only the sound of the officer's cuffs bagging on something medal on his belt as we walk to the doors to leave the school. My heart is racing now, as my breathing become shallower.

Mary opens the door and as the light floods into dark hallway it turns to static. I can hear the death bugs calling as the static consumes Mary walking right into it. I try to grab her to keep her from stepping inside but she is lost. I am so confused why should I care if she is overtaken? Good, right?

Deciding that she is lost I am sure I will not be taken back into that static hell. So, I turn to run but the officer tries to stop me. I push him back and he grabs my arms.

So, I kick him with all I have yelling at him to "Run! Don't you see it!"

This startled the officer. Looking confused and unsure he loosens his grip and I struggle free running down the hallway not sure where the static cannot go. In a sheer panic I crash into the single door separating the high school from the elementary part of the school. The door did not open just because I slam into it. For some unknown reason I did not see or recall it being there. I fall backward stunned for a second. Turning I see the officer coming, but it is not him that gets my ass off that floor in wild terror. The static is following him as the building behind him is eaten away by it.

I turn and this time turn the knob running through it hoping there is a door out. I see down the long hall double doors that likely lead outside like the ones on this side. So, I take off with all the speed I can muster headed for that escape route. I can only hope the static has not already gotten everything outside.

The cicadas are chirping full force and now the tires are hissing too as the static gains on me. I managed to get to those doors just in time before I am lost. Not even bothering with the handles I use my body to force the doors open ignoring the pain of my injuries from my battle earlier that day. The doors give in to my full force body slam and I am outside blinded by the full-on sun explosion as I emerge from the darkness. I cannot see a thing, so I just run not knowing which direction I am heading. At this point, I do not care where I am going. I just have to go, anywhere but here.

Hands grab me that seem to appear from nowhere. I cannot see the body they belong to. With sheer terror I being to yell as I fight them and kick them will all my might. They are too strong and now there are more arms grabbing me pushing me to the ground. Nothing is making any sense. The dirt tastes like fire as my face is forced into it. There is a weight on my neck as my arms are forced behind my back. I am then floating up. I fear I will fly off into the sky it is so fast.

A sudden burn to my face as I am slapped hard by one of the hands. My face flies to the side at the force of the smack. Then another as I see the static beat a hasty retreat backwards and colors begin to appear. Each second more and more world around me. I can taste blood and dirt in my mouth. The cicadas are going to sleep as the hissing ceases. I am so confused what is happening?

I close my eyes hoping this nightmare will end. My face is burning as I feel it swelling up even more than it was from the blows earlier in the day. Another hard slap comes across my face nearly knocking me to my knees, but somehow, I am being held up. I open my eyes. There is a man staring at me his mouth is moving. This man has a funny long handlebar mustache. That is funny as I watch it moving in the opposite direction of his mouthing. The infernal giggling rises up inside me and I cannot stop focusing on that funny mustache.

This man slaps me a fourth time. I am still laughing but now I am waking up. To my horror I am in handcuffs and a police officer is holding me up. This mustachio man is also a cop, he is in uniform. Short and heavy set with huge arms. He is saying something but not in English. I cannot understand his gibberish. He is very angry and red faced. I see him lift his hand again to slap me, I drop my head this time and he slaps my ear instead of my cheeks. I feel my teeth rattling as my ear goes numb.

"Boyd forget it, just load her in the back," I hear him say to the policeman holding me. His words suddenly are in English. Now I can understand.

Boyd hauls me laughing like a hyena and struggling to get away to the awaiting squad car. I look around at the scene which is now crystal clear no static at all to obscure my view. Students are standing everywhere watching this scene. They are looking afraid, and some are whispering. I think I can hear them, but it is gibberish. Mary is there too. She is embarrassed and keeps covering her mouth as I am forced into the back of the squad car. Her embarrassment is very funny! I really start to howl at that unable to control myself.

The police officers turn on the flashing blue and red lights as Boyd and Mustachio get into the front seat. The siren wails as I laugh madly in the backseat cage staring right into Mary's face as we pull out of the school yard.

Slowly, painfully slow, the laughing began to abate. I was so grateful. I hated that laughter as it was not me doing it. I felt like a prisoner to it unable to stem that noise coming from some demon inside of me. As I was finally able to quiet myself, I relaxed a bit to consider my situation. The events leading up to my ride as a county special guest was truly unexpected. I thought they would send me back to Mary and Bob. What happened there?

The cop called Boyd was at the wheel. The CB radio chattered with a woman's voice about the locations of various other officers. They had killed the siren but were driving at least seventy-five miles an hour speeding towards their destination. It was finally dawning on me that I am headed to jail. For what I could not understand, yet.

The mustachio cop picks up the CB radio control and reports our location to the chattering lady on the other side. He gives a time for expected arrival.

He adds, "Cathy, do you have the cell prepped? Better remove the sheets and anything not tied down for this one. Oh, and call Dr. Higgs tell him we got a live one." He hangs up the controller.

That sounded bad. "Are they talking about me? Why? Live one? Haha, they are wrong there. They have a dead one." I thought as the laughter began yet again over this little joke at the end of it.

I see Boyd's eyes look back at me in the review mirror with what appears to be confusion at my laughing fit.

Mustachio turns his head to the side saying to me, "hang in there, kiddo, we will have you there soon. A nice meal, a rest, and the Doc can get you all fixed up."

"What?" I think even more confused and upset then before, "Doctor? Did I hurt myself again?" I start to look over my body. My hands are cuffed behind me, so movement is pretty hard, but I seem to be in one piece.

I do hurt like hell all over, but I had just had my ass kicked by Kelly's goons a few hours ago. That was to be expected. I wiggled my fingers and toes, and they are there. Why do I need a doctor?

We finally arrive at the police station/jail house for this rural hell on earth county. I have finally gotten my laughter under control as Boyd opens my door and pulls me out. I let him. He has a gun, and I am not about to do shit without him saying so or doing so. The idea of being shot was not my dream come true to say the least. I was held by the arm and taken inside a cinder block tan building that had small window and almost no color other than white or tan.

Inside a woman was inside a box with cider blocks half-way up, then Plexiglas to the ceiling. Cathy was the dispatcher I heard in the car sitting behind a desk talking on a CB with phones and paper files to the sky. She was short and very heavy with very close-cropped black hair and friendly eyes. I liked her right away, she seemed nice I could tell.

I smiled at her as she got a look of horror on her face. She stood up and walked to the glass staring at me her mouth hanging open.

"Dennis, this is a kid! What the hell! How did no one report this? Look at her! She is skin and bones!

Where did you pick her up again! This is horrible for Christ's sake!" She was talking to Mustachio but looking at me.

I just smiled bigger to show her that we were friends. I did not know why she could not tell I was happy to meet her. So, I said, "Hi. You have the prettiest eyes I have ever seen!" Women love to be flattered. I knew that would make her feel better. I could tell she was not feeling well from her facial expression. Cathy was seriously sick to her stomach, and I knew what that was like.

My sudden speaking startled Boyd who still had my arm. He looked at Mustachio apparently called Dennis and said, "Okay, let's get her put up till the doctor gets here. I cannot deal with this anymore." Boyd did not like me apparently.

Dennis nodded then looking at Cathy who I was still moon eyeing and said, "Okay, tell the Doc to hurry. Call that girl's folks and tell them the charge needs to be dropped. If they give you any trouble, tell them we have pictures of the damage to this kid. Tell them we will press charges back for assaulting a mentally ill child." Huh?

Now that had my attention, who is he talking about? "Oh yeah stupid, you are in a jail house. He has lots of cases. Just be calm, sooner or later someone is going to tell you what is going on here and why you have been arrested. Until then, at least they have a heater." That made me start to laugh again. Oops, I would have to find a way to stop thinking before I broke a rib with all this laughing. It was really starting to hurt pretty bad.

I was led by Boyd still handcuffed to a small cell that was away from the usual cells that apparently had some residents already. I heard them talking to each other. This one had bars that separated it from the long hallway lined with cells in front of it. A small desk with a fat cop who looked thirteen he was so baby faced was at the desk reading a magazine with a deer on the front of it. He stood as he saw the three of us. On his belt was the keys to all those cells. I was still laughing. Now this really was funny.

Okay Keith, open the cell up and do not take your eyes off her okay. Cathy came through the door and joined us as the door to this cell was opened by Keith and I was taken inside. Once inside Boyd let go my arm and he and Dennis let Cathy pass. She stood there looking me over appearing to be pitying me as I chuckled.

"I got this Dennis. You boys give us some privacy will you, oh and I will need your cuff keys." Cathy said to them as they backed up. Everyone was staring at me.

"Be careful there Cathy, she is stronger than you think," warned Boyd as he took off my cuffs.

My wrists hurt but I just let my arms hang. I liked Cathy so I did not want her to know they hurt. She seemed so sad already. The males left the cell as Cathy began to pat me down finding my mad box and twenty dollars. She took them off me and put them on the cot beside her. It was the only thing in this white padded room besides a small toilet. She asked me to take off my jacket and shoes which I did without a fight. I did not know why she wanted them but whatever, she was the boss right? She then asked for my belt which made me giggle again, so I took it off and handed it to her. This game seemed very silly but not like I could do anything about it. Cathy then patted me down harshly. She grabbed my things she'd taken or asked me for and knocked on the now closed door. It was solid and padded hard to distinguish form the rest of the room. There were no windows, and a strange drain hole was in the center of the floor. Weird.

"Ready Keith," she said, and the door opened. She turned and said, "Get some rest kiddo. You look like you need it. When you are released, you can have these back." Then with that same sad look she walked out, and they closed the door.

That was good to hear. I looked around the cell. It smelled of vomit and mold. Yeah, kind of like home. I sat down on the cot which was bolted down. At least it was more comfortable than the ground I was used to. There were no sheets or blankets. I guessed Cathy took them like she was supposed to. There was a foam thing, flat without a cover. I assumed it was supposed to be a pillow. I laid down and without much work went right to sleep. It had been a long day. Whatever the hell was going on did not involve Mary or Bob. Far as I was concerned, this worked for me.

I awoke to the sound of a door opening and keys rattling. Groggy and confused as to where I was, I saw Dennis come into the cell.

"Okay kiddo, are you going to give me trouble? Do I need to cuff you or are you willing to come with me quietly?" He was looking stern but kind.

I nodded that I would come no problem. I followed him out of the cell as he led me down another hall (boy this place was bigger than it looked from the outside) to a small room with a big window where you could see inside it. I was wondering how long I had slept. The very few windows in the hallway to the outside world were dark. I assumed it was night but tonight or tomorrow night, I was unsure.

Inside this room sat a male of about forty. He had longer hair than the typically close-cut cops had. This man had huge glasses that strangely magnified his eyes. Although not that old, he already was silvering at the temples and in his well-groomed beard. He was wearing a sweater jacket with a button up shirt and tie. As we entered, he stood, and I could see he was wearing a pair of well-worn blue jeans. He smiled at me asking me to take a seat in the chair across from him at this small desk in the room. I looked around and there was nothing else in here. I did as I was told.

"Thanks, Dennis, I got it from here. I will yell if I need you" he said smiling at the officer.

Dennis said he would be just outside the door. Then looking at me said, "Behave yourself. Answer Doctor Higgs questions, okay?" He patted me on the head, and I pulled away. I hated to be touched and I am not a dog, damn it.

I saw this man called Doctor Higgs shoot Dennis a look and shake his head no. I assumed like me he did not like that gesture either. Good, me and this guy would get along just fine I decided.

Doctor Higgs sat there for a few moments looking at me pursing his lips appearing to study my face and clothing. Then after what seemed like eternity said, "I am Doctor Higgs. Do you know why you are here?"

I shook my head no. He sat back and took in a deep breath looking up at the ceiling. I looked up too. What the hell?

"You were picked up and brought here for an emergency twenty-four-hour hold. I am told the officers had come by to speak with you regarding a report you allegedly assaulted and battered using a deadly weapon earlier today at school. The police became concerned about your welfare after you demonstrated some very odd behaviors during their attempts to speak with you. So, let's talk about that, shall we?"

Huh? What the hell is he talking about? The fight? Deadly weapon? Odd behaviors? None of this could be correct. "You have the wrong person, mister," I said coldly, "Yeah, I was in a fight at school but there were no weapons, and I did not want to fight either. I had to because they started hitting me." Then I bitterly thought to myself, "Mary must be behind this."

"Oh, okay so you did not bite and break a young lady's finger during a fight today, is that what you are telling me?' he said leaning closer on the table. I leaned back further in my chair to keep my distance.

I nodded that I did do that while a smile broke out on my face with the memory of Kelly screaming as I did it. That made me giggle. Oh, shit not now. I managed to stifle the giggling, but it took me a minute. Doctor Higgs was studying me hard now. This had made him curious.

"You find that funny? You nearly bit off someone's finger and that is funny? Hummm, let me ask you about your make-up. Interesting look you have there. Want to tell me why this look?" He said staring hard at me.

I shook my head no, while staring right back at him coldly. I was done talking to this fellow. He was making me feel strange. Why all these questions? Does he mean teeth are a deadly weapon, really? I already knew if I pushed my stress level too high the cicadas would come. So, I pushed all thoughts out of my head and calmed my breathing. Losing it now was something I did not need for sure. I was in trouble already.

He started questioning me like a machine gun shoots a magazine, one right after another. I kept my mouth shut and only shrugged or nodded yes or no. Nothing of any detail. Somehow this guy knew all about the static and the shadows and that was scaring the hell out of me. I had never told anyone about them, how did he know? Unless they were real, and I was not going crazy after all. The more he asked the more uncomfortable I got till finally I was sure the death bugs would come. I was having trouble keeping it together realizing this had not all be just a bad dream, or sleepwalking. It was all real! The idea that this static was real was too much. It wanted to take me away and I knew that is what it was after. Now I realized it is coming for me and the shadows would consume me till I was no more. This thinking caused a swell of emotions to spew from my very core.

I stood up abruptly knocking over the chair. I grabbed my head; it was splitting right down the middle, and I needed to hold it together! My brains would spill onto the floor. I could hear the cicadas, but I was not going to listen, damn it. I paced back and forth telling myself "This is not real! This is not real! This is not real!" The laughter with crying at the same time began as the world felt it was caving in on my broken head.

"Calm down" I yelled at myself, "this is not real!" I was sure that any minute I would wake up and this bad dream will be over. The cold wind in my face and the stink of the outhouse in my nostrils felt real.

Doctor Higgs who was very startled, called out for Dennis. Dennis was there in seconds grabbing me as I tried to struggle from his grip. I heard Doctor Higgs tell Dennis to hold me as he went to get Cathy.

The room was laughing through the walls as everything was being devoured by the static. The static had come for me. I gave up struggling watching in horror as the world around me dissolved coming apart in every corner. Then suddenly a pressure and pain in my backside. Something had bitten me hard. I looked at Dennis to see if he could tell me what had bitten me. My eyes grew so heavy suddenly as the world darkened and the cicadas started to fly away to their dark hiding places. My body went numb, then limp as I could keep my eyes open no longer. I went on a vacation with the Sandman, a long deep and peaceful sleep far away from the static of my very confusing life.

I awoke to a sound familiar to me. The whirl of a hospital room. I was so sleepy, and my mouth felt like a desert, dry and foul. A nurse is standing over me with a friendly smile asking how I slept. Is she kidding? She offers me a drink of water and I try to grab it, but my hands are tied down. This was getting to be a habit I could live without. She helps me drink the water and I am grateful to have it.

I lay back and feel very odd. Something is not right, but what? It seems like things are going in slow motion. I am numb everywhere. I should be angry, scared something but I cannot feel anything at all. My thinking is as slow as cold molasses as I am barely able to even remember where I was last or my name. An IV is in my arm and the room looks like all the other hospital rooms I had been in. Wait, I thought I was in jail? Did I dream that?

Slowly, I recall the bridge swan dive. "Oh no." I think to myself, "I either nearly drowned there or maybe the fight? Did I get hurt during the fight maybe?" Oh. if only I could remember what is going on things would be okay.

I see Doctor Higgs come into my room. The nurse says hello and tells him I am finally alert. He nods and she leaves. I feel my gut whine. Last time I was alone with a doctor I got some pretty horrid news. All I can think is, "now what have I fucked up."

He smiles at me, "How are you feeling?" The doctor reaches down and lets my arms free.

I try to lift my arm, but it feels like lead. Everything is so slow. I sit up and drool pours out of my mouth down my chin to my hospital gown. What the hell? How can I be drooling, my mouth is so dry?

Doctor Higgs grabs some tissue off a hospital table and wipes my chin. I let him. I am so heavy and tired I could not stop him if I had wanted to.

He smiles at me. Then says, "sorry kiddo, you were having quite a psychotic break back there. I had to pop you with a lot of Thorazine to bring you back to earth. Don't worry, it will wear off soon enough. However, we do need to start you on anti-psychotics right away. Do you understand what I am saying?" He looks to see if I am listening.

I am but he is not making sense. Psychotic break? I nod anyway.

His face suddenly becomes serious, "I hope you do understand this. I have set up some appointments for follow up. I have told your guardian how important it is to keep all your appointments with your psychiatrist. It is very important you do not miss any of your doses of medication, okay?" He looks out the window, "I do not know if you recall our last talk. I assume you were too medicated to understand. Do you remember we had this discussion before?"

What? I look at him and shake my head no. I only remembered the police station. I tried to speak but my throat is so dry. I only mouth, 'what?'

Doctor Higgs looks sad, "kiddo you are developing schizophrenia. Do you understand what that is? We have run several brain scans and done some testing. There is no doubt. We can slow the progression maybe with medication but there is no cure. Medication will only help some of your symptoms. Some will never go away. You are going to be very sick, very soon. There is no way to know how bad this will get as it is different for each sufferer. As your reality breaks down you will need a lot of help. Probably for the rest of your life." he finished looking in my eyes to see if I understood what he just said to me.

What? What did he just say? Huh? I stared at him not sure if this is a joke. I shook my head yes

I understood but was thinking, "no, he is wrong. I am not schizophrenic that is just stupid. I mean really! Schizophrenics live on the streets, are dirty, talk to themselves, are paranoid, are socially inept, do not know who they are, hear shit that is not there, talk nonsense, have no friends, everyone is scared of them, and they dress funny. Oh wait....oh fuck me!!!! No, this is not real!" I try to get out of the bed. I have enough of this idiotic bullshit talk. He is trying to make me think I am going crazy. Fuck this noise.

"Whoa there, kiddo!" He says easily pushing my slow heavy body back to my bed, "I know this is a lot to deal with. You will have help. I have assigned you a very good counselor that will help you deal with adjusting to the symptoms of this disease as it finishes its onset. You can have a life, but you will need to treat your disease. This is a bump in the road I know, but many people with your illness lead happy productive lives."

Is he fucking kidding? What is this, an after school special here. Well, it is very clear he is full of shit. Schizophrenics do not have a life. Whew! For a second there I almost believed him. Now, see here, he is a liar.

I see Mary come into the room and for once I am happy to see her. This Doctor has gotten on my last nerve. She looks at me triumphantly. Oh yeah, that is right this stupid doctor probably told her the same bullshit. Well, she can smile if she likes. Just because someone says something does not make it a fact.

The speak briefly and finally Doctor liar leave us alone. She walks to me smiling that 'I have you now my pretty' smile of hers. "Guess we have finally found a way to keep you quiet. When they release you into my custody tomorrow, by the way, you will come home and behave yourself. If you give Bob and me any trouble, I can have you put away in a rubber room forever, loony." She chuckled at that little term of endearment she just hurled at me.

I just coldly stare at her drooling helplessly. I was too heavy and tired to move still. Doctor liar said the medication would wear off soon. Mary thinks she has me where she wants me. Well, we shall see about that. My thoughts may be slower, but the static is gone, and I am feeling clearer. A plan of action was already beginning to form, and Mary would soon rue the day she ever messed with me.

Well, that is plenty for this chapter, beauties. Somehow, I have gotten through this the hardest thing I ever had to admit in my life.

Now, understand this, I am Schizophrenic, but that does not define me. I did not believe it then. As you read on you will see that the diagnosis is correct. Some of you may not want to stick around at this point. That is fine. I have hidden my disease all my life as I suffered the ravages of this devastating disease and its stigma, along with the other physical problems I had already brought on myself in secrecy, fear, and shame. It has made my life very difficult with many falls, painful lessons, and even being taken advantage of due to a lack of understanding of reality.

If this knowledge bothers you or somehow leads you to question my ability to reason, then I would rather you go now with my love and blessings.

This story is going to tell you about my life becoming the Goth Queen you know today from a very troubled teen with a big disease.

I am tired of hiding and faking being well when the answer has always been right there. Some of you may have guessed it and some of you are in shock right now. Those who are not I say a heartfelt thank you. It is a disease like cancer, depression, or anxiety. Only I am schizophrenic 24/7, 365 days a year with no breaks or cure. The stigma of my demon is bad enough, but the treatment is something that after you are done reading this story (if you are still here), I still have to endure. This story is real not the delusions of some maniac. I feel this pain every day, and these are my real memories. I am not here just to joke and entertain. I am hoping you will gain some inner strength from my story to help you battle your own demons. So please be kind. Understand that the medication does not control all the symptoms.

Chapter 19: Frienemy Mine

Do understand, much of my story from here on out to the end was given to me by third party witness after the fact as that is not necessarily what I recall as I am slowly breaking from reality. Keep that in mind as I will tell you using both (what I have been told happened versus what I believe happened) to keep the story understandable for you. You may have some difficulty spotting the errors in my thinking at first, as I have only begun to break down but no worries.

Shall we continue? Great! Then strap on your electrodes, drool buckets and colanders as we are about to take one hell of a trip you will not soon forget (or will you?), as I introduce you for the first time to the psychotic who would one day be Goth Queen.

"It's hard to tell who has your back, from who has it long enough just to stab you in it...."
— Nicole Richie

As the day slowly wore on, I fell asleep often. Just as Dr. Liar promised, each time I awoke I felt less heavy and drooled a bit less. By midnight that night, I was feeling more like myself again as my thoughts and body were no longer heavy and slow. However, I still had a cotton mouth, as well as that strange feeling of nothing. I tried to think of funny things, no laughter. I then thought of Mary sure that would make me angry, still nothing. My emotions were devoid and empty. It felt very strange, but no matter, I had to think of a way out of Mary's grips. Emotions were of no consequence right now. In fact, I determined they may get in my way.

Mary came in from time to time to make sure I did not try a bold escape. She had nothing to worry about. I was going to escape her without having to cause a scene. She would glare at me or say nasty things about my alleged mental status like, 'sinners get what they deserve' but this was falling on deaf ears this time. Even mean old Mary could not budge my sleeping demons. I was wondering what the hell was in Thorazine, but no one would answer me except to say, 'it's to make the voices go away.'

"What voices?" I thought. "I do not hear voices! That would be nuts! These people obviously are the crazy ones." The only thing wrong with me was Mary.

I was certain Mary was behind all of these strange behaviors lately. She must have been putting something in the supplies she was bringing me. I had heard stories about LSD from school kids talking. I began to think she was putting acid in my supplies which is why it would come and go. She did seem obsessed with me taking drugs. After all, she certainly had a motive to try to discredit me. It all was making so much sense now. Mary did this to me. I was so grateful when I worked that all out as my mind cleared of the Thorazine.

Finally, I had an answer and now I could fix the problem. You know what they always say right? Like mother like daughter. Mary was using my mom's trick on me. Too bad for her I was on to it this time. I was no one's fool.

Mary came back into my room early that morning before Dr. Liar would be there to release me. She wanted to have a little discussion privately about our future arrangements now that her stupidity had put us on the law's radar. What an idiot. Bet she did not think it would get out of hand so bad, but now it has. I was also ready for a small chat when she came in looking both ways down the hall to make sure we were alone before she shut the door.

"Well, I have asked you be heavily medicated before you leave here sinner. I will not have you acting a nut in the car and upsetting Bob." She said eyeing me like a piece of shit she had just stepped in.

I smiled at her thinking, "You are an asshole." However, I said, "medicate me all you like. Bob will like that as I just lay there. It will remind him of you." I chuckled at that.

"Oh my God! Demon!" she spit at me, "You still act like a monster! They need to give you more medication! You are never getting to have my Bob! Do you hear me! You are a crazy fucking bitch!" (What? Wow, what a mouth huh?)

This made me laugh hard. If Mary cursed, she was really angry forgetting she was a fine Christian gal and all. I knew I had her right where I wanted her. Still smiling I said, "No worries, Mary, you can watch. Maybe I will show you how to keep your man happy, so he does not need other girls."

She came across the room and slapped me hard. My face flew to the side, and I could taste blood yet again as my back teeth ripped into the inside of my cheek. "Damn, what is with all the slapping people?" I thought and that made me chuckle a bit as I turned back staring defiantly at her. "So, you can avoid all this. Just drop me off where I belong and let things go back to....normal." I had to pause to find the right word there.

Mary snorted still angry and said, "You are sick. You are sick in your body, your mind, and your soul. I can't take you back even if I really do want to. If nothing more than to watch you suffer the torments of hell you deserve. I can't take you back because you have to see these doctors now or they will open a case on me and Bob, you fucking loon." She finished looking out the window and turning her back to me.

I rubbed my throbbing face. Slowly, I got out of the bed and went to where I had just seen the clothes I had been wearing when I got arrested laying on the visitor's chair. I began to put on my clothes waiting while Mary considered what was very obvious. I did not suggest it because I already knew Mary liked to be smarter than me and in control. So, to keep down the struggle I let her think. This was not brain science here you know. Whew! I sure was dizzy, what was that about? Stupid Thorazine. I pulled out my purse and began putting on my corpse make-up.

As I sat in the visitor's chair finishing my look, Mary turned around looking stern, "Okay, okay. I can take you back. But here is what is going to happen. You will take the medication. I will pick you up from school on all your appointment days get you there and drop you back off. You will not speak your vile words to me to or from the appointments. You also will not be fighting anymore at school, you hear me!" She waited to see if I understood the pact I was making with my devil.

I nodded appearing to look defeated. I knew she would get this. The only thing that worried me was that I had thus far been unable to keep my deals. Well, that was going to change as I was not going to eat or drink a damned thing from this crazy bitch anymore. I also was not going to take this stupid medication. It made me feel weird and dizzy. Fuck that noise. Besides, I did not need it once I stopped taking the damned drugs she has been slipping me.

The nurse came and gave me a dose of this unnecessary medication in a pill form, and I pretended to take it. When she and Mary left, I spit it into the commode. Yuck, it tasted like shit. Finally, Dr. Liar came gave me the same discussion of his delusion that I am a Schizophrenic or becoming one and I pretended to care. The acting job worked, and I was released to Mary with no incident. I was being very good and very calm. I just wanted to go home.

Mary and I traveled from the hospital in silence. I was given my mad box, belt, and shoes back, as well as my twenty dollars with my clothes. So, I was feeling pretty normal for a change. I was even starting to feel that weird numbness going away as what I perceived as happiness filled me with the first sign of my cemetery home coming into the distant view. Finally, home. The fight had happened on Thursday at lunchtime, so here on Sunday morning I was amazed at how much trouble can be crammed into just three days. I was considering the difficulty my very public arrest and melt down at school may cause me tomorrow morning as we pulled up to my home.

I jumped out before Mary even completely stopped the car. I had enough of her already and I just wanted to go to my outhouse and veg out to my mad box. I opened the gate not even looking back to wave by, taking out my mad box to set my earphones, as I headed to build my fire.

To my utter surprise Mary jumped on my back and sent us both face first into the cemetery dirt just inside the iron gate. My mad box flew out of my hands as I attempted to catch myself. All I managed to do was slow the face plant. The fall stunned both of us, but Mary recovered first and began to wail the piss out of my back and head with her fists. Okay, I admit, maybe I did have that coming for making such nasty statements. What was she thinking? Beating the shit out of me was not going to look good if I could not get to school tomorrow due to a broken skull.

I rolled over and managed to grab her flying fists as she was spewing obscenities at me that were too foul to repeat. She sure could cuss like a trucker. I held her wrists as she struggled to hit me again. I lay there on the ground using my weight to keep her off balance as she finally wore out trying to break free. At last, she stopped trying to hit me.

I laughed a bit and said, "You satisfied yet? Or do we sit here for a bit longer holding hands?" She shot me a look of hate.

"Let me go crazy bitch!" She pulled one more time, then I released her bracing for a blow in case she was not done. "I hate you," she spat, panting and winded.

Her hair was wild, and her dress now covered in dirt. I thought she looked better that way. I chuckled and got up to collect my madness box shaking my head at this unexpected battle.

"And people think I am crazy." I laughed while reaching down to grab my machine.

Mary got the drop on me again (fucking Thorazine) and wrestled the mad box out of my hands. She took it aimed at a nearby headstone and threw it hard as she could. It flew into pieces as I watched in absolute horror. I tried to grab it in midair but was far too slow. I landed on my knees staring now at the broken remains of my only company in my grey world.

"What have you done! What the hell have you done, Mary!" I started yelling staring in disbelief at that pile of junk. "Fuck, fuck, and triple fuck."

I grabbed it up and tried to see if it would turn on. I had my back to Mary and in my freak out I had completely forgotten she was even there. That is until something flew into the back of my head. This time it was not her fists. She had gotten something out of the car.

I turned to see a manila envelope landing on the ground with the papers inside scattering everywhere like falling leaves. "What the fuck!" Now, I am getting angry.

I stand up ready to plow this bitch. She can tell I am not going to tolerate another second. I see the look of triumph melt off her face as she begins to back up as I slowly walk toward her ready to rip her black heart from her dried up, old chest.

"Wait! You stay right there do you hear me! You touch me they will lock you up forever! Don't believe me, read those papers on the ground. You are too stupid to realize it, but I do not have to wait long.

You are never going to make it, you hear me! Your brains are turning to mush and soon enough I will be rid of you forever! They lock lunatics like you away from decent folks you know!" She taunted by rolling her finger around her temple in a 'crazy' motion while sticking out her tongue (well, that was childish).

"Fuck you, Mary! I am not crazy! Do not come back here ever or you know what, I will kill you," I yelled at her and began my infernal laughing.

"Mary, Mary quite contrary how does your garden grow? With silver bells and Cockle Shells but you come back I will kill you slow." I then said in a sing song voice. Now I was howling at that!

Mary screamed, "You are fucking insane" while pointing but running to the car. She did not look back and as so many times before peeled out of there throwing gravel and cussing.

"Gosh do I love these fine mother daughter moments." I said aloud to no one as I watched her car pull off. I laughed some more at that. "Oh no, but what about you?" My laughter stopped as I remembered my broken mad box.

I scooped it up and yeah, it was busted. The breeze began to blow slightly and the white paper doctor notes and brain imaging pictures that had fallen out of the folder when it collided with the back of my head began to travel around the headstones. I went and caught them all and replaced them in the envelop. It had my name on it written in pen on pieces of white tape on the tab.

I opened it up and there in a sharpie black pen written on the first page:

Diagnosis/Prognosis:

Axis I: Schizophrenia, Insipid-early onset, active, likely paranoid type.

See brain imaging/psychological testing attached.

Axis V: 20 at intake with best functioning last 12 months under 35-40

Prognosis: Poor: Will require substantial support. Retesting suggested after completion of onset for Axis I to verify paranoid type.

"Well, that is not nice, telling lies and pretending it is my lies." I said to no one as I looked at it intently. I did not understand most of it. "What to do with you?" I looked at the outhouse and decided to store it with the bible in my box of supplies. I could look up the stuff I did not understand later maybe. I did not like them saying things about me that I did not know how to defend myself against.

I went into the outhouse and other than some scatter from rats and other little beasties I room with nothing was amiss. I threw the folder and the broken madness machine into the supply box with a sigh.

Now what? Well, first I will throw out all of Mary's poisoned food and water, I think.

After gathering the whole mess into my arms, nearly dropping half of it. I took it, angry that I had ever fallen for it in the first place toward the road. You would think I had learned my lesson. Just hard-headed, I guess.

I walked out the gate and started to throw all the cans into the ditch but though if anyone happened by, they may see it and stop to investigate. I did not want that garbage in my cemetery so I took off down the road till I could not see even the walls and threw the whole mess there. Satisfied, that no one would be wise to my presence because of food evidence I headed back to the cemetery wondering where I could purchase another madness box and if I would have enough money for a new one.

I came back into my cemetery thinking I may just spend the afternoon gathering fuel for the fire as I told Marie's story of the fairy princess to my cemetery roomies for a laugh. As I walked into the outhouse, I was now telling my enthralled audience of listeners all around me of my stint with the Suicide Dive Team as an Olympic swimmer when I saw a sudden movement in the dark hovel too large to be a rat.

"What the fuck!" I yelled as Stephanie came out of the outhouse.

I fell back on my ass startled to dip shit status unable to believe what I was seeing. I blinked but she was still there. She was smiling that stupid sweet, innocent smile at me. She had two black eyes from the fight and bruises all over her arms. In her hand, I could see a manila envelope.

"Is this real?" I said now beginning to wonder if Dr. Liar was indeed onto something here, maybe I am crazy?

Stephanie laughed, "Yeah it is me, silly! Sorry didn't mean to scare you. I followed you here the other day when you beat up Kelly for me. I was too afraid to come in that day but after you got arrested, I came out here again and found your...uhm...house, I guess. I know that is kind of rude, but I thought I would help by watching your stuff." She appeared proud of herself for someone who had stalked me, then went snooping through my things.

"Okay, so now what the fuck are you doing here!" I said getting up. I was not happy. This girl is a plague.

She covered her mouth with my envelope (records) with only her bright mischievous blackened eyes looking at me over the top, "Well, I came back today and saw you and the woman you called Mary fighting. I got scared and hid over there by the wall. Neither of you saw me. So, when she left, I saw you go and get stuff and leave. I came in to wait for you to come back." She finished.

"You mean to see what I put in there you nosy asshole." I said disgusted.

She laughed and fanned herself with the envelope, "Now, now, let's not be ugly. I wanted to know more about you is all. Wow, what a read you know? You are kind of messed up, aren't you?" She said opening the folder and holding up a brain image and looking at it right in front of me. "Explains a lot!"

I snatched the whole thing out of her hands, "that is private! Mind your business." I put the scan back into the envelop and pointed to the gate, "Out is that way. Leave and do not fucking come back." I glared coldly at her.

Stephanie who was dressed in the same flower shirt and jeans from the first time I saw her grabbed the bottom of her shirt. She pushed out her bottom lip and kicking the ground looking down immaturely pouting, "Oh, you would not want me to leave now, would you? I don't think you want everyone to know about my latest gossip, would you?" She looked to see if I was getting her drift.

"Oh, I got it you little skank. You are blackmailing me, really? What is wrong with everybody in this shit town?" I thought but said, "What do you want, Stephanie. What do I have to do to get you to go the fuck away?" I sighed in resignation.

She had me. Those records may be lies, but kids can be cruel. I knew that if she told them about my bullshit diagnosis it could become really bad for me. Plus, it may encourage others to do what Kelly did and try to pick a fight. I stood there looking at her waiting to hear what stupid thing she wanted to make this all go away. Money likely. Goodbye, new madness box.

She lit up with delight that I was willing to listen to her demands. She pursed her lips the way Dr. Liar (Higgs, ok) had before and seemed far so happy for my comfort. "I just want you to be my friend, you know come over to my house and sit with me at lunch and stuff."

"Stuff?" I focused on that word. I wanted to know in detail what all she is asking.

"What is stuff?" I think. I never make deals with devils without knowing all the details and fine print, not anymore.

"You know silly! Girl stuff! We can go shopping and chase boys and gossip! It will be so cool!" She was truly excited about this 'stuff.'

I shook my head. She is for real crazy. Now, I could think of a million things I would rather do than hang out with Stephanie, chasing boys and gossiping. For starters, I was thinking maybe being locked up forever was not such a bad deal after all. Jail had been nice, even the hospital or the bottom of the lake. This little brain stem was getting on my last nerve.

"Get the fuck out. Go tell everyone. I don't care!" I threw the records at her and they fell on the ground as Stephanie tried to catch it, I watch it spilling its contents on the ground again. I chuckled and pointed to the gate again, "Leave or so help me I will make you leave."

She just stood there staring like a dumb cow at me in disbelief. Stephanie had misjudged me. I did not care. It might even work in my favor if everyone thinks I am bona fide crazy anyway. When she still did not go. I pulled back my arm and pointed again forcefully, I had enough. I reach over and grabbed her by her long pretty hair. I started walking to the gate with a large handful of her hair in my hand. Stephanie had no choice but to follow or be snatched bald as me.

She tried scratching my hand to make me let go but I was stronger than she was even though much thinner. I was a bit hardened and used to pain so I ignored her clawing and pleas. At the gate, I pulled her hair forward. Once, I had pulled her in front of me I opened the gate. With a shove to her chest, I pushed her out and slammed the gate between us glaring at her. She stood there holding her head where I had pulled her by the hair tearing up.

"Bye darling, been a real treat but do me a favor and get lost. Never come back or else. " I faked a big smile and waved while daring her to try to get back in.

Stephanie looked at me, finally angry now, "Okay, you are a stinking psycho anyway! What was I thinking wanting to be nice to you? I thought you could understand me, but you are just a bully like Kelly!" She stomped her foot and pointed at me, "I hope you do go Schizophrenic and spend the rest of your shitty life living in garbage cans!"

That made me smile, "Yep, okay, we done here? Best not to do too much thinking darling, I find it only gets you in trouble. For the last time, leave," I said still smiling as I waved again.

Stephanie turns to start walking. I watch her and can hear her sniffing. Relief that she had finally gotten the point had just started to fill me, when she turned back looked me right in the eyes and smiling.

"Well, I guess they will not like you living in a cemetery much. It would suck if someone told them about it. You know called and complained and stuff. Oh, never mind, see you at school." She then turned headed back toward the school walking away.

Fear made biscuits on my spine as I went cold. Would she really do that? Shit! I had not thought of the fact she had found out my secret housing arrangement. She had seen and heard the fight with

Mary. I swore I could kill Stephanie. What is her problem! While watching her walk into the distance I wrestled with my inner thoughts and fear of discovery. Finally, it was clear, she had my number. I was caught like a cemetery kid in a rat trap.

I pulled the gate open and took off after Stephanie. "Wait, okay! Deal fuck it, deal!" I yelled while running after her.

I saw her stop and turn around smiling. No longer a sweet innocent girl, but a dirty blackmailing asshole. As I reached her, I stifled the urge to strangle her to a heap of blood and bones.

"I thought you might see it my way." She said smugly.

"Yeah, let it go. What now?" I looked back to my cemetery worried to leave my home unguarded. Stephanie looked back too.

"Don't worry no one ever goes there, but your crazy ass. Okay so we are going to my house now to hang out and drink tea on the front porch. We can tell stories and oh, I have a tape player and earphones if you want them. I saw that Mary broke yours and stuff." She started babbling non-stop walking without even seeming to take a breath.

I followed even though I was feeling a bit uneasy. It felt like the space was too large around me. I was seriously pissed off at Stephanie about this. However, if she really had a madness box to give me, I would happily sit on some stupid porch and put up with her bullshit for a bit. I could always get home before dark after all. I would need time to think out some plan to get out of this later. For now, I really wanted that tape player.

Stephanie continued to blather on and on about people I had never heard of, nor did I care about. She talked about their private shames and made fun of their looks. In reality, I was thinking Stephanie was not a very nice person. She did not seem to have anything nice to say about anyone from what I gathered. I did not have to say a word. Stephanie did not want a friend, she wanted someone to be there for her to dump that garbage onto. Oh well, if I could just get that tape player, I could handle this just fine.

We walked past the school as she led me down one of the narrow town streets to a small white house with a long porch and a small tool shed in the back yard. It was a single level with a roof in bad need of repair from what I could tell. Right across the street was a small handsome church with a big multicolored glass window and a pointed steeple. The sign out from said it was Methodist Church. It was very funny, but the colored glass seemed to be pulsing which was sort of odd. I stood there fascinated by the sight as Stephanie continued into the house babbling. She did not even notice I did not follow.

I could not stop watching it, the pulsating colors bright and happy. Suddenly, they began to leap off the plating of the window and bleed into the sky. It was amazing. I had seen fireworks before, but this was better. I smiled in sheer delight at the show, what an incredible display.

Stephanie had finally noticed I was not with her. She came back outside to find me smiling and staring into the sky above the church. She looked up too, "What are you looking at?"

"You see it too! Isn't that incredible! How do you think they do that?" I was still in deeply enthralled watching my colors explode into the sky.

Stephanie shrugged, "I guess someone who knows that stuff. I don't care how they got that church built and you are weird. Come on, let me show you the house."

Her telling me to follow finally made the colors pull back inside. The show was over, so I shrugged too and followed her inside. The house was old and reeked of stale beer and dust. She had me follow her into her room which was small but comfortable. She has a single bed with an old metal frame, an old dresser with a cracked mirror and lots of ripped out magazine pictures taped all over the walls of female singers and half naked guys. On her bed she had at least a dozen stuffed animals. Everything was in pink or brown. This chick liked pink, go figure.

She dug under her bed and pulled out a basket. Reaching and still talking about bullshit (she never shut up) she found the tape player. Handing it to me she said, "It is still good, just a bit old fashioned. I got a new one so you can have this one. Oh, and here are the earphones."

She handed me a pair that would fit right into my ears discreetly. I will say, that despite her constant swamp mouth, I was truly grateful for the gift. I smiled at her as I took them and quickly hid them in my shirt under my jacket.

She then led me to their very small kitchen with very old-fashioned appliances from maybe the 1960's and made herself a glass of tea from a huge glass pitcher. I passed on that. No more drinking or eating for me! That is how they get you after all. I was thirsty but that is okay, it will pass I say to myself.

We went out onto her porch and sat in two old lawn chairs there sitting side by side. I was curious as to why we were doing this, but whatever. Better to have her on my side then blabbing that huge fucking mouth to anyone about my secret home.

She asked me again if I wanted something to drink which made me feel funny. Why did she keep asking that? What is her game? I shook my head no looking at her suspiciously. She was looking at me, too.

"Why do you dress like that?" She said, "I read the notes, it said because you are going crazy and stuff. Is that true?"

I blankly looked at her thinking, "what is she talking about?" I shrug.

"I have told you all about me. I want to know about you too. That is what friends do, they share stuff." She said leaning in as if interested in me suddenly. She smiled as she put her chin on her hand and elbow on her knee. "Tell me something cool. Like a secret or stuff."

"She keeps saying stuff why?" I start to think. Is this some code she is trying to get me to understand. "What is stuff?" I start to feel panicked as I try to remember what stuff even means. Why is she trying to put this thought inside my head? I start to shake my head staring blankly at her feeling my brains are about to blow out my ears as the word "stuff, stuff, stuff, stuff" keeps repeating in a loop.

I stand up and begin to pace, "Why can't I remember this word? Okay calm down, think what stuff is?" mumbling to myself.

I am becoming very agitated as nothing is making sense. I started hitting my forehead with my right fist, trying to bang it to work as I pace. I was trying to get the thoughts to stop scattering like that.

"The stuff is in the back. No put it in the back, but what is the stuff... in the back? Oh my! That is what stuff is. It is a definition or is it a stuff of things? Yes! That is it a stuff of things to come and then it will all make sense because that is what it is the stuff." I babble to myself in a string of nonsense trying to define the word stuff.

I believe it is a code, she wants information, and this is the key to it. My mind cannot hold on to the definition as I try wildly to understand it. Finally, frustrated that I am too stupid to know what this code mean I look to a now very upset Stephanie in absolute confusion.

I hear her say: "holy shit!" Stephanie says almost falling out of her chair, "What the fuck is this crazy shit, shit, shit and stuff and stuff and stuff."

"Why do you keep saying stuff!" I yell at her, "What are you trying to tell me, damn it! I do not understand stuff!" My heart is pounding. I am very afraid what is going on? Oh no, I know this feeling. The static is back.

I stop to listen. I can hear the cicadas coming. I look to Stephanie and ask if she can hear it. She looks afraid but shakes her head no. I look at the church for it. Yes, the static is coming, and it is moving fast. I ask her if she can see it, she jumps up and runs inside the house without answering me. My heart is really pounding now as I see the static coming for me and like Stephanie I want to run as the hissing begins but no! I am not running this time. This is never going to end so I will stand my ground. Let the static come and do what it may.

I close my eyes. I do not want to see it as it eats away the world. I feel my eyeballs fall deep inside my head. I am imploding. How is this even possible? The cicadas are so loud it is deafening, and the hissing is filling in the blank spots. My ears hurt it is so loud I reach up to hold them as my head begins to split down the middle from the sound. I fall to my knees and grit my teeth trying to keep my brains inside since my eyeballs are already gone.

I suddenly feel very cold, and wet. Now even colder, I open my eyes, they did not fall inside? Stephanie is there she has a big glass pitcher that is empty. "She drank all the tea?" Now that was funny, so I begin to laugh. The hissing and cicada are still screaming in my ears, but I cannot stop laughing at Stephanie drinking all the tea. She looks absolutely horrified.

Still laughing and holding my head together I say in a sing song voice, "You should be since you drank all that tea and stuff and stuff and stuff and stuff." Now I am howling at that statement.

I need to stop this somehow, and I remember the mad box in my shirt. I saw a cassette tape in it. I let my ears go hoping that my brains will not leak too badly. I fumble but get the earphones in my hands. Then quickly put the earphones into my ears. I am in agony as my head splits and my ears are bleeding. I hit the button, biting back the pain, turning the music full blast. As the music blares into my ears and it drowns out the cicada/hissing combo very quickly. I keep my head together until it stops splitting, slow at first then finally relief. I am very tired and can barely hold my eyes open, but I stand up and look at a crying Stephanie.

I cannot hear her because the music is so loud, but she is sitting cross legged in the yard with her head in her arms apparently weeping. I listen to a high-pitched woman sings how "girls just wanna have fun" thinking how odd a thing to sing about. I stand a bit watching Stephanie rocking there. So, I shrug and sit next to her. I have no idea what is wrong, but I have no choice but to do what she says, or she may tell on me. Wait, why am I wet?

Now that is funny, why am I wet? I begin a new attack of laughter. I am sure it was quite a sight to see. Two teenage girls sitting in the yard on a Sunday afternoon, one weeping and the other one laughing madly at nothing of worth. However, very soon Stephanie would prove to me why no good deed ever goes unpunished.

Chapter 20: Missed Opportunity of Miss Understanding

I hope everyone got lots of rest and properly took their medication. Come on down to the depths of the human mind as we get to look through my eyes at the world inside a world. Be very careful the fall is steep, the bottom unstable and do not wander! Stay by my side or you too could be lost forever in the furthest abyss of psychosis. Now, take a deep breath, as you go ahead and jump! No worries, I am already at the bottom waiting to take you on the tour!

"The most beautiful people we have known are those who have known defeat, known suffering, known struggle, known loss, and have found their way out of the depths. These persons have an appreciation, a sensitivity, and an understanding of life that fills them with compassion, gentleness, and a deep loving concern. Beautiful people do not just happen."
— Elisabeth Kübler-Ross

Time seems to stand still as Stephanie weeps and rocks back and forth. Whatever her issues are does not affect me, so I look down in my hands for something to do. I am holding my new mad box. I am fascinated by it suddenly. It was as if I had never seen anything like it before. Odd, I had one all this time and never noticed it's complexities. I turn it over and over in my hands marveling at the sleek smoothness of its surface and even the chips in the grey paint job seem of the most amazing substance. I look closely trying to discover its arcane secrets. It is singing to me of many things I only could dream of in a most fevered dance with the Sandman.

Stephanie's hand on my shoulder startles me from my feeling of becoming one with my new mad box. Her touch seemed more like a punch to my person. Only it is not to my body, but to my force field. I wince as it does hurt a little.

I quickly, shrug off her hand, "Keep your hands off me, bitch," I snarl. I am not happy she interrupted my latest discovery of...wait what did I just discover again? "Why am I wet?" I think as I see that my pants are darker in some areas than the rest. It seems that I have asked this before, but I am not sure, did I?

Stephanie is speaking I suddenly realize. At first, I thought it was only a fly buzzing around my ear, so I had tried to swat it away. I see her mouth moving as she is standing now over my sitting body. She is trying to tell me something, maybe?

"What just happened?" I finally understand, as she is now shouting at me moving her mouth slowly making exaggeration mouth movements with each word. I could not hear her over my mad box.

I flip off the music to hear her almost screaming "What is wrong with you?" She has dried tears all over her bruised-up face. However, she is no longer sad, she is angry, and maybe even a bit scared for some reason.

She is such a weirdo. I shrug my shoulders unsure what the hell she is talking about.

Stephanie reaches down and grabs my jacket collar with both her hands and starts shaking me. Not very hard as she is too small to do much other than rock me back and forth with her force. Her grabbing me caused that same odd sensation of being punched from a distance. I grab her wrists. I immediately let her go as electricity shoots from my palms that make contact with her skin. The shock startles me badly.

"What the fuck is this?" I yell and start to crawl rapidly like a crab backward almost knocking Stephanie down face first into my lap. She let go to save herself from the fall.

"Keep away from me! Don't touch me! How did you do that!" I yell as I manage to get to a safe distance and stand up ready to fight as I double up my fists. She tries that again I will knock her into next week.

"What is wrong with you? Are you going insane? Is that what this is?" Stephanie says looking confused and defeated unsure what to do with me apparently.

I do not understand what she is talking about, all I know is if she comes near me, I will beat her to death. She had better keep that crazy voodoo shit to herself.

My mind is whirling, trying to understand this phenomenon. Suddenly, a memory, the old woman.

I begin to think to myself wildly, "Oh! That's it! She is a witch! Damn, makes sense. I never believed in them but then again, never didn't either. Anything is possible, I don't know about everything now do I? She has put a curse on me. No wait, why is that tea pitcher empty? Oh my God! That bitch must have made me drink that whole pitcher. She is working with Mary! I am high on LSD, which is what is wrong!" Fear fills me as I think "between her and Mary they are trying to get me locked up forever!"

It is all was quite clear now. Stephanie and Mary need to be destroyed. I do not believe in killing but I had no choice. If I do not, they are going to try to put me away. No doubt I am scared to death but now I had an answer for this weird shit.

"Okay, the LSD will wear off so just play it cool and stay calm. She wants you to act crazy so she can call Mary. I am not going to let them win. Just breath, pretend you are okay and when we get out of here, we can make a plan." I explain to myself while I drop my fists and relax my stance of defense.

I close my eyes breathing deeply. "We can do this." I think with encouragement. "None of this is real, it is drugs, okay?" I nod my head and open my eyes.

Stephanie is standing there with her mouth hanging open. I smile at her to let her know I am cool, all is okay.

"Okay, this is too much for me, nutball" she says while breathing in deeply, "Well, what the fuck, just what the fuck? What are you going to do next? Start pissing on yourself and talking to God and stuff?"

Damn her, she is baiting me with that stupid word again. Still smiling I grit my teeth. Not going to let that bother me. Not again. I shake my head no. I knew now what she wants me to do as she just said. So, under no circumstance will I pee or talk unless she speaks first until I can get out of here and back to the cemetery. She may accuse me of speaking to God or peeing on myself. She thinks she is clever but nope. I got this.

"If you are done acting screwy, I need to make some dinner before my aunt comes home. You can come inside and help if you want." She said still eyeing me suspiciously.

No, I did not want to. I wanted to go home, away from this drugger. Stephanie walks back onto the porch and looks back while opening the door, "Come on in. I am sure the neighbors have had enough of a show!"

There is a show? Where? Now I am confused. Like a circus maybe? I look around and see nothing but empty lazy small-town streets and hear the distant sounds of televisions in houses from this neighborhood. A dog bark, a child yells, 'throw the ball.' No sounds of any 'shows.'

"Jesus Christ! Get in here dummy!" Stephanie yells at me breaking my confusion once more.

I can't remember what I was looking for. Oh well, I walk over and follow her inside. For the life of me I cannot remember why we are going inside either. What is wrong with me? Why am I wet?

I am brushing off the wetness on my pants as I walk inside. "Oh, sorry about that, there is a towel in the bathroom. I had to throw the tea on you because you were acting crazy." Stephanie says while pointing to a closed door, apparently the bathroom.

"Sure," I said. I walked into the bathroom but kept the door open. I was demonstrating I was not 'peeing' as I now recall she has given me LSD. Sure, it was tea, I must have pissed myself in a drugged-out haze and that is what she is talking about. Telling me this is tea is very clever, but I know what she did. She made me drink that tea. I am startled suddenly realizing maybe she wants to dose me up again. I need to get out of here while I still can, but how? I can't let her know I am on to the game. I could run but she will call someone before I can get this shit out of my system. I finish trying to dry off best I can while contemplating my escape.

Stephanie is making hamburger helper as I walk into the kitchen. I am working on some excuse to leave. She sees me and smiles telling me I look better already.

I smile thinking, "no thanks to you skank. You are so dead."

She begins to rattle on again about bullshit like before the whole...well whatever happened. I notice she keeps saying stuff and there is a strange echo in her kitchen as each of her words seems to repeat in a metallic sound then just hang in the air. I have to just stand there away from the appliances. I made the mistake of leaning on the refrigerator and got a shock in my force shield, like when Stephanie and I touched. I jumped quite startled. Stephanie did not see it, so I just backed off and stood with plenty of space between me and everything in that room.

"Damn this LSD is pretty potent shit," I think wondering how long I will be fucked up like this.

"Oh, you will just love my hamburger helper. I am the best cook, my aunt says." Stephanie turns to me with a bit of the concoction on a spoon wanting me to put that poison in my mouth.

I back up shaking my head no. She looks crushed. "Well, have it your way. You are missing out and you are so damned skinny! You know that if you eat you would look better." She says going back to her endless blathering about nothing.

Now I know there is something I am supposed to be doing but for the life of me I cannot remember what it is. I try to remember but all I get is an endless parade of Stephanie's echoing words and metallic scraping. Is this normal? I cannot recall. I look at Stephanie and try to focus on her thinking maybe this will center my mind.

She is talking and serving up plates of food. Three of them, it is the fork that is scraping that is what I hear. Okay now, why the echo? Is the house built funny or is it too empty? Is it the LSD she gave me?

"You going to stand there all night? My Aunt will be home in about half an hour and I want her to meet you. You are my best friend now! Come and eat! Let's cure you of that skinny mini look! You are almost as thin as the people that live out there where you are staying." Stephanie laughs at that.

"Wait, there is a cure?" I ask now very interested in this conversation. "You know how to make this stop?"

Stephanie looked up from the plate she is laying on the living room guest table in front of a very old stuffed easy chair. "Yeah, there is a cure. It is called eating. You should be able to put on weight fast as lightening and stuff." She giggles.

My eyes widen, "Why did I not see that? Lightening, electricity, static. Wait that is the cure! Static is not causing this. It is going to fix this!" I say to her, and she looks confused. "I need a piece of paper and a pencil before I forget, now damn it."

My sudden excitement startled Stephanie to action as she grabs a pad off the table next to the chair and a pen, "will a pen work? I don't have a pencil." She hands them to me.

I drop to my knees and using the floor to back the pad, I begin to write myself the note and equation code I am sure will save my mind.

'E is energy which is to be solved for X. Lightening is static and the charge is equal to E..." I write furiously sure I had the correct equation, now all I have to do is solve for X and I will have the cure.

Stephanie watches me as I scribble the nonsense equations on page after page babbling to myself about "the cure." She does not know what to do but stand there panicking as she knows her aunt is coming home very soon. She is suddenly aware she maybe should have read those records she found in my outhouse a bit more closely. Crazy is not as cool as she thought it would be and it certainly was not controllable.

"Please stop this. Don't go crazy right now my aunt is coming. They will lock you up and I will not have a friend anymore. She will call the cops! Oh, please stop," she cries out grabbing the pen from me and pushing me over onto the floor.

She has touched me again. Touching hurts. I have had enough of this brain stem. I stand up quickly furious as the room starts to breath and a woman screaming fills my mind. Without even trying to move I am on Stephanie hitting her and yelling with all my might to give back the pen and stop touching me. I decide to beat her to death. I need her to shut up and the dead don't talk...and stuff.

Stephanie's Aunt walks in on this little scene. I can only imagine what she must have thought. You work all day on the manufacturing line. Tired and hungry you open your front door to find you niece being pummeled by a girl that is dressed like a corpse. The corpse is the one doing the hitting but is yelling don't touch me. Plus, there is paper with strange writing strewn about your living room floor. Bet that was a bit unexpected. Oh boy, not good.

I look up when the door opens to see the biggest woman I had ever seen in my life. How could this be Stephanie's Aunt? Steph is tiny! The Aunt is at least 6 foot tall and had to weigh a good 300 pounds without the heavy rubber boots she was wearing. Her hair is black as spade and cropped at her shoulders with an unruly curl throughout making it look like a cow had licked her entire head. Her face was wide, wrinkled, and ruddy like someone who has high blood pressure. She was obviously beyond angry at this sight.

No way I was sticking around for this! I jumped off the crying Stephanie and ran straight toward the aunt. Her aunt surprised to have a wild-eyed, white-faced teenager running at her freaked and ran out the door in front of me thinking I was coming for her.

No, I just wanted to get out the only way I could see to get in. The Aunt stumbled off the porch and fell to the ground with a loud "grumpf" sound. I ran past her headed for home, not even stopping to look back.

"Shit, shit, shit, motherfucker," I yelled as I ran. Stephanie is going to tell on me, and this damned Aunt will contact call the cops for sure. Most of all I had lost the cure and I could not remember it already.

I stopped at the school yard. Winded and unsure what to do I needed to think. "Okay, what do I have at the cemetery of worth? Nothing. Okay, so do not go back there. They will look there." I look at the school, "what about school? Oh, what to do...wait, Mary that is where they will go."

I turn and head for Mary and Bob's home. She got me into this problem. She is going to get me out or so help me I will bury her in that graveyard of mine.

As soon as I was able to run after resting a bit, I ran again. It was getting late as I arrived in Bob and Mary's yard. The station wagon was gone, shit it is Sunday. They are at church. I am standing in the yard trying to come up with a new plan when Mary steps out the door looking confused and angry too.

"What are you doing here Get away. Bob will be home in a bit he cannot catch you here." She yells.

"I am in trouble." I was hating myself and wanting to vomit even saying this to Mary. "I need a place to hide. The cops are coming." my look is very pleading. If she did not help, I am screwed.

"Oh my God, what did you do!" She says horrified, "Did you kill someone?" She starts to back into the house afraid of me. I have to stop her.

"No! Stephanie put LSD in the tea and I am wigging out from the drugs so I beat her up even though she gave me the music she had and her Aunt came home for hamburger helper and she is calling the cops because she saw the cure and Stephanie she knows with the records and she kept saying stuff and she is going to have me put away and it is not my fault that she took my cure. I cannot go back and get it," I spew in an almost unintelligible gush of desperation.

Mary's eyes almost bugged out of her head. She tells me to wait there and do not move. She went inside the house. For the life of me I did as she said. I was so confused I did not know what to do.

She came back outside in a few moments and walked over to me. I stood there as she smacked me hard, "Wake up, damn you, demon!"

I felt the hit, but I also did not. It seemed like I was hit with a pillow as I was so numb. I looked at her after recovering, "what is happening?"

Mary smiled at me, "You are finished that is what is happening. Your brain is mush." She grabbed my arm and began marching me to the house next door.

I wanted to break free, but I was so numb. Nothing is making sense. Lights are bright and noises are amplified. Mary's hand on my upper arm is shocking me as I try to keep up with her rapid pace. Birds are chirping, I can taste them like dirt in my mouth. The very ground seems to be alive beneath my feet, warm and pulsating. Mary is saying something to me, but I cannot understand a word of it as she speaks in bits and codes like a machine.

"It is the electricity; it is the static that is the cure." I suddenly remember but I cannot remember what it is that I am supposed to be doing with that information. I just know that Mary is happy about it whatever it is and that is never a good thing.

Mary borrows the neighbor's car and pushes my babbling ass into it. I do not know where I am or who she is. I smile at her, I think. She is laughing so I laugh too, what is so funny?

The car starts and I feel it as my heartbeat begins to keep rhythm with its hums and life. I like the music it is making. Suddenly, I feel the urge to dance so I sway my arms with the percussion rocking in unison with its pulsating song. There is a woman here with me she is not dancing. She is pushing the pedal that makes it all go. She looks determined to make this song last as long as I like. I must be dancing beautifully. I do not understand why, but there are hands in my view, and they have on finger less gloves. I watch them as they gracefully flow in the air. It is so amazingly graceful I could watch them forever. I remember the story Marie used to tell of being a fairy princess in a castle. This is the princess. Marie got what she wanted. I am happy for her. So, I laugh in glee that there really is a happy ending to every fairy tale.

Mary pulls into the psychiatric clinic more than thirty miles away as I continue to fall deeper into psychosis and unreality. She is ready to have me put into intake no doubt. It will solve her problem. She parks the neighbor's car she has borrowed. Carefully, she removes her giggling and swaying granddaughter from the passenger side. She hurries inside the building sure to find help for this situation. Luckily, her passenger is not fighting. She is very passive and full of laughter appearing confused and unresponsive to any attempts to speak to her. No doubt the child is not there but somewhere else no one else can see but her.

The on-call psychologist comes into the waiting area and spies a giggling teen dressed like a ghoul and a very upset middle-aged woman. She is Dr. Scott, and she is a new mental health doctor only having finished her doctorate thesis two weeks ago. This is her first real job though she has done a lot of interning. Dr. Scott has never dealt with a Schizophrenic before, and certainly not with a very young one. She is scared but hopes her training is going to come in handy today. She is studying to become a psychiatrist but already has a Clinical Psychology license. Dr. Scott takes the teen and the woman to her office ready to call for help.

Mary explains to Dr. Scott that the teen has on setting Schizophrenia. That is already very obvious to the doctor. She asks about medication and is told Thorazine on emergency and a dose of Haldol at the hospital. Dr. Scott realizes this teen has not taken her medication at all since that shot of Thorazine. She questions Mary with a great deal of suspicion about the condition of this patient. Frail, thin, and very dangerously psychotic, the doctor suspects medical neglect. She suspects more too, but for now will let that go. Right now, it is imperative to stabilize this kid. She explains to Mary that when the Thorazine wore off there was a "re-bound effect" of the symptoms causing them to become severe very rapidly. She explains how important it is to keep all appointments and make sure medications are taken on time in the right dose.

Dr. Scott calls the psychiatrist at home. He tells her which medication to use to calm the symptoms quickly without hospitalization. Dr. Scott thinks hospitalization is needed, as she thinks the disease is being ignored at home, but he will not agree to it. The beds are full already with good paying patients and this kid is a ward of the state. No room for those who cannot pay unless the doctor can prove the teenager a threat to herself or others. Dr. Scott admits she cannot. The kid is passive, laughing, and calm. Not speaking at all or responding with violence. She is stuck. She hangs up the phone sighing knowing in her gut this is bad. She goes to the clinic drug cabinet and grabs the right samples in the right doses and a glass of water.

The doctor hands the kid the water and pills. No response. She is only giggling and swaying looking at the walls with what appears to be delight. The doctor asks Mary for assistance as the two of them work to get these pills into this very disturbed young person. Mary tills back the kids head with no resistance as Dr. Scott puts the pill in while opening her mouth gently. Water is poured in, and the patient swallows, no fight or acknowledgement of the act. This bothers Dr. Scott a lot. This kid is blown she thinks, but she has to let her go. She gives a large number of very powerful anti-psychotics as well as pills to help with the nasty side effects of these heavy hitting medications to Mary. She warns her that this must be given at high doses from here until they are due back for their appointment at the end of the month. Wait, the end of the month? Oh no, we will see her back in two weeks, we will make room for this one.

"Where am I? There is someone behind a desk talking to Mary. Yes, that is Mary." I think. "I have been having the strangest dream about dancing or something. What did they just put into my mouth? LSD, I bet." I did not fight them because I did not know this other person. The whole bunch of them are in on it. Mary, Stephanie and now this new woman. Well, I will not say a word and pretend I am sleeping. I will get Mary. I have had enough of this bullshit.

"What is this woman saying to her?" I watch them talking and realize it is me they are discussing, the dirty bitches. I watch them pretending not to be aware. I am aware, just not sure of what yet. Nothing is making sense so I will sit here until I can remember and watch them. No worries, I am going to go home and figure out a plan soon.

The woman is coming towards me. I just stare at her being careful not to let her know I am awake. "You will feel better soon kiddo. Just let the medication do its magic and take it you hear me? I will be worrying about you. I hope to meet the real you in two weeks." She smiles at me.

"Ah, finally an answer! This is not real. She just said I am not real! Oh my God! Now I understand. This is all a dream, and I am not really here! That explains the static, the visions all of it! I died that day when I took those pills! I am dead and this is just a weird dream my corpse is having. Everything is going to be okay now. No wonder everything is so fucked up. It is a dream, and I am a delusion! Hahaha! I fell for it! I always was a fool!" I think trying not to smile as I now feel much better. I am not real; this is not real. These delusions they keep talking about are me.

Mary is ready to go. She grabs my arm and leads me out the door. I continue to play opossum. I am so happy right now. Everything is going to be okay. I no longer have to worry. Maybe I was not supposed to know that I was not real, but now I do. So, I can handle this odd stuff. After all I am already dead.

Mary and I get back into the car. She starts it and I can now see that it is a car. Not a big music box. She is frustrated because she thought I was going to be locked up. Nope, sorry Mary. Fooled you. I keep my mouth shut for the thirty miles to return the car. She does not speak either.

Once in the car owner's driveway I open the door and get out. This startles Mary. She did not know I was aware or awake. She jumps out too, looking at me stunned.

"Where do you think you are going?" She is not sure what to do.

"Home, Mary. I would thank you for hiding me out till dark but go fuck yourself bitch. You owed me at least that one kindness. Sorry you did not get all you wanted there, but just like you, they do not care either." I laughed at that as I took off walking back home in the deepening darkness of night toward my cemetery home.

"Stephanie is not going to call anyone. Her Aunt won't either. No one gives a shit about a delusion. No one is coming to do anything. They never do. I am going to be fine." I say aloud as I am walking.

My mouth is full of cotton. I stopped by the school and drink water from the outside hose. No way Mary can poison the whole damned water supply there. No one would think of it I assure myself as I nervously drink deeply from it.

Once finished I realize I need to get water from somewhere. I doubt the school would be okay with me always drinking from the hose whenever I want. I think on that for a moment. I cannot store the water; Mary may get it while I am at school. I see an old garbage can in the parking lot. I dig through it till I find a suitable jug for water. I chuckled, as I thought of Stephanie's curse to 'dig in garbage cans' as I clean the jug with the water hose. I would just store a day's worth of water each day and pour it out each morning. That way it is always in my sight.

I arrive home very late, but everything is as I left it. I was right no one called anyone. My proof that I am not real. How else could I know? How else could I be in two places at once? That is because I saw the truth in the lake that day. I saw me on the gurney and Michelle hanging. I am dead and this is just not real. I am either a soul and this is hell, or my dying body is dreaming me up. Whichever, this is not real. It made so much sense I could not believe it took me all this time to figure it out. This delusional world is unstable, so of course things happen here that should not, like colors coming off of church windows. Those things are not important and need to be ignored. I will ignore them as now I understand they are just proof of what I just discovered. What is important is that in this delusional world, Mary and others are trying to hurt me like they did when I was alive. I understand that is my mission, to get those who hurt the real me. I get it now. I am on a mission to solve the murder of me. I think on this with new determination to avenge myself of my killers.

My mouth is still very cotton filled. I keep drinking the water and it will not go away. "Must be those pills, what was that all about?" I am so dizzy, and my stomach is cramping. I also have a headache. My body feels heavy with a slow feeling growing through me, making my joints feel jumpy. I did not bother with a fire tonight as I lay down to give into the horrid fatigue that seems to be overtaking me. I am just so tired. As I drift off, I chuckle that I ever fell for the whole lie that I am real. How stupid am I?

The morning light pours in. I am groggy and heavy. I have been drooling as my wig is all matted with it. I look at the old worn watch I have and realize I have to moving or be late for school. As I stand I almost faint. I am so dizzy. My knees are wobbly like a newborn colt.

"What is this happy bullshit," I yell out. I look at my clothing, it seems fine even though I have not changed since the arrest, unless you count the hospital gown. I check my make-up. All of my chin is clean of it. "Wow, what a drool fest, huh?" I laugh.

I fix my make-up and drink deep from my jug then pour out the water as I had agreed with me. I tuck the jug under my arm and take off for the school. No breakfast for me, but that is okay. I never liked to eat anyway. As I walk, my muscles cramp all over and I get that strange headache again. I open my mouth to relieve the pressure. It seems to be coming from my jaw. I realize I am clenching it unintentionally. Weird. I try to stop but it is like the jaw has a mind of its own. I arrive in the school yard rubbing my throbbing head with my jug under my arm, unbathed and still feeling weird.

As I walk to the doors leading inside, I notice you could hear a pin drop. Everyone is staring at me in absolute awe. Uh oh, do I look strange or something? Okay, stranger than normal? I go inside and the crowded hallway stops as everyone stars. Now I am scared. What is going on? I know that I am a delusion. Anything is possible. Did I just turn into a snake or a wolf or something? I rush down the hall as students back away to let me pass right to the rest room to check in the mirror.

I look at my reflection, nothing weirder than usual there. What is the deal? Stephanie comes out of one of the stalls and sees me examining myself in the mirror for holes. She is startled but then smiles.

"Well, well, look what the zombies' drug in! Hey there psycho, how are you feeling today?" She walked right up to me not appearing to be the least bit angry about yesterday.

I was not surprised she was not angry. This is a delusion and apparently, she is part of it. Going away is not going to happen. I have to get rid of her, that is the mission.

Looking right at her I smiled back and answered in a mocking sweet voice, "better."

She rolled her eyes. "Do not act like that. Did not you hear," she said excitedly.

I shook my head no, not really interested to 'hear' but I know Stephanie so I was about to 'hear.'

"Well, everyone thinks you are like a bad ass and stuff. Some people were here when you got arrested. They say you beat up like five cops and laughed as they beat you down with clubs, calling them pussies and stuff." Her eyes brightened as she relayed this very wrong story of the events of the arrest to me. "So, like everyone thinks you are so cool! You can have any boyfriend you want, and everyone wants to hang out with you. You are like the idol and stuff. But you are my best friend," she finished.

"Wait, what?" I stammer in disbelief. "I did what? I am what? Oh, and I am not your friend."

Stephanie did not listen to me only rattled on about how she had heard that crazy people were stronger than 'normal' people, but five cops is really amazing.

I stood there as she continued to talk thinking, "but it is not true. None of it."

"What is with the jug?" she finally took a breath.

I just shook my head and walked out leaving her there. As I walked back into the hallway, I found her story was correct. I was now the most infamous student that had ever walked those dusty halls. Every kid there moved out of the way nodding a friendly 'hi' and some looked at me adoringly. Some said my name in approval, dipping their heads. I hurried to my first class and sat down at my desk putting my jug next to me. The students did not pull their desks away today but smiled friendly and said "hey. That was really cool. You're a bad ass." Notes were passed to me the whole hour that I would ignore as they piled on my desk unread.

I was suddenly my dark delusional self's worst nightmare, popular. My head was killing me as my jaw began to grind on my back teeth against my will.

My stomach would not stop cramping and the whole damned room was too bright. I just wanted to crawl into a deep hole and die However, I knew I was already dead. Stephanie was still going to make me sorry I ever defended her apparently. I had no idea why I am feeling so horrid, but I am sure I have been poisoned again. So, without a shred of hope I continued to my next class when the bell rung. The hallway was full of my mistaken new fans.

Told you I would catch you before you hit the bottom, beauties! Now, I know this book may have been a bit of a hard read. I hope you were able to follow without getting too lost. Make sure to get a head count. If any of you are missing, well I am not sure there is anything can be done now. I hope all of you return to read Book Two entitled "Stop Calling Me Psycho", as we once again take a trip that even the entire fan base of the Grateful Dead would envy.

Alexandria May Ausman was born into a dangerously neglectful home environment. She was the helpless victim of numerous incidents of psychological, physical, and sexual assaults by her parents and peers. She dressed in an unusual manner to 'fightened' off bullies and to appear less attractive to sexual predators. Despite her cries for help her pleas for aid were ignored until she was finally placed in foster care at age fifteen. In her sixteenth year, her mental health began to deteriorate. Alexandria was quickly abandoned by her foster parents when she was diagnosed with Schizophrenia. While still only a teen, she was forced to battle this devastating illness alone.

Alexandria has struggled with lack of a support system, numerous psychotic episodes, exploitation, homelessness, and an uncaring mental health system.

Alexandria raised two healthy children. After obtaining her bachelor's degree in psychology she worked as a child abuse investigator and became a diagnostic psychologist while acquiring her Master's in psychology. Alexandria never forgot the experience of 'slipping through the cracks.' Her life's goal is to help people suffering abuse and/or mental illness have access to necessary services. In 2018, Alexandria's fashion expression gained notice. By accident, she became a model of 'gothic attire'. That summer she won the World Gothic Models contest. Henceforth, dubbed the Goth Queen, Alexandria didn't miss an opportunity to offer a helping hand to those in need.

She began writing a fictionalized account of her life experiences after a catastrophic return of psychotic symptoms. Today, Alexandria is retired, and homebound due to crippling symptoms of Schizophrenia. She currently lives in Tallahassee, Florida, with her loving husband and a loyal support dog.

Made in United States
Orlando, FL
13 July 2022